JC's Salvage

JC's Salvage

WJRIII

iUniverse

JC'S SALVAGE

iUniverse books may be ordered through booksellers or by contacting:

iUniverse
1663 Liberty Drive
Bloomington, IN 47403
www.iuniverse.com
844-349-9409

ISBN: 978-1-6632-3955-6 (sc)
ISBN: 978-1-6632-3966-2 (hc)
ISBN: 978-1-6632-3965-5 (e)

Library of Congress Control Number: 2022910028

Print information available on the last page.

iUniverse rev. date: 05/20/2022

1 January 2018

Dear reader
I am not sure this is the end
of this story but read if you will.
I find pleasure in not only putting down
my thoughts but finding, I have given someone
a minute or so of fun, reading. If that is the
case, you have thanked me. My hope is you will
pass this along, and if there is something I
could do more, let me know. I always
hope for criticism. That tells me, at
least someone read it. Thank
you for your time,
God's Blessings.

I would like to dedicate it to Emma, someone who has never received the proper credit deserved for her many years of service, working with the poor and marginalized. Many times, she was on the front lines while others were taking the credit. Also, to my family and friends who have pushed me to put these words down.

CHAPTER 1
Salvaged and repaired,
John Housler

His father had not returned from Vietnam and his mother had never quite gotten over it. She did work, and as a matter of fact, had a pretty good job. John had gone to a good school and done well.

Who knows or can say, just when these things start? A girlfriend moved away at a young age, his mother's needed counseling and constant wondering about what had happened to his father, his different interests in school and a lot of other things could have led to his problems.

John had left home at a young age. Upset, disgruntled, mad at the world, just walking away one night and never coming back, thumbing and walking, eventually finding himself in a town many miles away from where he was born. Getting a job was impossible as people asked too many questions, along with not having any papers. People would see this good-looking young man and offer him a dollar once in a while. As he and his clothes became more and more unkept, less people stopped to ask questions. Soon panhandling and stealing was a must. John Housler started stealing for food and cigarettes and soon he was stealing for other people. He had done a pretty poor job of stealing and after a number of arrests was given a four-year stint in the State prison.

In prison he made friends, learned to do drugs as they were so prevalent and along with drugs came all the other devices needed to keep to the addiction. Still, a good-looking guy, John had managed to lie and pout his way past the parole board and after only two years, was released to the streets, saying he was going to answer a help wanted add and stay with his mother while he took care of her.

This night, John was on a mission. He had learned where he had been so sloppy stealing in his past life and knew now, he was much better at it. A couple of stops tonight, not getting greedy but just enough to pay for his fix.

A car drove by, slowed down, coming close to the curb, someone throwing out a small, clear, plastic bag and almost at John's feet. This was the kind of bag, people often kept weed in. As the car sped off, John looked at the package and it was green but it sure looked like green money. Picking it up, he realized it was, money, and a piece of paper with it. Inside were several bills and pulling them out, threw down the bag. Separating the bills, he found ten, ten-dollar bills. A hundred dollars and just what he needed for his next hit.

He looked around to see if anyone else had witnessed the event and felt good that it was not busy tonight. There would be no looking over his shoulder tonight while he stole the high dollar children's clothes he had contracted to steal.

He would always need some kind of fix just to get up the nerve to steal and then it was never over quick enough. He tried to keep himself looking clean, even if he hadn't had a shower for several weeks. If you were poor, there were plenty of free clothes available somewhere to make yourself look clean.

He would go into a store just looking around, starting at the opposite side of the store from where he was going to steal. The idea was, that by the time he got to the merchandise he wanted, he figured they would be tired of watching him if they were watching. Wearing bulky clothes and leaning over what he wanted, He would grab what he needed, very carefully and fast, pull it under his clothes and ask to use the restroom. Just sticking his head in, he could always depend on the restroom being messy and acting like he suffered from mysophobia, say he was sorry but he just couldn't use that one and was going to go down the street but please, "I have a serious problem and very low tolerance for germs. I will be back. Maybe you could clean it up a bit before I return." That always threw off their attention but still, he would sweat until he was away.

Tonight, was different. Tonight, those rich fools could buy their kids clothes right from the store and pay the high price that everybody else paid. He almost ran down the street stopping at the corner. Maybe not smiling but upbeat anyway. Tonight, he had a hundred dollars and it was all his. Then something happened. He stopped at the corner as the light changed and changed and changed again, more than once. "why would?,,,, why him? Was the person a friend?,,,,, Did they know something about him? Was the money dirty in some way, maybe marked or who knew?"

He found himself walking back to the plastic bag that by now had blown into the street. He had to wait for several cars to pass. Picking it up, he took it under the street light and pulled out the paper which turned out to be a letter.

Unfolding and flattening the crumpled paper he read,

"This might be good or bad for you. I do not know who you are or if you are the person, I threw it at. I am not a rich person but once in a while I have a little money I can part with and I do this. I will never know if I did good or caused you more trouble but I will tell you this. We make our own way. It is always hard and it is just as hard to do it wrong as it is right. If you are a street person you already know that. When you do things right a lot more people respect and care for you. If you keep this for yourself it is because you need people to care for you. Money won't buy caring people but it might be what you need to find your way back. Be wise and be slow to spend it."

John looked at the money again and again at the neatly typed letter.

"This guy must be an idiot. Who is not going to spend it? Anybody who throws money out the window has to have a screw loose!"

Something was happening. What was it? Why? He had always just plodded along doing what was necessary to get to the next step. What was it? No one cared and no one even knew him. Oh, there were the dealers and some of the street people he would exchange a little information with, but so very little and well, it was starting to get to him.

There were few places to sit and even fewer to sleep. Benches had been rigged so sleeping was impossible and even sitting was uncomfortable, preventing the homeless from hanging around. Spikes had been put in places where a guy used to be able to lay down in the corner of an old building.

Down the street was a sort of soup kitchen. A restaurant owner had bought an old abandoned building next to his place, re opened a doorway connecting the two buildings and allowed the street people to sit in there while he was open. He would give them coffee and sometimes soup or leftovers. John didn't know the guy but had been in there a few times. Pushing his stash deep into his pocket he headed down to the soup kitchen. Luckily it was open and although there were no customers in the restaurant there were a few raged souls in the annex.

He knew the rules.

"Just go in and don't be a problem. If you obey the rules, I can give you a coffee."

It wasn't long before the owner came with a cup of coffee as well as a large kettle of soup. Hollering at one of the other street people."

"Chrissie, will you get some more cups and serve this to whoever wants some. I had it left and business is about done for the night."

The owner, Frans, setting a cup of coffee down for John, stretched and decided to sit down himself. Like he was talking to nobody, he rambled on about some of the customers and how lucky he was to meet so many great people. John just looked at him and for a minute their eyes met. John looked away but the store owner said,

"Son, you have something to say or ask. I don't know if I have any answers but I am here for a few minutes anyway. If you have something you want to say, don't wait too long."

John heard but it was like his head was spinning off his body. He had a lot to say but he had nothing to say. Finally, he picked his head up looking again at the Restaurant owner for what seemed like a long time. After a while he said,

"I just don't know, I just"

The store owner hollered for Chrissie to please bring some more hot coffee. Pouring John another cup and pushing it to him, he grabbed John's shoulder for just long enough to give it a squeeze and sitting back waited for whatever would come next.

John started again,

"I just don't know what is going on. Something, well someone, well I got something tonight and for some reason it has kind of confused me. You know from seeing me I just, well I'm no one or at least no one, anybody really cares

4

about. I don't know if I care about anything. I'm not even sure, those are the right words to what I am feeling."

A long silence and then the owner said

"I see a lot of street people in here and I know there is not much I can do for them. I had some hard times once and maybe that is why I do what I do but I don't think so. I think the reason I try to help, is because I always learn. People tell me about their lives and I can hardly believe they have made it this far. How they get through all the bad things that they have had to deal with is way beyond me. Son, the only thing I can tell you for now, is what you are experiencing is, you are thinking. You have put aside all of your usual activities long enough to think. Someone or something has given you an opportunity that is very special. As for advice, don't stop thinking. Hold on to that for as long as you can. If you fall away, try hard to come back to thinking."

The store owner gave John a plastic travel cup, someone had left, filed with the last of the hot coffee and announced he had to close up and John got up and slowly walked back out on the street.

'What was he talking about? Did he mean, I was thinking about changing?" John had no intention of changing. What did all those people have that he needed? Fancy cars, clothes, warm houses and did they seem any better off, then he was? They still complained. He would hear them. They still needed more things, didn't have any time, always working or running here or there. So many times, he would hear them talking about things they thought they knew and they were so stupid. Why would he want to be like that? They had been nowhere. They just didn't know a lot.

It was cold but tonight was not the night to go to the shelter. He just walked. When you are homeless you don't suffer all the things people think you do. As for the cold, one gets used to being outdoors and is able to tolerate a lot more than most who have homes. The body weathers and although it might not be comfortable, maybe one forgets what comfortable is.

So, John plodded along and not because the restaurant owner said so, he was thinking. He just couldn't stop going over so many things.

Was he even considering a different life? What makes him think he could ever get back to a life, some people thought he should? He would have to change so much and where would he start. Right now, he sure could use a drink or just a small hit. Ronnie Fender was going to have some samples tonight and he could walk there in twenty minutes. Heck, he had money and he could take the trolley. He could take a cab, but he would never spend money on transportation. Not that kind of money, and here he was, walking in the wrong direction of any kind of high. Where was he going. It had been a long time since he had walked in this part of town and he was actually walking towards the outskirts. He stopped finally, sitting on an old phone pole that had been taken down. He pulled a granola bar from his pocket and sipping on the coffee that by now had gotten cold, he thought some more. Getting up he went at least a mile more, coming to a walking trail and headed up that just as if he knew where he was going. Finally, he stopped and looked around. What was he doing? He had no idea what was around this part of town and it might just be the kind of place he could be relieved of his cash. A beating is one thing but one doesn't come on a hundred dollars every day. A bridge had been built over a small creek so John looked around and sliding down the bank found a comfortable place under the bridge. There was cardboard and newspaper around and soon he had gathered enough for a bed. He had done this many times in other places. Taking the small plastic bag of cash from his pocket he found a place in the ceiling of the bridge to slide it in. A very small and most unlikely place for anyone to be looking or expecting to find a hundred dollars. Curling up in his little cocoon of paper and cardboard he was plenty warm.

He couldn't help but laugh to himself about the fact that he was comfortable while people in expensive houses, would be complaining about the cold. They would never understand and a good thing because there wasn't that much room under bridges. He was off to sleep in no time, waking to the noise of a tire spinning. Climbing up the bank he spied the creator of the noise.

Down the trail where it met the street, was a truck, stuck in a low spot just off the pavement. John walked up to the truck where a man was trying to rock the vehicle back and forth, almost but not getting out of his predicament and only slowly digging in more.

John motioned to the driver and going around back signaled for him to go forward very slowly. Putting his shoulder against the truck, it almost leaped out of the hole. The truck pulled forward and drove off. John could see it moving away in the distance. "Not even thanks or a pack of cigarettes." Usually, a good deed could at least get him a pack of smokes.

Eventually the truck's brake lights came on. Turning around and coming back, the driver gruffly told John to get in.

John had been around and by now had taken rides with every kind of nut out there. It didn't worry him as he had nothing to lose and could always jump out. He had done that before too.

Climbing in, it was nice to feel the warm and almost too warm. He wanted to roll the window down but knew that wouldn't do. They drove a short way, just back to the edge of town and pulled into a drive, passed a house into the back yard pulling up to a small barn. The man got out and not saying a word, walked back to the building, opened the side door and went in. John sat there a few minutes and not sure what to do next, but finally followed the man in to the barn.

Was this guy going in to town where John hung out? Should he say thanks? In fact, the guy should be thanking him.

The little old barn was actually cheery inside, if a barn can be cheery. It was warm, lighted, and neat. Lots of tools, parts and pieces and a kind of kitchen in one corner with a couple of old chairs.

The man pointed to a ragged but cozy looking chair and over his shoulder, told John to sit. A wood stove was putting out lots of heat and on top was a well-used old coffee pot, already steaming and he poured John a cup. Pulling some eggs and a foil wrapped thing from an older chipped and banged up refrigerator, he started breakfast on a two-burner contraption with a hose leading to a propane cylinder down the way a bit.

"I need ya ta hep me lift an engine on ta ma truck and then I'll take ya where yer goin".

The hot breakfast was unbelievable. Eggs, sausage taters and toast. Simple to most pallets but it might have been the predicament or the fact that John hadn't eaten in a couple of days but more than that, there are times when the worst coffee can taste like heaven and a tin of water out of a cold, fast running stream, is better than the most expensive bottled water made.

After breakfast they loaded an engine on the truck. John was impressed at how strong this little guy was and between the two had no trouble lifting it. There was already a pile of scrap on the truck and it was easy to see what was going on, even if there was no conversation.

Slamming the tailgate up, they were back in the truck and on their way.

John had told this guy he would be going down town but they pulled into a scrap yard before they got very far. John said he would unload after the weigh in and the man could go to the office for the information. The truck was reweighed empty, cash collected and back on the road. Hardly a block down the road, they pulled in behind a gas station and up to a pile of scrap car parts. John jumped out and had most of the pieces loaded before Karl could get to them. The driver, Karl went inside the station for a few minutes and was back climbing in. He looked in and asked John if he wanted a job.

Just like that, "do you want a job?"

John almost laughed.

"And where would you pick me up, at my house? Should I ask my accountant, if it will interfere with my vast income Would it affect my taxes? Should I send my tuxedo to the cleaners? No, I don't want your stupid job, what would you want me to do, your dirty work?"

But John didn't say that. Maybe too embarrassed but he just said *"sure"*

The man said his name was Karl Lewis and he was a scrap metal man. He could use the help on most days as he had more business than he could manage.

"I usually gets up early, says ma morning prayers, gets the stove a goin in the barn an puts the coffee on. Than, I do a short run, roun the area ta see what I might find an I come back an have a bit of breakfast."

Karl had figured John to be homeless and said he could stay in the barn nights but he couldn't bring any friends around and any drinking or drugs were off his property and don't come in drunk.

A decent cot was arranged in the barn, plenty of heat, food and books to read. John fell into this quite easy and found himself staying.

Karl would go into the house at the end of the day and would come out early in the morning, have the coffee, John had taken the liberty to make and pretty soon John was making breakfasts.

On a few occasions John had wandered down the road to a small store, buying a few cans of beer with the money, Karl had advanced him, but not so often.

In a short time, they were learning about each other. Karl was born in the same house he lived in now. He had been in military service, later married, lost his wife to leukemia stumbled around for some years and finally picked himself up. Tried several jobs but never was able to deal with the work place regiment. Hard work was not a problem but the constant bickering and back stabbing was more than he wanted to deal with. He found he could pick up scrap, make smell investments, watch his spending and get along well enough.

For John, this was the real stuff. It had all happened so fast. John had moved into the house but most of their goings on were still in the barn. They put a shower out there and it helped keep the house clean and in order. John was satisfied to have a friend and a place to stay. Not like it was anything he would have ever asked for. It just came and he was riding along. No one had to tell John he would have to give up his addictions. Seeing this clean life and how well it worked, made him just want to clean himself up. Sweating out the addictions in the grit of the job helped a lot, keeping his physical self, busy, while keeping his mind busy.

In the past, John had picked steel and cardboard many times piling it in a grocery cart and pushing it to the scrap dealer where he might get some change and on a rare occasion a dollar. Once he found a catalytic converter and scored twenty-eight dollars. Something about platinum or whatever was in it but John was just glad to get it.

They went from boss and helper to partners, to business partners in a little more than a year. Both had a decent education, understanding the necessity of knowledge and help from others. They looked into what other scrappers were doing and what parts of that, would work for them. Both were tight with their money and John started a bank account. John fell off a couple of times, picking up a bottle at the party store, staying drunk for two or three days and then back on the wagon. Karl never said too much but then he didn't have to. John felt bad enough.

The business went along smoothly, sometimes working together, sometimes apart. One might be picking scrap while the other was in the library or at an attorney's office working on the business part of it. Right from the start both understood the importance of team work. Picking up, or heading off work for the other guy. They understood, by themselves they were just a single body but working together they were as good as three or four. Once they bought their first dependable truck, they started making some better money. As soon as they could they hired a driver and helper. They would go in to a business or old falling down buildings, farm fields and buildings being remolded. They went anywhere they could, to pick up scrap. There was no such thing as quitting time. They would get their rest but if there was something to help their business at three o'clock in the morning, they would be there. Sometimes, a business would have scrap after some remodel or demolition and needed to keep the construction people busy during the day. Rather than get in the way, John and Karl would offer to do their pick up at night. They did their best to accommodate the customers and it didn't take long for the word to get around. In the beginning they had given the customers some of the return from the scrap but now people were so glad to get their efficient service, they would pay a percentage for the hauling away and gradually hauling became most of their income.

The more they did, the more people wanted them and the more they gave. Taking very little from the profit and always buying better and more equipment.

Around this time, John decided to try and find out what had happened to his childhood sweetheart. Maybe he wanted to brag to her a bit or sometimes curiosity gets the better of us. After some searching by a friend, he acquired several phone numbers in the general area where he seemed to remember her family moving. Five or six calls later and he found her. Luann was beside her self that he was able to find her, much less want to talk to her. Spending a long time on a number of phone calls and exchanging a great deal of information, one day they decided, Luann would fly in to see him and go over old times. Although her return flight was paid for it was never used and the rest is, as they say, history.

By now they had three children, with one on the way. Karl had married young, so by the time he met John, his two children had gone off to school and were taking care of their own lives. It all just fell into place with its problems but few compared to the good times. There must have been an unwritten rule creep into all their lives.

"Prepare for the worst but work for the best"

When problems came along it was as if you had put too much salt on your food and you just toughed it out. Ate the food and knew the next would be better. In business as well as their family life, there were days when one or the other couldn't do anything right. Together they would work it out laughing their way through.

Holidays and any visiting days were always fun, integrating the play time with work time. The children would be doing some small chore allowing the adults to handle the necessary daily routine. Quitting early there would be a meal with a variety of leftovers, new recipes to try and special things, brought from a distant place. Everybody mingled and at the same time, respected each other's place.

A large parcel of property had been purchased where scrap was sorted, a large building was constructed and vehicles were kept clean and working well. People were hired, paid well and so they grew, somedays, never leaving a desk or the property but always working at something for the business.

They put in their own scales, sorting and storing their salvage scrap in large truck containers. The containers were weighed, photographed, locked and set aside ready to deliver at the best time or in some cases picked up by a salvage dealer at the most convenient time. This kept the drivers from having to wait in long lines during peak times as well as selling, when scrap prices were high.

Employees were treated well, with good wages, profit sharing and reasonable benefits. Working for K&J was a much-coveted job and once you got it you were not anxious to lose it. Respect and togetherness were not only encouraged but insisted on.

Early on, they had started brain storming or maybe just talking and learning a lot about each other and about each other's ideas. It was easy to see as long as they continued along this way, not getting greedy, anxious or lazy they would continue to do well. Their combined experiences caused them to feel satisfaction from pleasing customers, more than profit. Still, the profit came, and did it come!

John had contacted his mother, moved her close to him and put her to work keeping financial records. With the help of Karl and some of his friends they went to work on finding out what they could about John's father. New material and information, was available and they were able, after some time to contact two of the men from his father's squad. Stories were told and remains brought home but that is a story for another time.

It is enough to say; his mother was a changed woman. Changed for the better.

Both Karl and John cared a great deal about the poor people in their area. John was more expressive but Karl although not so anxious to say so and acting tough, cared just as much. While John had been on the street with many, Karl had been in service, seen some bad times, seen drugs and addiction, lost some friends and coming home had to deal with a lot of things, many of his military friends weren't able to deal with. Consequently, they too became kind of lost. More than once they had talked about it but mostly tried to do something by giving a person a job or just buying them a meal. They knew that was not only not enough but more like throwing a crumb out for a mouse and making him more exposed and venerable to the cat. Poor people needed healthy people to care about them. Not to take them home, not to babysit them, they needed people, just to care.

After considerable research, talking with others who had tried to help the poor, sharing the stories of the poor they knew, Karl and John came up with a bit of a plan.

There had been a small old airport just on the edge of town and it still had some buildings. It had a large airplane hangar, overgrown with weeds and trees, but with room enough for their plan. The property had been idle for some time and purchasing it, was easy. There would be some rough things to deal with along the way but for now it was perfect.

They didn't ask or wait for a lot of praise from the community, knowing most people approved of accomplishments long before dreams.

With the help of many of the poor, friends and their staff they cleaned and moved a lot of left behind junk. Some of which became scrap to be turned into cash.

There was no such thing as an opening day. John and Karl turned the few attached offices into combination work places and bedrooms and often stayed nights themselves with some of the needy.

The street people and poor loved to have a chance to do something and it was easy to see quick improvement. This was poor-man's therapy. To the poor, this was their place and no one argued the point. While it was getting things done, maybe not as good as professionals, it was getting done and it was cheap.

John and Karl had cleaned up and fenced in the scrap business, landscaping and dressing up buildings to the point of getting local awards for community improvement. They knew what it would take to make this place work and although fancy won't pay bills, it makes for good public relations. That part was easy. Some simple outdoor cleanup and a trip or two to the landscape supplier and considering its location, they were looking better than anything around.

The place took shape in record time. In the very first days of purchasing the building, poor people were coming in and eating from donated cans of food. In a couple more days, there was a stove, running water and three meals, a day, being served. Sometimes it was soup for breakfast and cereal for supper but something. Sometimes only cold water while a heater was being installed. Like so much in the building, not perfect but more than perfect to the people being served.

Being salvage pickers and demolition haulers, didn't take long for them to stock the place with a lot of what was needed. A bed or chair, refrigerator, desk, gallons of paint, shelving, building material, lighting, restaurant equipment, all used, sometimes broken or dirty and many times, ready to use or repairable. Sometimes they would haul in pieces which turned out to have no value. It would be dismantled, taken apart and sent to the scrap yard or recycler.

They would see a person walking the streets, looking like they had no place to go, ask him or her to help, explaining what they were trying to do. Not always, but sometimes the person would stay and sometimes work out well.

The place was soon crawling with volunteers, some just curious, some with a real desire to help and some glad to find a place they could call home.

The town officials and businesses were more than glad to work with them, as it would help keep the (tramps) off the street. Karl and John would just bite their tongue and be thankful these people weren't working against them.

No two people could have been better at creating this place. Along with family members, they were not afraid of work, dirt, rust and broken things. People would marvel at how they could turn what appeared to be junk into serious dollars. Like many of the people who had been thrown out and now coming in to their place, there was great value in tangible items, others had thrown out. John and Karl knew they couldn't fix every appliance or fixture they picked up and they knew they couldn't fix every street person who came in but that didn't stop them from trying.

Soon donations came, and as people could see their small donations create so much good will, they couldn't help but make even more donations.

A wood heater was installed to more or less use up some of the wood scraps while supplementing their regular heating system. A system for heating water with wood was created so they would always have enough hot water at a very lean cost. Eventually wood cutters and landscapers would leave some of their cuttings.

They became great environmentalists, without ever trying. Recycle, reuse, call it what you want, it was all money and they made it work.

One day, a minister called to enquire about their place and in conversation asked "what was the name of their homeless place?" They really hadn't thought about a name but being lost for words, John just said,

"Karl and I thought we would just use our fist initials."

"So, your name is John and you run a salvage business. What did you say the name of your partner is? Carl? You are going to call it JC's Salvage, with a J and a C? I think that is absolutely marvelous. Who would have ever thought of that.,,,, That defiantly had to be inspired?"

John tried to say he was almost correct and that Karl was spelled with a K but never could get it said. Before John could get any more out, the minister thanked him, said he would be talking with all the church leaders in the community and there would soon be donations and people to help on whatever was needed. He hung up and John just sat there.

About that time, Karl came in.

"Sit down Karl with a K and we need to talk. I may be calling you C for a while."

John told him the story over a coffee and they both laughed till they cried.

"So, Karl, what do you think"?

"Well," Said Karl, *"I don't see me changing my name at this point considering, all it would take with the business and not only would there be a lot of Bibles to rewrite, I'm pretty sure, Jesus isn't ready to make a change either, but I must say. J C's Salvage has a great sound. We are, trying to salvage some of these folks and this business has been his, all along anyway. So, J C's Salvage it is."*

Old laundry equipment was the easiest to find and it seemed there was always a volunteer, day and night doing laundry or just supervising laundry. Salvage electrical wire was strung up for a clothes line, from wall to wall and lager pieces, like blankets, sheets or curtains would be air dried while the clothes would be done in the dryers.

Old wooden pallets were collected, taken apart and with the help of a retired wood worker, visitors were taught how to make everything from bird houses to rustic, tables and chairs.

The right person had agreed to do what he could with all the donated paint. He was turned lose to mix as much as he could, considering type as well as decent colors and painting was going on everywhere. A street person who had never painted before might come along, be offered a paint roller and a wall to cover. When he had done what he could, a more trained person merely straightens up the work and everybody gained. The street person did something positive, creative, felt good about it, probably for the first time in many years and J C's, got a wall and many walls painted, free paint and free labor.

People with no place to go, could come in anytime of the day or night, given soup or something to eat, staying in a kind of staging area until they could be interviewed and informed of what was expected of them while they stayed. At, 9am, they would be processed in, assigned a bed area, consideration given to their position a`1nd needs. If they chose to go only as far as the staging area, they would be on their own for laundry, food and other services. At no time, were they allowed to be rowdy or disrespectful of other people.

The main areas were divided up into rooms of anywhere one, to five or six. Walls were portable and could be changed as needed. Men, women, safety, personality and addiction issues would be addressed and as some of the visitors became more senior, would be asked to be a sort of captain of a room or area.

The people coming to stay would often have baggage, cans, bottles, radios, excess clothes, and medications/drugs. Rather than try to control all of it, they would be required, as part of the rules, to leave most everything locked up outside of the main living area, in plastic bags with their names. As long as they didn't abuse their use, they would be escorted and supervised while they grabbed what single item they needed and the bag or bags, locked back up.

Some of the homeless people had been given or allowed subsidized homes, long before JC's, came along, and although they were happy to be in a place of their own, really weren't ready for them. Being lonely, they would invite their friends, often people in trouble like themselves. People would come in with pets, personal hygiene was overlooked and trash wound up everywhere. If there was a drug man around and there always is, he would be at the house in a minute, dealing and making promises. You wouldn't put a child in a place and expect them to fend for themselves and many of these folks had never had a chance to learn home-making. Putting them in an apartment or house can be like putting an elderly person who has never driven, on the freeway with a new Corvette. There is going to be a crash. Poor people don't need, yet another let down, by being thrown out of their home because they didn't keep up to the rules.

JC's, decided to do as much as they could to invite these people to visit and visit often. They would work with them, encouraging them to sit through some training for anything that might help them keep their home and gradually move forward. They would be taught about care and cleaning and how to accomplish things with the least amount of pocket cash.

Things like being thrifty, reasoning out discipline, cleanliness for the sake of health and just having a place to be proud of when some of the volunteers came to visit.

The same volunteers would be taught to fawn over all improvements weather a single flower in the yard, a painted wall or just a clean room.

Professional people were encouraged to come in to JC's and do interviews, advise people about their rights, fill out paperwork and showed, how to make contacts, and what they would need to move on to better conditions. Military, mental and physical disabilities were addressed as well as protecting any income they might have coming.

People came in doing amateur entertainment, serving special meals, cutting hair, giving talks about everything from history to cooking, sewing, construction, race car driving, wise shopping, personal hygiene, and more. A game room was available during approved hours and with consideration being given to all involved. Personal electronic items were allowed but only as far as the staging area and locked back up when not being used.

Any continual violation of rules would put a person back to the staging area but more often the person would be ambushed by a volunteer and encouraged to quietly think about respect and needs of the majority.

Nothing is perfect but Karl and John had been through a lot so they expected little but even so, the return was tremendous. One of their duties was to constantly be innovative and explorative, looking at new and suggested ideas, and like the salvage business, using what they could and throwing out what didn't work. They were working with precious human beings here and nothing but their best would be considered. It wasn't so much to buy a new coat but to notice when one was needed.

John's mother became involved, getting some of the lady's she had come to know at church, involved. Different groups would take on special projects and so the operation like their scrap business started to more or less run itself. The more people volunteered the more they got to know not only the homeless and the poor, but the more they became familiar with how to use the rules and what to expect. Everyone eventually learned the return value of being a foot washer.

Frans, the restaurant owner, John had talked to, the night of the hundred-dollar gift, had been contacted. After volunteering over a number of years, Frans made arrangements to develop a restaurant at JC's salvage. A year and a half in its development and opening, people were dining and getting to know many of the street people. Frans served those who could afford to eat there and JC's kitchen, served the street people for free. JC's, became a poor man's community center, constantly growing, with one service working with another, to cut costs as well as hire as many as they could. Some of the same food, same cooks and wait staff and some of the same prep devices made it easier to accomplish. Getting everyone to understand and appreciate the concept at first, was not easy but as time went on it was considered genius.

The blending and melting, growing and learning, moving to the new Frans place, for not only the street people but the customers and volunteers as well, was a good thing. Frans's JC's restaurant turned out to be an important part of the operation.

John and Karl began to realize, they had built a kind of factory, turning out productive people who instead of being concerned about new, bigger, and fancier things than their neighbor, were able to feel good about learning and experiencing their own growth and independence. People were taught that, simple happy lives, were far more achievable and far more satisfying. JC's may not have solved all the problems with the poor but their success was much higher than the national average.

As the success with the street people and the poor grew, it naturally got into the news and soon people from all over the country were coming to visit and copy their strategies.

There were business problems, family problems, weather problems, and you name it. Maybe not as many as some people but a lot and they learned to take them in stride.

When John first met Karl and gone into his barn for breakfast, he had noticed a cross and sort of small chapel with a chair and place to kneel. Under the cross was a large empty glass jar. After a few days, John had to ask and was told,

"We didn't have a place to go to a church when I was in service so we built a simple chapel where ever we went. Someone decided to put a ration can under the cross for us to put our troubles in. You just tell your problems to the can and when you come back it is always empty."

The story had been printed and posted at every property, they owned, and you could find a small chapel and a vase or container of some sort, always empty.

There were always road trips, making a sort of vacation day, work day combination. One or the other would have a mission and someone would go along. It might be the partner, one of the grandchildren, John's mother or one of Karl's children. One-day Karl cornered John.

John had told Karl about the hundred-dollar stash and where he had put it so many years ago, and so Karl said to John,

"I'm going to go and steal your hundred dollars from under the bridge. Do you want to go?"

Together they drove out that way, talking about all the water under their own proverbial bridge and how happy they were, giving all the credit to God.

Getting to the spot, they walked slowly up the old grassy trail and stopping at the bridge, John decided to look, just for fun. Crawling down the bank, it was obvious, many strangers had been up to the same sleeping arrangement, under there. He slowly moved to the small place he had tucked the plastic bag and low and behold, it was there along with a rather large abandoned wasp nest. He pulled it out shaking lose the mud and dirt and carried it up showing it to Karl. So hard to believe it is still here. I guess we eat tonight, and they both laughed. Driving on John asked Karl to stop at the party store where he ran in. Coming out he had a small bag.

"Have you got a pen in here?"

Taking a small plastic sandwich bag out of his store bag and a pad of paper he wrote something and tucked it into the clear plastic bag along with the hundred dollars. Karl didn't need any instructions but just started down town and getting there cruising up and down until finding a target. Pulling close to the curb, John threw the package almost on to the foot of a guy, ragged and staggering. Instantly Karl dove away, only to turn in an alley and backing out to watch.

The man kept walking but then stopped, looked back, slowly, almost like he didn't care, picked up the package. Looked at it and looked again. And now looking around up and down the street, he pulled the contents out a bit and quickly stuffed it into his pocket again taking up his pace down the street but seeming to walk a little steadier but not so much with a destination. He seemed to be thinking.

January 24 2018

I wrote this story, at the end of 2017. I know I am not a writer, but enjoy doing what I do. I never start a story with an ending, or even a middle. That just comes as I go along.

Something happened when I was in Florida from January 10, 2018 to January 20, 2018.

Rented a car and it was new with 700 miles. Not a car, one expects to have problems with.

On my second day after leaving 8:00 Mass the car was driving rough. A quick check and I discovered a flat tire.

Called the rental people and it was going to take a while so decided to make the change to the spare, myself. The spare was what we often call a donut and not designed to be used a long time.

Pulled out the jack and spare and started to jack up the car, and a small pickup truck pulled in. The passenger jumped out, pushed me out of the way and proceeded to change the tire while giving the driver instructions to go back home and get the tire repair kit.

After the driver returned and while the passenger was finishing the repair and pumping up the repaired tire, I had a chance to talk to the driver. He told me the other guy was homeless. Something I had already guessed. The part that threw me was when he said, "the homeless man was LIVING IN MY BARN".

I don't know how common it is for a person to be living in a city barn or for that matter just how many city barns still exist. When I wrote in my story, John started out living in a barn. I just pulled it out of the air, or so I thought.

I do know, there are no coincidences in God's world.

CHAPTER 2
Sheds for threads
and weary Heads

As the concern for the poor and needy became a larger part of what they were doing here at JC's Salvage, more storage was needed. Storage for donated food as well as storage for clothing. There was the need to store things that had been picked up, such as old appliances, wood and supplies for other projects.

Sometimes a project would wait until enough of what was needed, could be collected or other times a project would be done, thought up, discussed and accomplished simply because there was an excess of materials. A pile of donated cement blocks could be stacked safe and neat to make a temporary picnic table in the yard. The cabinet of a stove, washer or dryer could be stripped, painted and maybe trimmed out with wood to make a storage place or cabinet.

Early on, when John and Karl were just starting to take in homeless people and get people to volunteer, one of the volunteers asked if she could build a storage shed with some of the salvage materials collected.

A bit apprehensive, a meeting was arranged, Julie Prater showed some drawings as well as pictures of sheds she had helped on and more than one she had done completely by herself. The group, impressed, decided almost unanimously and she started with a little help and as it started to show promise more of the guests became involved.

The building turned out to be an eight by ten-foot box, ten feet high, with almost the entire front having doors, opening for access. Some old wooden billboards had been donated and they were cut to make most of the structure. A flat but slightly sloped roof with a rubber covering, using material left over from a large roofing project in the area. A well decorated parapet gave the building a serious side. The facade was done to look like brick. Pallet wood had been collected, cut to a scaled down brick size, treated and stained and applied with construction adhesive and staples to a grey background. Fake windows and a door were cut in and painted to look like a working part of the building.

The building was completed in a relatively short time, due in part to other volunteers taking on a small piece or part of the project. As people seen it coming together, everyone wanted to get involved. Old Coach lamps were found to decorate the outside and someone took on the electric for a project. Lights were cleaned up painted rewired and all was arranged so a single extension cord could be used to give the building light when needed. Someone else had volunteered to paint the outside while another took on the inside. Much paint Had been donated so it was just a matter of finding a color and amount needed, sometimes mixing compatible types and coming up with a color to do what was needed. A mural was painted on one side and pictures were painted on the walls inside. A large storage shelf, at the seven-foot level had a ceiling fan painted on its underside and around the inside of the building a frog and a couple of lady bugs painted on walls.

From the outside, looking like a business, with an upstairs apartment, the building was not only practical for storage but just the thing to draw people, curious to know how JC's was going. Built to withstand weather and use, strong enough to last many years, capable of considerable storage, while at the same time an artistically fun thing to gaze on. Built on skids, it could be moved to where ever it was needed. The building became a popular subject around the area and brought a lot of much needed positive conversation about JC's salvage.

Julie turned out to be a great designer, and very artistic, helping when she could. She was the right person to get people involved and after seeing this storage building come out so well, it was obvious this wouldn't be the last. Eventually other storage buildings were going up. Someone would say what about this or that kind of building, a small committee would meet, Julie would do the final check and suggestions, deciding whose idea this time, by pulling one out of a hat. A church with a steeple became popular, actually using one for a small outdoor Chapple and selling a couple. There was a hospital, post office, little factory, a bakery and butcher shop with their products painted in to look like these things were being seen through the windows and doors. Houses with chimneys and various style roofs. The ideas were endless and in time JC's had a bit of a storage building village and selling one or two as time went on.

Wendy Dower showed up one day with a request. Wendy was a psychiatrist and interested in many of the same people JC's had coming in. In spite of being skeptical at first and advising against any support of JC's salvage, she was now on their side. She soon could see, "It wasn't perfect but more and more people were spending more time there and so, more of the needy were spending time there and off the streets. It was not just a place for a meal and a bed but a healthy miniature community, with volunteers and helpers coming and going at all hours.

She would encourage her clients to visit, get help or get involved. Spend some time talking with a lonely widower or mother who had lost someone and was volunteering. Grab a coffee, go off to a quiet secluded corner just sitting and relaxing in a safe place. They could play cards or put a puzzle together. Help with some of the construction or repairs.

Many had taken her advice and had found a home. They would go through a kind of informal training, be advised as to what society expected and how to avoid being taken advantage of. Occasionally a lecturer would come in and a person could go and listen but most of the training, "if it can be called that" came by way of experiencing healthy people working together at something they enjoyed.

This day, Wendy was on a mission. She had been advised, by the police, of a young man living in the woods, a couple miles out of town and not doing all that well. There had been some reports of miner thefts and a couple of store break-ins. He, the young man, had refused to answer any questions, to the point of being belligerent and their only recourse was to leave him alone, at least for now. The next time they got a call, and if he refused to leave, they would have to hand cuff him and bring him in. They had told her, that he wasn't looking all that well and didn't appear to be accustomed to living outdoors.

Wendy told John the story and asked if he would accompany her, trying to find this guy. Of course, John agreed and the next morning, dressed in old, well-worn clothes, from JC's closet they started out almost before daylight. John said, based on what they heard, that would likely be the best time to catch him off guard. They went to the general area driving around until John seen what he wanted to see. Parking the car, they walked to an area Wendy hadn't noticed. Some trash and worn-down weeds led into a thickly wooded area and an obviously recently used path. Following the path for, about three hundred feet they came to an opening and some debris, a kind of fire pit, card board boxes and one being used by someone for a sleeping area.

John said "hello" and the man in the box came alive in a bit of a jerk and quickly rose to a sitting position, eyes wide and looking like he had seen a ghost. John had talked to Wendy and asked to let him take the lead at first. He just said good morning while Wendy found a piece of half burned log to sit on and pretend to watch John. He scrounged around picking up pieces of paper some sticks and whatever else would burn. Reaching in a bag he had brought and pulling out a piece of fire starter he soon had a fire. A little pot. Two old pop bottles of water and some powdered chocolate, three unmatched and chipped cups came out. In minutes, he had things ready, taking a cup over to this guy still sitting and staring. John set the steaming cup on the ground in front of him and turned his back, talking to Wendy as if they had some kind of plan to go somewhere. After what seemed like a long time, John turned and looked at the man,

"Hi, my name is John, do you have a name you want to give me."

An unsteady, *"Robert"*, came back and John got up, pouring the last of the hot chocolate in Roberts empty cup. John poked around at the fire slowly burning up the leftover coals and then reached in has bag pulling out three sandwiches. He put two of the sandwiches in front of Robert and the other shared with Windy. Once again, his back to Robert he could tell by the Russel of the papers, the sandwiches were being consumed at light speed. They stayed for a long time saying little but telling Robert to hang in there. They would be back tomorrow, but for now they needed to get some business done. Without being asked, they said they would not tell anyone about this great spot and he should stay here as it was safe.

John left the raged back pack there telling Robert

"You can have all that is in the bag. There is a lot more where that came from. Just save me the bag."

Off they went, neither saying much.

Wendy understood as much as John, Robert wasn't ready to go with them anywhere and for that matter wasn't ready to tell them much. That would take a little time.

For most of three weeks they went out, sometimes twice a day, taking hot meals, an old raincoat and other assorted gifts. Eventually they started telling Robert about JC's place and how they would like to have him stay with them for a while. John showed him pictures and talked about the many projects. There were no locks and at least for a little while, he would stay for free and maybe eventually find something to do to earn his keep if he decided to stay. John said we have a hotel that is empty right now and you can stay there all by yourself. We will see that you get plenty to eat, as long as you clean up a bit and take care of yourself and your area.

Robert said he was seventeen and some of the other things he told them were not things they wanted to hear. It was sure, Robert wasn't ever going home again and it wasn't sure how long it would take for him to feel safe around anyone.

After church one Sunday, Wendy in spite of being warned by John, "not to go alone" went out and visited Robert. She went out like a mother, taking him fresh baked donuts and hot chocolate from the bakery, a wonderfully aromatic apple pie. Several bottles of water and as many peanut butter and jelly sandwiches. Four pieces of fried chicken were in a container to keep them hot with a small dish of mashed potatoes and gravy.

Robert sat there eating, fried chicken in one hand and a donut in the other. Wendy had brought a cloth to spread on the ground, making it look like one of those magazine pictures, picnics. She sat there with him, talking about this or that telling him about what was read at church today and how important God was in her life. She talked about places she had seen but did her best to avoid talking about family things. Wendy stayed for about three hours, by now feeling like she had made some progress. When she left, she gave Robert a small stuffed bear.

"This is just a stuffed bear but it is to remind you that where ever you go, someone is always with you, even if you don't see him."

John went to work very early the next morning and found Wendy's car in the parking lot. Wendy was sitting in the front seat just staring. Pulling up beside her he got out and went to the window tapping to get her attention. She jumped and seemed to come out of a dream, rolling down her window.

Why didn't you go inside? People are always glad to see you and more importantly need you.

"Sorry, John, it just wasn't a visiting morning and I just couldn't share this."

Oh, oh, this wasn't good. Something was wrong and he would go slow.

"I need to go inside to check in and get a coffee. Would you like one?"

"I'd love one but you don't have to ----------"

In minutes he was back, two coffees and fresh rolls baked by one of the homeless at Frans's "JC's" restaurant.

John jumped in the car passing her the coffee and opening up the bag of fresh bakery, smelling, rolls.

They sat there a minute sipping coffee and tearing small bits from the rolls.

"What's up?" John asked and almost wishing he hadn't asked.

Wendy squeaked out,

"I went to visit Robert yesterday"

Accompanied by tears and sobbing, sniffling, head shaking.

John Just sat there, nothing to say, nothing to ask but just a time to wait and above all things, listen.

"Thank God, I have a wonderful family or I wouldn't be able to do this. I got a little more of what Robert's home life was like and well, you know I can't tell you much more than you already know from him. I'm sure his parents will eventually be arrested. I have to think of them as very sick people and depend on God to handle that part of it."

She sobbed some more and it seemed she would never be able to compose herself.

"I believe Robert is almost ready to come in but he will have to be handled very carefully"

Once again, she started crying and through her tears,

"I just wanted to hug him so badly. No one should have to go through what he has gone through."

By now, Karl showed up and although he knew most of the story, was glad to hear the recent information.

"Do whatever you can and know I will be here to help. You know, my barn apartment is still available and he wouldn't be bothered there."

John said,

"I think I have a bit of a plan and I will call you and explain but right now we better get. This young man is used to a time when we show up and if he doesn't see us, gets pretty emotional."

They drove out to the place where Robert was staying, stopping for a hot chocolate and donuts on the way.

By now, Robert was anxious to see them. He still didn't say much but by all indications he had been preparing for their visit. The area was cleaned up, trash and scattered papers gone, most likely to the fire which was cleaned up to some kind of order.

Soon they got to the point and Robert said he would go with them. Every part of his being spelled fear.

"I won't have to ride in a car, will I?"

"No"

Looking at Wendy, John said.

"Wendy is going on ahead with the car and I want to walk and enjoy this beautiful day."

It turned out to be a pretty long walk, just poking along, not wanting to give Robert any more reason to be afraid. They talked about the weather, fishing, animals and anything John could dream up to avoid Robert's family life. John had told him, days earlier, about his own life and how Karl had rescued him from living on the streets. That had perked some attention and John brought a bit of that up again, reminding Robert of the care and kindness that was there for him.

About a half mile from JC's salvage, they found Wendy waiting in the car. Seeing them, she jumped out and said,

"I want to have my time walking with Robert"

As if it were some, kind of privilege. John relinquished his partner position, jumped in the car and traveled to JC's in time to make sure all was in order as he had requested.

He had advised as many as needed to know of the situation or at least, just as much as they needed to know.

27

By now, privacy was well understood at the center, and the less you said, the less likely you were, to say the wrong thing.

Soon Wendy showed up with her patient, walking past the main buildings and back to the storage units as John had suggested. The area had been cleared of most of the staring guests and volunteers and other than a couple of harmless, hellos from a distance not much was said. John met them in front of one of the well-done sheds. On the overhead sign it said "Friendly Hotel" and on the front porch a bench, small mail box, plastic flowers in a trey of peat, a four by five-foot landscape, turquoise painted kidney shaped pool with a miniature "No Swimming "sign was just in front.

No more than ten by twelve feet, the building had a real door and real scaled down windows. It was the second in its style and size, the first designed by a volunteer and delivered in two pieces, to his house and used by his grandchildren.

"This is the hotel I promised and although it probably isn't what you might have thought, it will give you as much privacy as you want for as long as you need it."

Inside was a cot or single bed, easily used for a couch, a single chair, small tables, pictures hanging on walls and all set up to be used for a fun play house or quickly turned into a storage building.

There were lights but no running water. Some shelves, a few books, naturally one being a bible, paper, pens, walls well painted and clean. A single sign on the wall.

"No one has ever become poor by giving" Anne Frank.

In they went, John caring a case of bottled water, paper towels and a small box of snacks. Wendy came in carrying the wild flowers they had picked on the walk in, taking a bottle of water that John had drank from, putting it on the table with the wild flowers.

Wendy said *"I have to go to work"*, wished Robert well, not waiting for a response and slipped out.

John was pretty sure the tears were flowing the minute she left the building. This time they would be tears of joy, she deserved for arranging to bring Robert in.

John stayed a little while, seeing that Robert would sit down and giving him necessary instructions.

"We will arrange for a wash station for you and there is a portable bathroom outside used by the people when they are in the yard. It is maintained on a regular basis and when we get you your wash station you can dump the waste in there. You will get a regular delivery of food and whatever else you need twice a day. You can leave notes on the porch and your delivery's will be left there. Whenever you feel up to it, you can come to the main building where there is recreation, food, talks by people who want to help and a whole lot more. There are no locks here and you are free to come and go as you please".

John left and soon returned with a quickly assembled wash station which wasn't much more than a large water bottle, wash basin and a five-gallon bucket, the crudely built stand smelling of freshly cut lumber.

Clean clothes, from the clothing shed were brought. Soap and personal hygiene products which had been donated were brought.

The next day Wendy advised Robert, he should be checked by a doctor and it would be private in his own room and no one but the doctor she knew would be there. She knew a doctor who would come out and do a physical just like he would get, going to school. Robert looked at her like she had suggested he set his foot on fire but after a while, quietly said his "OK".

The next day the doctor came out and after the exam, called Wendy at her office.

"I think it is safe to say, you saved him from starving to death. Whatever he had been eating was not doing him much good. He has been deprived of nutrition for so long it is a wonder he is still alive. Anyone else, I would insist go directly into the hospital. For now, I will give you a list of foods which will bring him up slowly and especially juices. Also, I'll send you a prescription for antibiotics with instructions on a controlled diet for starters. There will be issues with parasites but with medicine are easily taken care of. I hope he can adjust to the regiment. As for other things like why he left home, just call me when he is ready to go to court. I will be there."

Over time, more and more conveniences were arranged and while everything was being used as instructed, Robert showed little sign of moving out of his hermit state. Food and other things would be left on the porch, unless Wendy or John and eventually Karl who had been introduced, came with the delivery. They would ask to be invited in, chat or share a hot chocolate or a pop, for a short while and say their goodbyes.

When Karl was introduced to Robert, he asked if he could call him "Bob". A bit of a nod and a whispered "OK" and from then on it was "Bob" to Karl.

There wasn't a soul at the center who hadn't heard of Robert and all understood what privacy meant. The police had stopped back and assumed Robert was still in the woods. They were just told he was safe where he was and for now shouldn't be bothered. Wendy told them, her and John were visiting him on a regular basis and for now he should be left alone as much as he needed, never divulging his move to the center. The police never asked much and knowing what the law had to offer wasn't as good as what JC's Salvage might be able to do and were content, he was not causing trouble to himself or others.

The three of them worked with Robert as much as they cold, filling him in on some schooling, helping him read and write better than he had and trying to bring him up to date on current affairs. Robert was always receptive but still not talking much and still not ready to be among a lot of people.

Months went by, Robert always cleaning up after himself and keeping to himself. They would see him out sometimes at night when the rest of the area was quiet.

One day it was reported that the breakfast food which had been left for Robert was still there at noon. John went out and finding the apartment empty and it left as someone expecting to return but no Robert. Everything was clean and put into boxes and bags, neatly stored under the cot.

When Wendy heard, all three of them went out to the wooded area where he had stayed and although it looked like someone had been there, Robert was not to be found.

A few days passed and no Robert. No great surprise as this was a common ending to these situations, with the guest, maybe showing up much later or never showing up again. Of course, they felt bad, but life goes on.

Karl and John had to go out of town on business for a day and used their time to accomplish other things needed. When they returned, they would go to the Police and tell them what had happened and once again they would hear from at least one person, "You don't have the right to keep these things from us. We have the right to know. You are not the law."

It rained the next day and both John and Karl decided to sleep in. They had arrived home from out of town in the early morning and were exhausted.

About one in the afternoon, a call came into Karl advising him to get down to the center. I can't tell you what is going on now but you need to be here. The frantic caller hung up with no more information. Karl called John and Wendy at her office, giving them what little information, he had and sped off to the center.

All three arrived at about the same time and looking out toward Robert's Hotel they could see a crowd. Their hearts sank. This could only be Bad. The first volunteer they passed on their way could only say, I'm sorry but you will have to see it for yourself.

Breaking through a crowd of volunteers, guests and staff, they found Robert. Sitting on the bench, talking with another guest and offering cookies to others. A table had been set up with a decorative yellow, paper table cloth. Paper ribbon decorated the sides of the table making it look pretty fancy. On the table was instant coffee, A pot of hot water on the little camp stove, Robert had been loaned, a container of lemonade, several boxes of cookies, some hard candies, tooth picks, Styrofoam cups, packets of sugar, creamer, hot chocolate were all in a neatly decorated cardboard box. There were donuts, some small sandwiches, and more. Cement blocks had been gathered for seating.

Above it all on the building was a hand painted sign, "No one has ever become poor by giving"

Wendy met Robert's eyes and said,

"Robert, can I talk with you?"

Sheepishly Robert walked out a way from the gathering with Wendy, John and Karl.

Sternly Wendy said,

"How did you do all of this and what is this all about? You know how we feel about stealing and how it can bring us a lot of problems."

Robert looked up at her and quietly said,

"Yes, and I know what you think. I didn't steal. I see all the nice things you do for me and Mr. Karl told me once that when you give, it makes you feel

good. I knew I needed to feel good about something so I planned this party. I have been on my own for a long time and I learned some things. I had a little money buried in the woods where I was staying so I went back and got it. Also, I looked for returnable bottles late at night when everyone else was sleeping. Some of the things I saved from the meals you brought me. I haven't drunk any coffee, hot chocolate or powdered drinks because I wanted to save it. The last couple of days I have been at the library typing out my life story because I think the police will eventually want to know why I left home. I'm not good at typing so it took a long time and at night I just stayed in doorways or alleys finding what I could to eat. I hope I didn't upset you too much but I had to do these things first."

There wasn't a lot to be said or was anyone capable of saying anything and it was the right time for a big group hug that seemed to last and last.

Once more Robert started in, still talking quietly.

"I know Mr. Karl was right because now I have friends and I feel real real good."

Robert or Bob as he was being called more these days was introduced to the main building and after a while learned the whole place. He was given chores and you could depend on him to do more than his share.

Sooner than they would have liked, the court date came around. Then more dates and more time in court, much of the testimony in the judge's chambers. There had been two older children, a boy and a girl but as near as anyone could tell, they had left home a few years before and neighbors had not heard from them.

The story came out in the paper with limited details but a horrible story just the same. JC's had been credited with the rescue and it didn't hurt to have many donations pouring in. Some with Robert's name and a trust fund was set up for him. Because of this, Robert was set pretty well, financially and the right people immediately set up private schooling and mentoring as he could handle it. Tutors would be paid to come to the center and talk with Robert, teach him as needed and if he chose, others could sit in.

When the trial wound down the judge ordered any properties be turned over to JC's as they or rather Wendy, had become Robert's guardian.

The center had received a couple of estates in the past and they were able to deal with these things rapidly and efficiently getting the most benefit from the gift.

The house was not in the best of shape but in a good neighborhood and with the skills available to the center it would be up to the best standards in less than a month.

Robert had said he would never go back into the house and asked if he could leave any of that to his friends, Wendy, John and Karl.

The three went through, boxing up anything that might be of value or reused, careful to set many things aside for disposal as not wanting to remind Robert of his pain later on down the road.

Most was left to be shipped to a recycler several miles away.

When they felt satisfied, they had done what they could, it was turned over to the center remodeling committee which was also the painting committee, cleaning committee, building committee and wore a few more hats. Pretty much, anyone who was willing to be involved was on the committee, choosing one person to decide on the best plans.

In no time at all, it was a nice house almost unrecognizable by any former visitors.

Karl had some friends looking for a place to rent as they were both working and on the road a lot. Dave and June could afford its miner upkeep, had heard the story and figured the house, in the area they needed to be in, would come up.

The rent would cover any needed expenses with legal business as well as physical repairs. All went into an investment for Robert and only withdrawn as needed for the house.

When Dave and June moved into the house it was all cleaned, painted, carpet replaced, looking and smelling much like a brand-new house.

Several months after moving in they decided to replace the carpet in one of the unused bedrooms installing something more to their liking and use the room for guests. Dave decided, on a day off, to tear up the existing carpet and in the process had discovered the original vinyl underneath. Although it was in fine shape decided it was time for it to go. Underneath that was a floor register he was sure had been missed in the cleaning. He removed the one loose screw holding it down and in the heat pipe, found a treasure trove of not only dust but, a couple small toys, papers a small book. Some small change and a picture all tied up in a box.

Karl was called immediately, coming right out and between the two, went through the contents of the box over several cups of coffee. The contents were catalogued and put back into the box, after some study. The box and as was any other things found would be put into storage, safely kept for whenever Robert was ready for it.

Karl and John didn't see each other as often or at least every day as they had in the past, keeping busy with so many things and as for Wendy, working in her own office away from JC's was seen even less.

Karl called an informal meeting as soon as the three could agree on a date, looking forward to brainstorming with his friends again. He had a guest set up a private room for them and asked for a coffee pot and some things to munch on.

Once they were together, John asked," what's up? You look serious."

Karl volunteered,

"This may well be serious and that is why I have called you two in on it. I didn't want to call sooner as I needed time to do some of my own, seat of the pants, research".

He went on to tell them about the find in the bedroom heat vent, of Robert's former home and that he needed time to see how all of this would be received by the court system or if they even cared. He had talked with the judge, not showing her any of it and she had said it would only bring more to the media and not do Robert any good. As for his parents, they were not going anywhere for a long time so it would do nothing for their position.

"We, the Judge and I have come up with some ideas that will have to be sorted and tested and that is where you two come in."

By now, they were all ears. They certainly hadn't forgot about Robert but didn't see him every day as they had, knowing he was doing well and moving up. Also, they knew they couldn't afford to have any one guest attach themselves to just a single person or group and Robert was learning to socialize quick.

Karl pulled out a well wrapped and taped box from under the table while John and Wendy looked on. Unwrapping and opening it, he slowly handed out the contents.

"Before you look at this, I have to warn you, some of ------"

"We understand Karl. Some things have to be done".

Passing the items around and trying to maintain some kind of composure, Wendy started in. "These two people in this picture with the baby could be his brother and sister. The picture has been torn, so you can guess who was torn off. I believe Robert is ready for me to approach him with some of this. At least I can ask him about the box and its hiding place and see if he would be willing to tell us anymore. I think it would be best to only show him the picture at first and if he is ready for that. I don't see his writings being of any value to him at this time as he has enough to try and move past."

Karl said,

"I was hoping you would do that and John and I will follow up with whatever we can come up with. If these are siblings and if Bob agrees, we need to work on what it will take to try and find them"

Wendy found Robert, Bob to his friends now, taking a short walk so they could have some privacy.

She told him the story and said she didn't think he needed to go over the things right now but could when or if ever he thought he should.

It was easy to see he had forgotten the treasure and for a minute thought he would cry. He stopped and said, *"just one more step moving forward like John says. I will be alright and you are probably right. I don't think I need to go over those things".*

Wendy mentioned, a picture had been in the box and was it his sister and brother?

"Oh, yea, I remember the picture well and yes, that is them."

"How would you feel about us trying to find them?" Wendy asked.

"Do you think you could ever do that and how would you do it? I would love to sister and relatives if there have a brother and are any".

By checking records at the court house, John was able to determine the length of time the family had lived in the house. Neighbors were not reliable as they had moved in much later and it was best not to include them in any of this.

John was able to find where they had moved from and with the help of some of his wife's friends living in that area found that they had only lived there a few years. The third address seemed to be a good one to use the family name without it being connected with the recent trial. They didn't want the news people to get ahold of the story and bring more grief on Robert.

Adds were placed in the local paper of the city they formally lived in, with minimum details and one of their friends, doing genealogy, posted some of the same information being careful, not to give away the circumstances.

In a meeting with Robert, Wendy told him of where they were with their investigation and told him it might take a long time if anything did come up and it might come up with some bad news.

Robert assured her; he had already thought of that but was anxious to hear anything.

One day, about two months later, Karl received a call from June.

Before she could start, Karl asked, *"How is the new house and how is the job? I suppose you called to complain about the grass or the plumbing"* laughing, knowing she would never complain and had always thanked him for the wonderful house.

"I had a visitor, Karl. He came asking how long we had lived here and wanted to know what had happened to the family who had been living here. Before I knew it, I had told him when we moved in, John, and that the family living here had gone to jail. I am so sorry. He caught me off guard and it just slipped out. He seemed to be a little surprised and quickly drove off before I could get any information. I'm not even sure I can tell you what he looks like."

"Don't take it personal." Karl said, "these things are bound to happen. It may have been something or nothing. If you hear or remember anything else, please let us know."

Later on, the next day another call came in from the police saying a man had called asking for information about Robert and his parents and of course, we couldn't tell him any more than what was in the papers. We don't even repeat that for privacy's sake. The man had hung up abruptly and they couldn't tell any more.

Two days after that a call came in from the library. Someone had called them asking about old newspapers pertaining to the incident with Robert and his parents and all they could tell him, was to come in and do the research. They would help where they could.

By now, Wendy Karl and John were frantic. Could this be a lead? They were starting to feel like real investigators and were drinking too much coffee and not sleeping a lot.

John decides it was time to take this a little further. With Robert's understanding and approval, a ragged search party was assembled. With what information they could muster, a poor description, Roberts last name and not much more, street people were enlisted. Encouraged to say little but just watch and ask only a few questions, off they went. Volunteers became involved and of course Wendy, Karl and John along with their families got involved. A day passed, two days passed and in the middle of the third day, one of the guests, Billy K, came to the center, moving much faster than usual.

"I got to see John, I got to see John."

John happened to be in an early morning meeting but when he was told of the message, he said he would have to leave for at least a couple of minutes. If a guest was frantic and this one, Billy K didn't get frantic very often it could mean something he needed to hear.

"You know I drink wine Johnny and you know I drink too much some time. You know I don't have a lot of money but I'm not dumb. It's hard for me to get money for wine. People won't give money to a drunk"

"Please, Billy K, can you get to the story. I have a meeting I just left and a lot of people are waiting for me."

"Well, a few years ago, I discovered that sometimes people don't finish their wine and throw away, almost full bottles".

By now, John was having a hard time holding on.

"I found out that they throw almost full bottles, in the dumpster in the back of the hotel down town. I don't tell anyone else because than the owner would stop me from going there. It's kind of my own secret. I get there long before daylight."

Billy, John Protested, "I need to go"

Billy K pulled out a crumpled and dirty envelope and handed it to John.

"I found this in the dumpster".

John looked at the envelope that was sent from some place out west. Opening it, found it empty "what am I supposed to do with this?"

Quietly and almost spiritually Billy said,

"Look at the address"

John said, "I did, it's from",,,,,,, smoothing out the envelope and reading the name of the person it was addressed to, he couldn't believe his eyes.

It was Roberts last name and not a common name to be taken lightly at this point.

"Which hotel? and go inside and tell the staff to call Wendy and John. Give them the same information you gave me just don't take so long doing it. I love you Billy K, you son of a gun. You and I need to talk more. You did a great thing but I need to go and see if this guy is still there."

"The big hotel down town, next to the city bank and don't worry John. I took care of that." Billy said. *"He will still be there".*

John didn't even want to think of what that meant as he ran to his car.

As he pulled up to the hotel, he noticed a couple of his guests standing around. As he looked further, he could see homeless people everywhere. In front of stores, leaning against poles, sitting on benches and in the parking lot.

One of the regular people who lived at JC's came up to John.

"When Billy K told us to watch to see if this guy left, we just passed the word. I have been here for an hour and more of our friends keep showing up. I think we got people from other counties."

John went inside and knowing Jimmy, the manager, asked about the name.

"You know I can get in trouble for this, but I remember when you guys helped me out so here is the number of the room, he is in."

Thanking him, John ran up the stairs to the room. When the man came to the door, John introduced himself and quickly spilled out enough of the story to make his point.

"Wow"

the man commented *"I think we may have a lot to talk about. Please come in."*

It didn't take long for John to be convinced that this was the right guy. Not only did he look like Roberg, same hair and color, same eyes, older but seemed to have some of the same characteristics. He asked if he could use the room phone.

Calling Jimmy, the manager, he told him to get ahold of one of the street people; "tell them there is going to be a big party at JC's tonight and it is starting now. All the pizza they can eat and anything else we can muster up. You know the routine. Call all the other people to get this thing rolling."

He hung up the phone and said to Marcus, "for now all you need to know about that, you will learn in time."

He sat there with Marcus and as much as they went on, had no doubts this was the missing brother.

Marcus told John about Evangeline his sister and said the two were in constant contact. Both had gone through extensive therapy and now, had healthy families. They had wondered and worried about Bobby and even if they knew of where their parents had moved would be afraid of what might happen to Bobby if they tried to contact him. They had not heard of anything at the time of the trial and might not have thought it related if they had read it, as it was so far away.

When Eva seen the information on a genealogy sight, they got excited but apprehensive. Mark decided to go and do what he could, to find out if they were related to this Robert but by now really wasn't sure where to go next.

He paused long enough to call Evangeline and through tears, said she would be there as soon as she could.

Mark gave the phone number of the hotel and the name and said she would be able to contact him as soon as needed. John interrupted the conversation and insisted on her having Wendy's number.

"When can I see him, and can we go there now?" Mark asked.

"This is the kind of thing I need to go over with Wendy, Robert's psychiatrist and councilor. But I am sure it won't be too many days." John said.

They talked a little longer and a knock came at the door.

Opening the door, Wendy charged in. Grabbing Mark, she gave him the biggest hug she could.

"I'm guessing you are the brother and You have no idea, what this means to so many people who have worked so hard. I hope you are not too busy for the next few days because it will take at least that long for all of us to get acquainted."

John jumped in, *"Mark was asking how soon he could see Robert, and I told him …."* *"Well let's go"* Wendy interrupted, *"I have already talked to*

Robb, Robert, Bobby, well I have already talked to him and he is ready. My diagnosis is this is something he has needed for a long time."

Mark asked if they were sure, it was safe to go out this early. He had been intending to go out for an early breakfast someplace and found a lot of unsavory looking people just standing around looking in his direction.

"Fear not," John said, *"those are the Merry men of Sherwood. As long as they are around you are safe."* Chuckling to himself as Wendy gave him that, *"I can't believe you just made that up,"* look.

Down the steps, John pausing to whisper something to Jimmy at the front desk. Then, out to the car and down the street to JC's. All along the way people were walking, some in twos and some alone. They seemed to know Johnny's old car and they all waved.

When they got to JC's it was a buzz with, things going on. A fire was going in the large fire pit. Seats of every kind were being brought up to the pit. Music was coming from at least three radios and a pizza wagon was dropping off pizza.

As the driver was leaving, he stopped.

"Pretty early in the day for pizza John but when Jimmy called me at home. I figured it was important. Besides we like the business. I will be back with the next load pretty shortly and you will have to tell me when to stop."

Robert was there waiting at the door of the main building and when the two met the whole place seemed to stop and just watch. Not too many words were exchanged as that would take a bit.

John told Markus, *"When something important happens, we usually include a trip to the chapel"*

Both Marcus and Robert were in agreement and off they went hand in hand shoulder to shoulder, Robert pointing the way.

John went back to the meeting room and was greeted with, *"don't even think of apologizing. When we heard of what was going on, we were glad you went and when we heard it worked out to be the right person, we just sat here feeling like someone had just won the lottery."*

"Thank you, I don't think I deserve such patience and someone **has** won the lottery or something greater, but for now, let us get to business so you people can get to what you need to do."

The meeting finished taking less time than usual to come up with final decisions and exchange information. Out on the yard people were moving around talking and enjoying the day. Markus was being introduced to everyone by Robert. Wendy was there talking with among others, the Judge who had postponed court, after hearing the news. The police were there talking with the people and assuring them this was a friendly visit. They had seen an exceptionally large group of street people down town and were curious of the reason.

Later in the day, a small private jet flew over and seemed to be lower than usual, heading toward the new airport about thirty miles out. Sometime after that, A helicopter flew over coming from the direction of the airport. A large cardboard sign was dropped, almost landing in the fire. One of the guests brought it to John.

It had a shoe tied to it and *"I love you Brother"*, had been written with purple nail polish. In smaller writing, *"please pick us up at the hospital heliport"*.

John showed the sign to Marcus and Mark said,

"I think I know what this is all about. For now, we need to get to the hospital and pick her up."

Wendy heard the conversation and asked if she couldn't go alone with Robert and a driver. The hospital was less than three miles away and they would be back shortly.

Seeing John was still puzzled over the whole thing Mark explained, *Eve's husband was a businessman owning more than one place. His work and contacts had him flying all over. He probably was in the private jet that flew over earlier. When he got to the airport, he would have called ahead for a helicopter to bring him closer and sooner. The hospital must have given the pilot clearance to use their heliport to land for a few minutes.*

When Wendy returned with Eve, she confirmed Mark's guesses. Eve had called Her husband and there had been a kind of plan, discussed for years, hoping that one day Robert would show up somewhere. Almost immediately they were in the air, leaving instructions for their children. They had called a close uncle. He would help the children, find a place for the pets, make as many contacts as they could and help them to get to their flight on time, arriving late the next day.

The party lasted for three more days, with the children as well as other relations showing up. Wendy, Karl and John's family naturally got involved, and there were outings, things to see and so many stories.

Meeting so many of the people at JC's gave them a whole new perspective on the word marginalized and they all felt it was a tremendous lesson for the children.

A trip to the woods, sitting on a log, with hot chocolate and donuts shared, at the place Robert had stayed.

The Shed/hotel Robert had stayed in was admired and photographed. With the children's insisting and Mark's agreeing, July Prater agreed to send a blue print as well as material list to replicate the Hotel/shed which would be used for a play house.

They had all talked together and Robert would go back home with them. It would be good for him to get away from the area, at least for a while and if he ever needed, a phone call would bring him back. Wendy felt sure he was ready and John and Karl were sure he would be a great help around two homes with parents who were away so much.

He had developed many skills, in the short time with them at JC's and had the desire as well as ambition to go a long way.

Eve's husband commented, I know he has missed a lot and it will be a while for him to be where he should be scholastically but I can't help but see how he is way ahead of us in his attitude and demeaner. We are going to get more out of this than we can ever return. We can't thank you enough for,,,,, well, salvaging Bobby.

Just before leaving they made a trip to the little outdoor chapel. Marcus took out his wallet, removing several bills and started to put them in the empty jar. Robert stopped him and said,

"No, I have already put enough in that jar for all of us".

"But it's empty" Mark said. Robert just looked at him and smiled.

"It sure is, and I want it to stay that way. I will tell you all about it later".

CHAPTER 3
George Remembers

He remembered being chided by his parents for his coming home late, the condition he was in and later that day overhearing them laughing with friends and talking about how drunk he had been.

"Junior did manage to make it to the bathroom!" From his mother.

"Oh, don't be too hard on him, I remember you, talking about spending some time in that cool oasis yourself, with the white ceramic wishing well". They all laughed.

"And I was wishing I could die" From his father. Another uproarious laugh.

His parents had tolerated a lot when he was young. It seemed to have started somewhere so far back. Someone found a half empty bottle of whiskey. Another time a few cans of beer from a parent's party when no one was looking or counting or maybe not even caring. Long before he got to high school, he had been impressing his friends with his drinking stories. In high school he carried on the same and by that time had a tolerance for alcohol that amazed the best. He was invited to all the crazy parties or just crashed them. Smart enough to get through high school even if it meant finding someone to cheat for him. College was the same and there always seemed to be someone to overlook the drunkenness, pills and drugs. *"He was such a great sport".*

A decent job out of college and so it went. He had not married although he had a number of chances and always the wrong one. Georgie Lyle just couldn't see himself tied down. After a number of missing clients because of his drinking, his boss came to him and said, "we are running a business here. You are going to have to make a decision. Either you give up the drinking or we have to let you go." His boss told him that they needed him and would do anything they could. He was a great asset to their business but the drinking was causing problems. It was obvious to everyone, George had a problem and needed to get help.

That worked for a little while and he actually slowed down but soon one more and one more and he was right back in the same boat.

One day George just didn't go in to work. Didn't call or talk to anyone. Slept late, went out and bought a bottle and tried to forget it all.

From there it didn't take long. A quick exit without giving a forward address, no rent money, no place he was appointed to go but just slide off to anonymity. Someone, he had told he was out of work, in a bar, bought him a drink and was telling him about jobs in South Carolina. "As it turns out, I have a friend who is going there tomorrow. He drives his own truck and is always glad to have a passenger".

A night in a shelter with an early coffee, grabbing an apple to disguise the licker smell before they sent him on his way, he was off to meet his chauffeur. Pleasant enough ride sleeping a bit or faking sleep to avoid too much conversation George was now in a warmer part of the country. Taking his drivers name and address, thanked him and promised to stay in touch.

South Carolina turned out to be just like so many other places with all the suckers and do-gooders offering everything from shoes, blankets, clothes and money. He was given personal hygiene products and pain pills for his reported wounds he had received in the war. If George wasn't anything else, he was a good talker and a great, straight-faced liar.

One of the gimmicks he had learned early was to carry a small tattered journal and ask people, who had offered him things, for their names and addresses, so he could thank them. That always got him even more.

He would only stay a short time in one city or town depending on size. Even though he was drinking most of the day and night, he would try to stay with a kind of plan. Try not to appear drunk when panhandling, and stay as clean as possible. Staying clean was easy, changing clothes every time he visited a place, "This poor guy has been through a lot. Let's help him out!" He could get clean clothes and that was everywhere. Rarely would anyone question his stories and if they did, he would just move on to the next place and he would be given a whole new wardrobe or at least enough to last a few days of sleeping out of doors. Shelters, thrift stores, churches, organizations, and just gullible people seemed to all be ready, like fall apples to be picked. Even better, he wasn't doing anything illegal.

On a cooler day he was walking in the country. He had just left a city where he had done well for a couple of weeks but felt it might be a good time to move on before someone figured him out or maybe made trouble down the road. He chose a small gravel road from a map at the library. Poking along, occasionally taking a sip from the bottle in the coat he was carrying and talking to the frogs, snakes, and all the other moving things, his eyes hit on but then, on the very edge of the road, just where the grass was covering some of the gravel, he noticed something leather. So much junk on the roads these days, he thought as he passed by, but then about twenty feet further he thought, *"What if?"* I am not exactly late for anything and he walked back. Almost missed it coming from the other direction. Pulling it out of the tangled weeds, making it obvious it had been there for several days if not weeks. It was a woman's wallet.

Opening it he found it had several green bills and they were not all singles. Looking around he tried to think. Normally the thing to do is grab the cash and get rid of the rest quick. All the "what if's" started coming to mind again stuffing it in with the whiskey bottle, it could wait until he knew he was away or hidden from anyone coming by.

A couple more miles down the road, he was getting a little hungry and seeing a little shack of a house decided to check it out. Ditching the bottle and wallet in a low spot under some brush he went and looked around the house. No car in the drive and no phone line running to the house but they probably had a cell phone. He walked up the lane to a little porch and a door that looked as worn as the rest of the place, knocking lightly on the door. A woman probably in her late twenties came to the door. George told her his story.

"Stopped to ask if I could get a drink of water from your hose if you have one. Someone ran me off the road, beat me up and stole all I had. I was headed to some relations about ten more miles down the road and I intended to surprise them. You see they didn't know I ever got out of the POW camp" he lied.

"Yall just come on in. Got some iced tea in the fridge and yall sure welcome to that."

She sat him down in a broken but clean old chair and a clean quart fruit jar with Iced tea. The jar rattled from the ice when she had brought it and normally George JR. wouldn't be caught near a drop of Iced tea but this was hard to resist. It went down surprisingly easy as he sat there checking his surroundings. Pretty easy to see this person was poor or at least doing a good job of making it look that way. Sparse is hardly a word for what he was seeing, yet it was apparent she was and had been living here for some time.

While he was lost in his imagination, she had put together some food for him.

"I'm sorry this is all I can give you right now, and I must ask you to move on. My two children will be getting off the bus in a while and they don't see a lot of people often, not to mention what the bus driver will have to say."

Startled he just said *"yes mam, you shouldn't have done that. I'll do alright"* and he almost felt guilty and wanted to tell the truth, that he was just another drunken panhandler. Instead, he realized he had to rush out before being seen so he just left giving her one more weak, *"thank you"*. Retrieving the lunch and down the road a way's and out of sight of the house he had just left, he moved sideways into the brush and a wooded area. There he found a place clear and dry to sit back against a tree and relax. He opened the brown wrinkled bag she had given him and found two sandwiches wrapped very neatly in clear wrap and with a couple sheets of paper towel. There were two homemade oatmeal cookies and an apple. Along with the food was a note.

"Thank you for being my opportunity to give. There are not enough of them."

He ate one of the sandwiches and it was still in his hand when he fell asleep. He felt like he had slept for many hours when something woke him. Slowly opening his eyes, he seen a long-tailed weasel eating the remains of the sandwich he had been eating. For a while he watched the little guy through partially opened eyes. When the weasel started for the bag, he shoved him off, the weasel gone like a bullet. As soon as he had chased the weasel away, he realized what he had done and wanted to cry.

This poor woman, whoever she was took him in, gave him food and drink and sent him away better off and even thanked him for letting her serve him. He just shooed off one of the few creatures who would come around him, for the sake of a few crumbs he didn't even need.

He sat there holding himself saying "God help me, God help me, God help me." It might have been timing, exhaustion, hunger, some reaction to the location of the stars. Repeating over and over "God help me" eventually he fell back to sleep. When he woke it was late. A bright moon was up and that was good. He could see that the weasel or someone else had finished off the rest of the lunch and he wished he had taken better care but then he remembered the little guy he had chased off. Laughing to himself he whispered, *"Thank you for the opportunity to give. There are not enough of them."*

Getting up, the stars were out bright, he backtracked down the road to where he had hidden the wallet and his bottle. Picking them up he quietly and carefully headed in the direction of the little house.

When he got to the house, he set the wallet on the edge of the porch where he was pretty sure it would be seen. "Who knows, he thought. She might be able to buy some food or whatever she needs for a few days and what good was it going to do him.

Without thinking any more about it he hurried off and down the road, walking the rest of the night, slipping back into the woods in the daylight for a little more sleep and then back down the road. Sometime just before noon he came to a small town. Having a little money in his pocket decided to hit the grocery store for whatever he could get with his bit of change. He had only been in the store for ten minutes or so, when someone approached him. Quickly George said, *"hay, if I'm a problem I will leave".*

"No, no I'm the manager and I need something. You look a little hungry and I need someone to help unload a truck for me. You can eat while you are working and as much as you want".

George knew he could eat quite a little and what cash he had wasn't going to buy enough to bother.

"Sure, let's give it a try"

While he was working, Fred the manager helped when he wasn't called away for some other duty. George started in slowly but seemed to pick up steam as time went along. The work became methodic and a kind of rhythm made it go along pretty fast.

The manager brought him sandwiches from the deli. Hot coffee and plenty of iced tea. Fruit and vegetables if he wanted. Pieces of pie. He was encouraged to take a lot of brakes and at least an hour lunch. A table and chair had been set up outside the truck and the table was loaded with food for him to devour.

This was a very large truck and the unloading lasted into the dark hours. Fred explained that he generally used the fork lift from the hardware store. Basically, the town fork lift and it was out of order and the trucker couldn't wait for another day.

When they were done unpacking, sorting and shelving some of the product, Fred thanked George although he never knew or asked his name. Fred told George that if he hadn't come along, he would have to send the product back even after he paid for it and most likely it would be dumped. "I tell you friend, that would have been a lot of money out of my pocket. I am also the owner. He went up to one of the cash drawers and pulled out what looked like a great deal of money. *"This is not near enough to pay you for what you have saved me, I want you to"* "Stop right there. The deal was I would eat my wages. If you feel the need to part with some of that, there is a small house about twelve miles out the road where a poor young lady lives. She has at least two children and I believe she could use some of that."*

"I know the place and didn't resize anyone lived their full time. I will check it out myself and do whatever I can, but you need to be paid" Fred said.

George came back with, *"OK, while you are crunching the numbers, I am going to use your john if it is all right."*

"Don't be too long, Misses Fred thinks I love this place more than her"

George Lyle JR went back to the bathroom but instead of going in he just slipped out the back door, filling his pockets with some of the food they had left next to the truck. Outside he managed to vanish into the shadows and being a small town made it easy to be gone and down the road quickly.

Once more, back on the road and carrying the same bottle, realizing he hadn't had a drink in many hours. What was going on? He seemed to feel,,, he seemed to feel,,,,.

For several more days he moved along, picking food out of store trash dumpsters at night and exchanging clothes in thrift stores, who were willing to listen to his stories and outfit him for free. Sometimes shoes were a problem but he would take them and if they were too big, fill them with newspaper or weeds to make them fit. An extra pair of sox stuffed in the toe would work at times. After a while he got rid of the bottle. He hadn't taken a drink since the little old house and the sandwich lady.

In one of the thrift stores he visited, there was a speaker talking about AA meetings and although he had known they were not for him, decided to go and see just for fun. Not that he remembered anything about fun. While he was at the meeting, he heard from one of the other guests about a place up north called JC's Salvage and how they had a loose program that you could go and just cool off. Sleep all day, get drunk or get busy. You were given what was needed but you had to make the choices. Stay there for ten years or ten days and do pretty much as you pleased. Just stay out of trouble with the law and don't bother those who were trying to move up.

George heard it but like so many things we hear it takes time to get to that part of the brain that really analyzes it.

It was at least a couple of months before George decided this might be a chance for him. He had stayed away from drinking, Went through the withdrawals by himself in the woods. Stayed sick for weeks but was on some kind of mend.

What about this place called JC Salvage? He had looked it up at the library and found a few comments about it on line. It sure didn't sound like heaven and no one was promising gold streets but, but,,, there was that feeling again. George had been stopping in churches once in a while. Not so much for a service but just to sit in the back, alone and think.

One day a young priest came in the back door. The church was not lit really well but enough for him to see George. Coming over he welcomed George and said, *"I am father Mat and if you ever need anything I am here."*

They shook hands and Father Mat walked up toward the front.

"Wait"

George hollered as it echoed around the empty Church. Then, a little more quietly *"I mean,,,,,,,, Yes I want to,,, Can I have a word with you?"*

Father Mat said

"Of course, and if you don't mind, we could go off to the side up front, where it won't sound like we are in a concert hall".

George met Father Mathew half way up the isle and together they strolled the rest of the way to the side, exchanging just a little information.

George was surprised to be able to talk so freely and at the same time not be asked a lot of questions. On the other hand, both he and Father Mat would understand that Father Mat would know most of his story without George telling it. He asked Father about JC's Salvage, with father Mat saying he had heard just a very little about the place but would check into it for George if he would like. George agreed to get back to him and they parted.

Every day after that George found himself in the same place in the same church. For two weeks no one showed up other than a couple of older ladies lighting candles, staying a bit to pray and leaving. George was lost. What to do now? Just some crazy idea of this pie in the sky shelter. About now a guy could use a bottle. Leaving the church, he notices a sign "Office" with an arrow, pointing to a small building on the side. He thought about it and thought what's the use, and walked away. Then he remembered going back for the little hint of leather that turned out to be a wallet with money. Turning around he marched back to the office and as he was going up the stairs a woman was just locking up.

"Can I help you?

"Oh, I was just looking for Father Mathew and"

"I'm sorry but Father Mathew is gone".

Like a hammer in the stomach, he wanted to run but could hardly breath.

He had made a connection and it had taken all he could do to open up to someone. How dumb could he be? The world is not some place for dreamers. It is all about survival. Get what you can, get drunk if that helps and move on. No one cares and no one wants to care. The world is just one dark dark fog with vicious creatures lurking everywhere. Fight them off when you can and get high so you don't have to think about them the rest of the time.

"He'll be back in less than an hour."

George woke from his thoughts.

"What", I mean "What did you say"

"Father Mathew, he has prison ministry every day at this time and he will be back shortly. He loves working with the prisoners and never misses a day. I can let you in to the waiting room if you like".

"Does he come in this way? I can just wait on the steps."

By now he was shaking and just needed to sit. She moved away saying, *"it shouldn't be long. He is only allowed to stay during a certain time."*

George had his head down when a slight touch on his shoulder startled him. Jumping up

"Father Mat,, I thought,, I've been here I,,, I."

Looking at him Father asked if he had time to come in and have a coffee.

Unlocking the door, both went in to an already made pot of coffee and some fresh rolls.

"Cream or sugar?"

"Black will be fine"

and slowly George got out, what had happened and that he had been here every day waiting in the same place at the back of the church.

Father Mathew sat down, sipping his coffee and it seemed he waited a long time before he spoke.

"My dear friend., Some might find this almost funny. For me and for you, it is far more serious. I don't know if it is good serious or bad serious but I believe it is up to you and please give me time to explain. OH, and by all means take one or two of those rolls, they are not near as good stale. One of the church lady's makes them."

"As you may have been told,"

he continued on,

"I have a prison ministry. Because of all the prison rules, bureaucracy, and selfish non-caring people I can only go to the prison during certain hours. I can only have small groups in the chapel and so I go every day and still don't get to see all that want to be seen. I have talked and fought for more and better times but so far to no avail. I have proved that security is not an issue. They have cameras and extra guards as well as plenty of locked gates and doors.

"I don't know why I am telling you this but the day, I met you in church was a rare day. A main water pipe had broken and with all the repair people coming and going, the warden had ordered all the prisoners to be kept in their cells and I was turned away. That is the only reason I was here that time of day. If you hadn't come to the office, today, if you hadn't met my secretary, Janet, if you hadn't stayed, you would never have known that. Now, you can make a big thing or a small thing out of that. To me those are smaller miracles and I just sort of save them in my memory."

"One more thing. Don't think I didn't look for you every day, never dreaming you would be at the church early. Had I thought of that, I would have put a large sigh on the back seat asking for the loud guy to come and see me in my office later."

He laughed and asked George if he could give him a hug. George got up and as this was something, he had not done in a long time gave Father a rather uncomfortable hug.

"Good, the hugs will get better with time" father said.

Father Mat told George that he had checked and even called JC's Salvage and from what he could glean it would be a great place for George to start to reclaim his life. They had told father that they would have some kind of work for him if he wanted and it wouldn't pay a lot but would help pay back for food and whatever services he used, while building a small nest egg.

I have hardly gotten to know you but will hate to see you leave and by the way, we have a spare room with a shared shower you are welcome to use until and if you decide to go north. You would be expected to do your own laundry including bedding and we have laundry machines. It is simple but it is what works for me. Breakfast is at 6am and you are welcome to come. There will be a knock at the door but only once. If you don't respond you are out of luck.

How could George refuse? He was up for anything. It was like his brain was disconnected and he was on a leash. Everything was coming at him and he hardly had to make a decision. Was this good or bad. Some kind of trickery? Going went to the room that had been pointed out and found it the smallest room he had ever stayed in. It had a simple bed, small writing table and a lamp. That was about all. Almost immediately he went to the shower and there hung a kind of heavy robe you pull on over your head complete with a hood. A note said, *"tonight you can be a fifteenth century Monk. Wear it until you have laundered your clothes."*

The shower was great and he felt like maybe he had stayed too long. Watching the dirt and grime go down the drain he wondered how long he could stay clean. Clean inside as well as out and would he be pulled back to his old ways? This was fairly easy now, when you were being treated so well but what about tomorrow and next week and next year. He had been out long enough to see a lot and knew it wouldn't be easy. How many had he seen fall back. What made him think he was any better? Somewhere bells were ringing. Father Mat had told him that bells would be ringing for various things but he hadn't caught any of that. Well, it brought him out of his depressing thoughts, so that was good.

Back in his room he found a small plate with a sandwich a large beautiful apple and a beautiful engraved and steaming tea pot. He poured the black tea in the provided matching cup, sipping and savoring the cut pieces of sandwiches. Setting the cup down he settled back on the hard bed. All of a sudden, he heard a single knock on the door and the lights came on.

What the????

He didn't remember turning the lights off. He didn't remember falling asleep. He was sure he would find a tooth brush and tooth paste in the shared bath but, oh well. Off he went in his Monks robe and sure enough tooth brush and paste he badly needed. A little handmade map of the layout of the building and where breakfast was being served. He was ready for some food and off he went, finding the breakfast room and Father Mathew with another priest. Looking up they greeted George and the other priest started laughing out of control.

Looking at George he said

"I'm so sorry but I Just couldn't hold it in. That robe fits you a lot better than it fit Mat here when we were doing the children's play"

George looked at Father Mat and realized on him it almost hit the floor and Father Mathew was at least a foot shorter. Recognizing the fun, he responded with, *I'm too new here to say much but at some other time I might have just as much trouble keeping it in. I'll bet the floor was kept clean"*

Father Mat pretending to be put off by the remarks said,

"What say we thank the lord for this meal and while we are at it thank him that I had something to cover this giant."

Another laugh and prayers were said. More prayers than George had ever heard at a meal but for some reason comforting and welcome like something he would like to have said.

The meal was porridge or oatmeal as he had always called it with fruit on the table. The expected pot of tea and that was all. They ate quietly and shortly the two priests excused themselves and disappeared.

George found the laundry with the hand drawn map and found reading material while doing his wash. Out the back was a small enclosed garden and carrying a book with him, found solace in just being here. Somewhere around noon, the secretary found him and said,

"There is a lunch prepared for you in the dining room."

And off she went before he could say thank you or no thank you or anything.

Once again in the dining room was a sandwich of some kind of meat minced and a cheese he had never tasted before but good. Some fresh vegetables were cut to a handy small size and of course the tea pot.

Later when supper time came the food was a little heavier and a bit more filling. The prayers were longer and conversation went on for more than an hour after, while enjoying tea and some special homemade cookies. George would find out that the people of the church were responsible for all the great food and wanted to bring in more but were asked to hold off as the priests wouldn't throw out the left overs and couldn't afford to put on the weight.

One day father Mat said,

"They would have us eating pizza, lasagna, and spaghetti every night and a full breakfast every morning. We love them and we also love how they cook but wearing it is difficult"

This style of living, went on for several days and one day Father Mathew came to him.

"I have a ride for you if you want it. You will be taken a good part of the way and I feel sure, between the Lord and you; the rest will be easy."

George knew this would not be easy. The day had been decided and one day before breakfast a note came under the door,

"Your ride will be out front in thirty-five minutes. We will not be saying good bye but only know we pray you do well and would love to see you again. God's speed"

it was signed Your brothers in Crist, Father Mathew and Father Terrence.

George tucked the note in his pocket. That would be the only thing he would have to remember them by.

Out the front door was a large delivery truck. The man at the wheel looked like he was anxious to be moving along and as George had his journal in his pocket but didn't have anything to carry or pack. It was easy.

"My name's Cal and Father M says you usually wear a Monks robe but you are going In-cog-ni-to today. You church people sure don't carry much when you travel."

George just laughed saying, he had plenty where he was going. The ride went well talking about farms and farm animals, Cals family and how lucky he was to have all his grandchildren healthy. They talked about a lot of things but never got into what George did or why he was on the road. George could only imagine what Father Mat had told him.

The rocking and noises of the road soon had George sleeping and other than a stop for lunch found them moving along very well.

When they arrived at the place where they had to part Cal said,

"Let me get your bag."

Out from behind the seat he pulled a small bag. Handed it to George, said his goodbyes and pulled away, leaving George in the middle of nowhere. None of this had been rehearsed so George could only just go along.

He had a pretty good idea what he would find in the small travel bag. Opening the bag, he found a lunch, two apples and sandwiches, a few cookies and of course the brown monk's robe. An envelope with Father Mathew's address and a note,

"My prayers will go for the happy monk; I believe your future to be full of love and caring".

Nothing more said but in the envelope was a cross and chain.

George put the chain on and it made him feel a little better. Up the road was a small store and gas station. He still had a little money and could at least buy a candy bar. He was surprised to find this small place open this late but walked in. Much to his surprise, the store owner called him by name."

You George? Got yer ticket right her, bus-el be long shortly. Guy called, said you'd have a cup a tae"

George sat there at a tiny little table eating a sandwich with a wonderful cup of tea.

"Hant many folks dink da tea naw-days. Wife makes it an says hant but one way ta makes it".

"Well, I think it is about the best tea I ever had" George said. *"Please be sure and thank her."*

"Oh, Hant nutin, She makes it fer all the bus riden folks. Says it's her way a passin long some love".

George asked the man for his address and was given a handmade business card. About that time, the bus pulled up and blew the horn. George grabbed his bag, the store owner handed him a warm Styrofoam cup with a sip lid and he was off. As he was leaving the store, he noticed a cross above the door and a sigh,

"Pass along the love, where ever you go".

He looked back at the store owner and pointed to the sign,
"I will, I promise I will".
On the bus he sipped the warm tea and ate the other sandwich from his bag. This had been a long day and he put his head back, thinking it might be a long night.

The bus driver woke George up saying *"this is your stop sir".* Shaking his head to wake up and climbing out of his seat, asked the driver,
"Have you ever heard of JC's salvage?
"Straight down that road and a little to the east. You'll see the old radio antenna. Used to be an airport. It's about twelve miles from here, just outside of town. Tell em Hank the bus driver said hi. There's a phone in the gas station if you want to call a taxi."

George grabbed his bag and climbed down out of the bus to a pretty chilly night that he wasn't dressed for. He had no intention of calling a cab, even if he had the money and the walk would warm him. By now it was ten o'clock at night and he felt like he was in good shape. Off he went in the direction of JC's, just putting down one mile after the other. After a while his long day and little food started to ware on him. He felt himself slowing down and pretty soon he just wanted to stop. He staggered a bit on the dark road as a car drove by and blew their horn.

"Hay, where you goin man. You crazy man? You gona get runed over man."

A voice from off by the woods, as three rough looking young men approached him.

"I'm sorry but I don't have much of anything" George said.

"Hay, it ain like that man, Rico, this man's walkin in da streets man. Hes gona get runed over. We gots ta help him man."

George told them he was just going down the road about eight or ten more miles but just needed to get a little rest and he would be all right.

They told him they had a place in the woods a ways off the road, and he was welcome to join them. They were just going down the road like him and stopped but figured it was best to be somewhere out of the way, where people wouldn't think they were trouble makers.

Against his better judgement, George followed them, quite a way back into this thick wood. He was so cold and so tired he felt this was his only choice. Stopping after a little way, George pulled out the robe from his bag. It was easy to throw over himself and it made him much warmer. A little further on, they came to a clearing. A small fire burned and two other men sat there poking the fire and heating something on a rock.

"Hay you guys, we found this gringo trying to get runed over on da road." The other two fell to their knees and said, *"un sacerdote"*. The three who had been in front of him when he put the robe on. turned around and with wide open eyes, *"lo lamentamos mucho, we did not know, lo lamentamos mucho padre"*

George was puzzled for just a minute and then, maybe because he was tired or maybe because it was the right time, started laughing, he laughed and laughed and when he could he explained to them where and how he received the robe, they all laughed some more. Even after the explanation they seemed to have a great deal of respect for him. They were making tortillas on the fire and offered a couple to George which he devoured quickly along with several gulps of warm coffee from a shared cup. They talked a bit and realizing he was tired, together they made him a place to sleep gathering and walking down some weeds. He was amazed at how handy they were and working together could accomplish so much.

He laid down is this weed cocoon. they had made for him and was asleep in no time.

When he awoke in the morning it must have been pretty late. He looked over and there was some kind of small animal roasting on a stick. When they realized he was awake they pushed the community cup to him with steaming coffee. Sitting up he grabbed the cup and it felt so good to feel the warmth in his hands. Sharp sticks were tearing off small strips of meet from the roasting animal and George was given a piece. He remembered himself many years before, sitting in a fancy restaurant drinking wine and eating prime rib. He thought that prime rib, couldn't have tasted near a good as this.

When breakfast was over, they cleaned up. He marveled at, how efficient they were and when they left to walk out to the road one could hardly tell that anyone had been there.

One of the Mexicans had a bow over his shoulder and some arrows or at least sharp sticks tied up in long grass. When George inquired, he was told, *desayuno, breakfast.*

They were only on the road for a short time when a slow-moving van pulled in front of them. A middle-aged man jumped out and asked, with a laughing, giggling voice.

Is one of you George? And more laughing. "Hi, I'm Tom Sparrow, when they called and told us you were coming, I had no idea you would be so easy to spot. That robe does you well, but you might want to take some of the weeds off of it. Makes you look like a woolly mammoth," and he laughed some more. George didn't want to leave his new-found friends but this was the time. No one plans these things but he had to go with this man who obviously was alerted to his coming.

"I hate to leave you guys and I sure wish, well what can I say. You guys probably saved my life".

"We understand parting. You go and maybe someday. We are off to see Jesus Salver and he will take good care of us. He is a good man. Confiamos en Dios"

George jumped in the van and waved as they pulled away. It was hard to relax thinking of leaving his new friends. All of a sudden, a thought came.

"Stop the car, stop the car."

Tom was more than a little startled but pulled over.

"Would you please go back. I need to talk to my friends".

As soon as Tom got back to where the five Mexicans were George jumped out. *"Where did you say you were going"* One of them pulled out a worn and wrinkled paper. It was a tattered business card and on it he could just make out JC's Salvage.

JC's Salvage George said.

"Yes" Miguel said "Jesus Salvar".

"We are all going to the same place, George said, *and if Tom won't let us all in, we will walk the rest of the way."* There was a big group hug laughing and dancing, Tom saying he would make room no matter if someone had to ride on the roof.

In they piled, a little snug but inn. Tom got on his cell phone and called the office. *"I'm bringing in Friar Tuck, Robin Hood, and a bunch of merry men. Do what you can to ready some showers and enough hot food for six men who are used to living in the woods. We don't want them to ransack the castle".*

With that he hung up and they all laughed.

When they pulled into JC's some of the guests as well some employees were waiting. Cameras were snapping pictures and the group was more than glad to play out some pretty corny but laughable pictures.

All were brought in without formal introductions which was always left to the individuals. Quickly they became acclimated with the surroundings and they became an Iatrical part of JC's.

Stories were told about their travels and all the miracles that contributed to their safe arrival at JC's Salvage.

George found it easy to work toward getting the good part of his old life back. Prayer, hard work, and good friends to share with and work for.

Miguel and his friends found many things they could do around JC's. John had heard from a friend at a shelter in San Antonio, about five young men who did landscaping around their shelter. Their shelter was very crowded and hoped maybe JC's would have some work for them, until they could work into the community. John knew they would be a big help to JC's fledgling landscaping business and so they were.

Bendicipon de Dios para todos

CHAPTER 4
What's in a gift?

When George Lyle showed up at JC's Salvage, he had a lot to think about. He had been a drinker and a user from the time he was in grade school. Managing to stay within most of society's standards, he had made it all the way through college. He had found a great job and was well-liked. Always the life of the party, there was very little to slow down his desire for more of whatever it was going to take to make him happy. He was very good at his work but after a while showing up late or not showing up at all, and a number of warnings about his job, he just quit going to work, soon thereafter finding himself on the street. Being on the street, does not take very long to learn what it is going to take to survive. Survival means number one, supplying the addiction by using people or whatever means available. Food and shelter were secondary and those needs, were much easier to satisfy. Cardboard boxes, a warm doorway and maybe a shelter if there were not too many rules. Food was usually available from organizations intended for that purpose and if they weren't, there were plenty of garbage dumpsters that were bound to have something still edible.

One day, after what to some might have appeared as a series of circumstances, George decided it was time to turn his life around if he could.

He had gone through withdrawals from alcohol and drugs. He had met a lot of new very helpful people and felt he needed to give a lot back. In fact, he knew by giving back he would gain a great deal. Sure, he would do his best, work hard and try to move up to a more responsible life but could he ever get close to where he once was? Along with That, how could he ever begin to pay back all those who had helped him? George knew he needed money, and that meant a decent job. He could depend on JC's just so long and at some point, he needed to be paying them back. Paying them more than just his work and services.

JC's taught him that giving back was easy. The hard part was having the faith to believe that you were doing some good. When we give, we like to be sure that our resources are being used well. The art of giving is working hard to find someone or some place that can be trusted to disperse our gift wisely.

"When we give, whether it's a large amount of money, food, clothing, our time or just holding the door for someone, we will probably never know just how much good, we have passed along".

He stayed with JC's for more than a year, doing what he could for them, with his investment skills as well as a lot of manual labor. The two seemed to work together helping him heal and get stronger both physically as well as mentally. The office work came easy but the physical work was much harder and he loved watching himself get stronger.

He thought about calling his old boss. Mostly because the people at JC's Insisted, he try to recover some of his past and do his best to mend bridges. Talking it over with staff, they suggested he not call but go and visit. The idea of "a picture is worth a thousand words". They might be glad to hear that he was recovering, but would they believe it? Face-to-face was the only thing to do.

So, it was. Off he went with a little money he had earned at JC's and saved with JC's blessings. "We are always here for you" they told him. "Don't forget that and don't forget us".

George's old workplace was about 200 miles from JC's. He had chosen a day when a delivery truck to JC's would be going back that way. Four hours on the truck and a short taxi ride put him at the front door of his old workplace. Nervous and feeling like he wanted to run, George Lyle just stood there. Soon an unfamiliar face came by and asked if he was going in or if he was going to buy the place. A bit of a chuckle and George followed this young lady in. Walking to the familiar elevator taking in all the sites, some new, some old, and all of the time, wondering what on earth he was doing here.

He thought about all the things he'd been through and all the people who had helped him. He could not let them down, and he had to do this. He wasn't expecting these people to welcome him back with open arms or for that matter, want much of anything to do with him. He had more or less left them to find someone to fill the rather important job he had been doing and had left them without a word. He was hoping that at the very least he could get a bit of a letter to use as an introductory letter for some other job somewhere. They wouldn't have to praise him or say all kinds of great things about him, even if they were true but basically answer to the work that he had done and the fact that he had been there for a number of years.

The elevator doors opened up on the third floor, much quicker than he had remembered. It was all coming back more and more clearly over time. Straight to his old boss's office he walked. Knocked on the door and walked in.

"Can I help you?" came a voice buried in paperwork? George just stood there saying nothing and slowly his former boss Todd raised his head saying

"Can I?", and stopping halfway, just starring.

"Oh my God; George Lyle, where in the world have you been and what are you doing here? Everyone thought you were; well never mind. Everyone will be surprised. What are you doing now?"

Slowly George said,

"Yes, I am alive and in a lot of ways I'm doing very well. I have a lot to tell you and if you are really interested, maybe sometime we could go for a coffee when you're not so busy."

Todd reached around and grabbed his suit coat off the hangar and said,

"You appear all of a sudden, out of nowhere, I have absolutely nothing to do for the next two hours and our coffee shop is just waiting for us, I just know this is going to be good".

Off they went to the coffee shop passing a few staring, half waving, people George had once known. They ordered coffee and rolls and found a quiet corner. His former boss seemed to be smart enough to know that this was a time to listen and not a time for a lot of questions. Often times the questions are answered with the listening and making for a lot less questions.

George just sat there staring for a minute and then saying,

"it was very hard for me to come here," and *"I want to thank you for being willing to hear what I have to say."*

Todd sipped his coffee and just nodded. Again, George started in right from the beginning, how he became more and more addicted from the time he was a child and how he had eventually wound up on the street. How and why, he wound up in South Carolina and all the miracles and wonderful people that brought him back here and had contributed to him cleaning up. He talked about how easy it was to get drugs and alcohol and how he had suckered so many people into giving him things that he could sell for more drugs and alcohol. He talked about getting food out of garbage dumpsters and drinking whiskey from half bottles that he would find. He talked about all the people that he had taken advantage of and a young lady living in the shack who was willing to give more than what she had. He told about the rides that he was given no questions asked. He told about the grocery store and how he was rewarded for just helping unload the truck. Told about living back in the woods where no one would find him while he went through withdrawals. He told about the Priest that he met and how he had allowed him to stay there at a time when he needed it so bad. He told Todd about JC's and the way their program or lack of a program, worked and how much help they had been.

Todd just sat there saying nothing as if he was spellbound. Even when George told him about his escapades in the woods with the Mexican men, meant to make him laugh, Todd didn't even smile.

Finally, George was through, sitting there wondering if he had said way too much. *"After a few minutes of terrifying quiet Todd got up.*

Stay right there and do not move a muscle. I have a few things to get together that are yours and I will be back."

A lady came by with a lunch tray and on it some mixed fruit and crackers and another coffee. You may not know it she said but you ordered this. A little laugh a smile and she was gone.

George sat there picking at the morsels and thinking he should run out of this place. Anything of his, that was left here was just more flotsam and jetsam that he did not have a place to store anyway. How many envelopes of his legal rights did he need?

After a little more than a half an hour, Todd came back with a folder and sat down.

George started in.

"I was just hoping, well maybe I could get just a bit of a letter."

"Stop right there," Todd broke in; and George knew he was crazy for even trying.

"George Lyle," Todd said, *"if even part of your story is true, you have a place right here and in fact a number of places for you to choose from. Your story impacted me so hard, I had to go into the John and wipe my eyes for at least 20 minutes. Every day we suffer some kind of a loss because of addictions. If not one of our own employees, a relation or friend of one of our employees. You could do a lot for us by not only sharing your story but encouraging our employees and letting them know that help is out there. Things have changed in the time you have been gone but if your skills are anywhere close to where they were when you left, I don't think it would take you very long to catch up. I'm not saying you're going to be able to just walk in here and be right where you were when you left. You left a big hole and we can't afford to have that happen too many times. We will take you back on a trial basis. In 30 days, in 90 days and in six months there will be certain goals that we will expect you to achieve. If that works out and if you agree with this you have a job."*

George couldn't believe what he was hearing. All choked up he managed to spit out, *"As soon as I can, well of course, well how soon, will tomorrow, I need to find."*

Once again Todd chimed in; *"Sean, over in marketing has a basement apartment for rent right now and it is only two blocks away. You can rent that for a week at a time or until you find something better. There is no reason that I can't take you over to meet him right now and while I'm at it, introduce you to the rest of the staff. You did a great job when you were here before and they will be glad to hear you're back. You don't have to share your reasons for being gone but I think you'll find that problem is more common today than we care to admit."*

"Before you leave, we need to go over this file. We tried very hard to find you but you had seemed to just drop off the face of the earth. Anyway, from the very first day you started working here back in college through your payroll deduction, you allowed us to invest some of your money. That money hasn't just been sitting here waiting for you to come back. It has done quite well for you

in spite of a recession." He handed George the file opening it and pointing to some of the figures. George looked at the figures and looked at Todd.

"*Yes*" Todd said, "*that's correct, I told you, your investment did well for you. You could go quite a number of years without going to work with this amount of money but we hope you don't and we want you to come work with us.*"

The rest of the day George felt like a six-year-old child at the circus for the first time. He met old friends and made new friends, he laughed and cried, talked about plans and things he must do, told what he could about his experiences and he met Sean. George talked about the apartment with Sean, they agreed on the price and the rules, later walking home with Sean and meeting his family.

Sean's wife Emily said,

"*Sean called me earlier and told me he was bringing home a friend with him who might be staying with us for a while. I have arranged another place at the dinner table. Dinner will be in an hour and you are welcome to freshen up. I think you'll find what you need in your shower downstairs and if there's anything else, please let me know.*"

George went down into the basement and found it a lot more than what he anticipated. It was finished well, not real fancy but space was used efficiently. There was a bedroom, large enough for a double bed and a lamp table with a lamp, reasonable bathroom with a shower, a small kitchenette with apartment size appliances, the front room with a small library and a walkout to a lower backyard and enclosed solarium, complete with a small wood stove. Part of the basement was unfinished but had some shelves that he might use for storage.

Emily had left some sweats of Sean's with a note for George to use them. In and out of the shower and some of Sean's slippers, George was ready to go. "*Come and get it*" Emily hollered from the top of the stairs, "*We're ready if you are*". George could not fight back tears while they were saying grace and when the three children asked, George just said, "*I've got so much happy in me, that it's bubbling over.*"

After dinner George asked to use the phone. He called JC's salvage, advising the person on duty of his situation and asking them to pass it on the next day. "*Please tell everybody that I am doing much better than I could've ever have dreamed. It is all a miracle, and I will get back with them with more information as soon as I can."*

The children soon became infatuated with George and he loved them but they had been cautioned to let George have his own private time.

On his lunch hour, George arranged to use a small portion of his investments to open a bank account in the nearby bank. He was given a credit card he could use at the ATM machine and use Sean's address for a contact place.

George had no trouble completing his 30-day expectations and pretty well completed his six-month expectations at the same time. The company was very happy with George and Todd told him more than once, that he had personally gained from bringing George back.

He used his time wisely, studying manuals and various reports to bring himself up to speed, studying on his lunch hour and at home.

George appreciated his job and wanted to do everything he could to let them know that he appreciated it. Along with a cell phone, expense account and a few other things, they had given George a laptop computer. On many days George would merely work from home and probably gave them more hours than they expected.

Though by now he could well afford a fancy apartment, he was more than satisfied with his basement apartment and Sean and Emily appreciated the extra income. The second washer and dryer were put in the unfinished part of the basement and George insisted on paying a little more, to cover the cost of the utilities.

Through all of his travels he had managed to hang on to his journal. Its original intention had been to impress the people when he was panhandling so that they might think he really cared about them and was taking their phone number or address to pay them back. Now he was ashamed of what he had done and his reasons for having it but he was glad to have it so that he might connect with some of these same people.

He put together a letter.

"Dear friend,

Some time back our paths crossed. I lead you to believe that I was poor and homeless and needed help and you responded by helping me in a way you thought would make my life better. The truth is I used whatever I could get to trade for what I needed for my addictions. The dollars you invested in me

I traded for pennies worth of drugs and alcohol. For that I am attempting to apologize. I am willing to pay back with interest whatever you invested, be it money or a pair of socks.

I have come a long way back and closer to what society recognizes as a responsible person. I am doing well and I want to share more than anything my story and be able to inform people like yourself how they can really help. Giving clothes, money, food, to someone coming along who appears needy, all too often works in reverse. Anything given should be done in a way and to a place that is trusted and the gift can be dispersed so that its value can be appreciated fully.

These are critical times. Homelessness as we often call it, is at an extremely high level. Taxes, federal funding, generous organizations, churches, groups and individuals, are spending many millions of dollars, putting together shelters, apartments, soup kitchens and lunch counters, clothing collections and so much more. Is it really doing any good in your area? People are dying, some refusing a place to live when offered, some taking gifts and a place to stay but not having the means or the know-how to keep it or use it properly.

As a survivor I would love to share my story about what works and what does not work. Yes, we badly need caring people like yourself but the care needs to be funneled to where it can do the most good and you can feel the good results.

George sent out many letters, not only to people that had helped him along the way but to churches and organizations around the country. One day the church he was attending asked him if he would speak to their congregation. He was surprised at the response he received. It was uncomfortable for him to speak at first but he found that just telling things that he had experienced in the way they were, was what people wanted to hear. He told them, how clever he was, at lying and how he would try and keep himself clean and neat and that seemed to give him an edge. He told them some of the stories, he had made up about being hurt in the war, about losing his family in a tragic fire, about his family being in a terrible car crash with him looking on, about his sister and brother being hit by a train, and many other stories he had made up.

After he spoke, they naturally wanted to know where they should donate or how they should donate.

He told them about JC's and although it might've appeared a rather crude operation, was in fact quite extensive and had accomplished much.

"JC's is not only allowing everybody to come in but goes out and looks for the needy and the poor and asks them to come in. They do everything they can to show them a clean, honest, responsible environment and only ask them to leave when they feel the person or persons are able to make it on their own. Some of the time, the guests give back as much as they have taken away and more."

He talked about Father Matthew and the difficulties that he was encountering with his prison ministry. He told them of the few other organizations that he had heard about but continued to emphasize that the giver needed to do their homework.

"If you find the right place to give, you will get a lot more back. This is an investment in society and those of you who understand investing will do your best to get the best return".

After about a year, George asked his boss if he could take a road trip. He had gotten a new driver's license and bought a decent car, he could work from wherever he was with his laptop, and there were various clients around the country that like to see a human face once in a while. It was easily arranged and off he went.

One of the first places he wanted to go was back to that little shack of a house where the lady lived who had given him the sandwiches and the iced tea. Getting to the town that he had been in before heading that way, was easy. Finding the road was not so easy. Some of the gravel roads had been paved by now. More buildings had been built in various places but after a while by driving a few miles down each one he gradually came on the cabin. Pulling up in front, the place looked even worse than it had and in fact it looked more deserted. As he went up to the door and knocked his heart sunk. Scraps of paper lay scattered on the porch and the mailbox was full of what appeared to be advertisements. He tried the door and it was open. Not a soul around and nothing moving anywhere in sight so, why not go in. He poked around inside and it was obvious that whoever had been here, moved out leaving most of what had been there, as there was nothing really worth taking with them. He found a newspaper that some animal had been chewing up for a nest and a pencil circle around an address in the want ads. Grabbing what was left of the paper he went back out to his car. The phone number was still legible and he called it. A female voice coming on the line, "can I help you".

Now George's thinking, *"how do I do this? What can I possibly say that she will listen to? ma'am, my name is George and I'm inquiring about someone who helped me out a great deal quite some time ago. I have very little information to go on and all I can tell you, she lived in a kind of a small rough house in the country"* Giving her the name of the street. *I believe she had at least two children."*

"Well guess what, you have called the right place, I have no idea where she is or how to get a hold of her right now but it has to be the same lady, we hired quite some time back. Obviously if I did have more information, I really couldn't give it to you because that would be private. I'll tell you what I will do. Is there any more information you can give me?"

George thought and out loud he said,

"I don't know. Not much. I was only there just a few minutes., She gave me iced tea. She made me some sandwiches. She rushed me out because her kids were coming home from school and didn't think it would look very good to them or the bus driver, and that's about it. Oh, one other thing, I left an old wallet on her porch but it was dark by then and she might not know that I left it."

The lady on the other end of the line said if anything came up or she heard from this person she would tell them what George had said and pass along whatever information he wanted to give her.

George gave her his cell phone number and his email address and asked if it would be all right if he called back in a few days to see if there had been any response. The lady said that would be fine and hung up.

From their George traveled on to the supermarket where he had helped unload the truck. Found the owner, manager, Fred, fortunately at a slow time in the store and sat and talked with him for over an hour. Told him some of his story and told him how the hard work he had done, contributed so much, not only to his sobriety but to moving into a much better life. He asked Fred if the town had ever gotten another forklift.

"No," Fred said, *"but one of these days. The one we got is still reliable and lots of parts are available. I suppose there will always be parts available, but it seems to break down on days when somebody needs it pretty bad. We chip in and help each other out so it's okay."*

George asked Fred if there was a hotel or a place to stay in town and Fred told him about a room over the top of the hardware store.

"It's not used very often and I can't even tell you when the last time it was used, but I know it's clean and Dennis will rent it to you pretty cheap."

"Do you deliver?" George asked,

"Yes of course I deliver. In fact, I remember delivering some groceries for you. I think I still owe you money for working that hard."

Once more George said,

"I think you and I have a little more to talk about. Can you tell your wife you will be just a little late and if she would, put together a couple of those great deli sandwiches with a thermos of hot coffee when you close tonight? And. If you will, just bring them up to my room. I'll be waiting."

Fred just said, *"you are one strange fella but I'll call the wife and if she hasn't got some other chore for me, I'll be there. Look for me about 7:15."*

At almost 7:15 on the button, there was a knock on the door.

"Come on in Fred."

George had borrowed a large card table from the Hardware store owner, Dennis and when Fred came in, George and Dennis were sitting at the table looking over George's laptop.

"Here's your dinner with a little more than what you asked for and might I ask, what you two hombres are up to?"

Well, Dennis and I got talking about your forklift problem and Dennis has been sitting here showing me the good and bad, about forklifts and a little more than I thought I ever needed to know.

"Right there, that one you got on the screen right now, that's a Butte," Dennis said. Fred said, *"Dennis is an even a bigger dreamer then I am but I guess it don't hurt to dream. One of these days we'll get us a new forklift. It sure won't be that Cadillac but it'll serve our purposes right well."*

"You mean to say that one's not good enough for you?" George asked.

Not good enough? Fred said, *"Tat's way too good for this town, but what are we talking about anyway and just exactly what was it, you wanted me to come up here for."*

Well George said, "if I could've done this without your knowledge, I would've preferred to do it that way but because I don't know anything about this kind of stuff, I'm going to buy you a forklift and I need your input"

"Well, you can't just, where you, no, no, no, no, what are you and Dennis hooking up here?"

Dennis sat there wide-eyed and looking at Fred, finally saying, *"I have no idea what he's talking about."*

George broke in. *"Unless you can give me a good reason not to, I'm ordering this forklift tomorrow morning. I will give them both of your phone numbers and you will arrange where it is to be delivered and I suggest you put pressure on them anyway you can, to get it here as soon as possible. I will pay for it over the phone with a credit card with the stipulation that the card does not pay off until you see the forklift. That should put a little rush on it. There is no doubt in my mind that you will be getting a call from them shortly after I call them. I know right now you're trying to figure out if this is some kind of a scam and you probably won't get any sleep tonight wondering. All I can say is you two guys need to get the heck out of here so I can get some work done. Get some rest and we'll see what happens tomorrow."*

Dennis and Fred could hardly say a word. On one hand, they should be thrilled to death to be receiving such a large gift but on the other hand there was just no way that they could justify this expensive gift if,,, it is real.

Off they went closing the door behind them and George went right back to work. In a little while he ate one of the sandwiches that Fred had brought him, had a little coffee and found himself nodding off. Took his Bible out and managed to get through about a half-hour but then he lay down on the bed and went right to sleep.

Morning came and it was a little later than George had planned. He grabbed the thermos of coffee that was still at least warm. Poured himself a cup, checking the time again. As soon as 8 o'clock rolled around he called the forklift company, insisting on talking to the owner. He explained the situation telling him of the company he worked for and in fact telling him about JC's salvage and how they had a couple of forklifts that may need to be replaced one day.

The owner just said we don't get a chance to do Christmas this time a year but I think you've convinced me to follow up on this. If that credit card is real and it's got enough on it to cover this machine, this'll be the fastest delivery we ever made. These are the kind of things that make good advertising for us, so I hope everything you are telling me is true. Tell me the phone number one more time, and the address of the place where it's going.

George gave him all the information he could, along with his own cell phone number in case there were any problems.

Jumping in the shower he felt pretty good. A quick shower, clean clothes, grabbed his laptop and his small bag and was out the back door to his car. Out on the front street he heard some banging. It almost sounded like a shootout and he thought he'd seen a flare go over the top of the building.

George pulled around from the back the building and slowly up to the main street and here was the grocery store owner Fred and hardware store owner Dennis lighting all kinds of fireworks, people gradually coming from everywhere to see what all the fuss was this early in the morning. When they seen George pull out, they hollered at him and he rolled down his window.

"George, we just got the call, there bringing it as soon as they can. It should be here by tomorrow night. We can't thank you enough. Dennis brought all his old fireworks over so the whole town can celebrate. We are going to remember you, George."

He just waved and gradually drove out of town trying not to hit any of the pedestrians that seem to be coming from everywhere. He wouldn't be buying large gifts like that every day for people but it sure felt good to know he had done something that was going to profit so many people.

A little further down the road and about 15 minutes later, George received a call on his cell phone. *"Mr. Lyle, we want you to know that we appreciate this opportunity not only to make the sale but to serve these people who obviously need this piece of machinery. If you don't mind, we are going to use this story in an advertisement and I expect you want your name kept out of it. You mentioned this JC's salvage place and we already have an associate looking into it. If their story is as warm and solid as yours, we will be making a large donation there this year. Please do not hesitate to call us if there's anything else we can do."*

From there he drove on down to see father Mathew. *"George, it is so great to see you. I have so much to tell you and so many things I want to ask you about your travels. First of all, thank you for writing all the letters and getting all the people to petition the warden and the governor to work out a little better program for my present ministry. With a little encouragement they started to recognize its value and how it would help them keep better control.*

I hope you can stay for at least a couple days because we are having a special speaker." "And just who is the special speaker" George asked.

Father Matt chuckled, *"You are the special speaker. When I heard you might be coming this way someday, I realized that there would be nobody better than you to speak to our volunteers. We have people stay in the old gymnasium on cold nights and we have volunteers to help out. We all know, that is not the best situation and are looking for something better and I think a talk from you would be a great help."*

"That is not what I came for, George said, *and I had not given that the glimmer of a thought but that it is exactly what I would like to do. There is so much need and we are only beginning to understand how we are going to deal with the problem."*

George stayed for four days, communicating with his work at home, taking care of what he needed to take care of online, visiting a client in the area and giving his talks. On the fourth day, he was in the Church Garden, trying to decide whether he should stay for a few more days in this most comfortable setting that allowed him to get a lot of his work done. His cell phone rang and a female voice asked,

"Is this Mr. George?"

"Yes, ma'am I'm George, what can I do for you?"

"Oh, Mr. George, how long I have wanted to talk to you. I am the lady that lived in the little house and gave you a couple of sandwiches. How are you doing are you all right?"

George was a little startled and said, *"I am doing quite well, how are you, I hope you're doing well."*

"Mr. George I can't begin to tell you how well I'm doing. Is there any way that you can come and see me or I can come and see you? I will travel anywhere."

A bit taken back, George said slowly, "a, a, a, sure, I can probably come and see you one of these days. Do you have an address?"

She gave him her address and phone number, telling him that it would be just too difficult to explain all over the phone. She would look forward to seeing him and would appreciate a call an hour or so before he got there. She would like her three children to be there when he came.

He hung around for one more night but was kind of anxious to find out just how this run-down cabin lady was doing. Had she run into somebody who had made promises but was just using her? Was she on drugs or some other addiction? He would know soon enough and like too often, maybe is this case, not be able to do anything about it.

Saying goodbye to father Matthew, after agreeing to more future talks, he drove back north a little sad. Always difficult to leave good friends and hoping to make more new ones.

The address she had given him was nowhere near the address in the newspaper want ads, he had seen in her cabin. This address was more than 200 miles from where he had called. As it turned out it was North in the direction he needed to go toward where he was living. Also, he was able to visit a couple more clients on the way. After two more hotel room stops, he came to the town she was living in. Called her on his cell phone from a coffee shop he found. Giving her the name and address of the coffee shop, she said, *"yes, I know the place but I would rather you came to where I'm living. The children will be out of school in about a half-hour and if you wouldn't mind waiting that long, I am very anxious to talk to you."*

He waited more than half hour and gradually found his way to the address she had given him. He found himself in front of a long, long driveway going up to a huge estate but there was no question about the address. Still apprehensive he slowly drove up the driveway to a door that was swinging wide open. Two children ran out asking if he was Mr. George.

"Mom and Kenny Are waiting inside and said for you to follow us right in." Across the walk and up a flight of stairs across a large porch and in. There stood the young lady, woman he had met in the cabin, or at least, somebody that looked like her. She was dressed far better than the woman he had seen in the cabin. Her hair and everything about her, looked like a lady of class; Upper-class. Also, in the room was an older lady and gentleman looking pretty classy themselves.

There was a small dog romping, the three children nervously moving around, and then the moment was interrupted with the older gentleman saying,

"I would like to introduce you to everyone."

Introductions were made round and soon the story started.

The young lady, Janet Walters had found the wallet that day when her kids came home from school. She had just stepped out on the porch and there it lay. She ran out to the bus driver telling her that she had found a wallet, going through it, found an address and asked the bus driver if she wouldn't contact the address. Not thinking much about it the bus driver sent a note off to the address and that the wallet had been found and where it was. In the meantime, Janet had answered an ad in the newspaper, telling of a job that needed a cleaning lady. It meant taking the children out of school and moving them to another area but it paid well and the place where she was to be a cleaning lady, had a small apartment that they could use until she found something better.

It'd taken a while for the owners of the wallet to be contacted and to find out where Janet had moved. When they found her, they were fascinated by her situation. They always were looking for a family that they could help and although the people where Janet was doing housecleaning were not very anxious to let her go, bragged her up and knew that she would be better off with someone who could help her more than they could.

Her new friends had arranged for the children's schooling, transportation, and more than enough field trips. They had put Janet to work cleaning their house but limited her to one day a week. The rest of the week was for her schooling and she was already quite handy on her new computer. Saturday and Sunday were days off and she would spend that time with the children, sometimes taking little trips with her new family.

Mr. and Mrs. Richards said that the Walter's family had given them a whole new life. Mrs. Richards jumped in asking why George didn't keep the money that was in the wallet? Did he have any idea how much money was in it? "There was enough to make somebody happy for several days", she said. More importantly to her, there were so many important papers and phone numbers, in the wallet and a lot of things that could have caused them trouble trying to replace credit cards, bank cards and so on. Mr. Richards chimed in again.

"You may think you did just a little thing by putting that wallet there but that started a beautiful pin ball rolling and it is still rolling, ringing bells and sending out rewards."

George appreciated the complement and of course thanked him but he couldn't help but think about all the people that were not as fortunate as he was. Mental illness, drug or alcohol addictions, or just plain poor and not having the ability to begin to move up. How could he ever tell people what it was like? How could he ever explain to them, that it wasn't money or gifts but simple touches of kindness, thoughtful kindness, that had helped him begin to move up. If people could only know that they were cared for they could start to learn how to make it on their own. "How did that go?

"But the greatest of these is,,."

There seems to be a kind of notion that putting up a building or finding one and allowing what we are calling homeless stay there for a few hours, solves a problem.

Know before I go too far and for those who will want to challenge what I have to say, I can only say don't waste your time. If you really care, come up with something better and move on it. Put your name on it, take credit for it, get your picture in the paper but by all means do something more than what is being done presently in far too many places.

Shelters and subsidized housing are great ideas but then what?

Poor and homeless need training. Weather they are invited, coaxed, coerce, tricked or just taught by example they most often need training. Training to make a bed, training to have some kind of order, training to listen and at the same time showed the value of these things. If you lost a pet, would you be content to know it was given some food and a nice place to sleep and nothing more? Would you hope someone was giving it some attention? If you happen to care about animals, would you build a nice house for a stray somewhere where it would not be a bother and tell all that you had solved a problem?

I hope you are in a place where you are getting that good feeling that comes from helping.

CHAPTER 5
The Reconstruction
of Chad Taylor

*H*urt in a construction accident, Chad Taylor had been living at home for a couple of years. After some time, he was receiving a disability, and because of his bad back he could do nothing, or so it was said.

At times, someone would see Chad, lifting or moving around with a project he wanted to do but that was rare. What they weren't saying and everyone knew, Chad was a drunk.

As all so often the story is, although he denied it, Chad knew exactly where he was and how much of a burden, he was to his family even though he never told them. He hated himself, he hated the drink, he hated being on a disability and he hated the fact that he couldn't tell anyone just how he felt. Secretly he knew he was capable of some kind of work but something, just something seemed to be keeping him captive.

How many times had he told himself he was going to change, he was going to seek help but then something just got in the way? He still had friends in the bars or at the party stores, who were more than happy to leave him with the impression he was doing the best he could and with his accident and all, "so what if he had a drink once in a while". He deserved at least that much out of life.

Alcoholics Anonymous was using a room at JC's salvage and one day, Chad was invited to a meeting that happened to be at JC's and after several more invites he attended one. It wasn't the first meeting or maybe not the next two or three but eventually it stuck. He started attending more often and not only listening to but being around others who had been in the same boat as he was, well it was hard to ignore so many of the things he had been ignoring.

Now he remembers his last day of taking a drink. Chad remembers Fred Holzer inviting him to a meeting just like he himself, invites people now.

It all took time; Chad didn't find detox and the withdrawals easy but with family support and seeing the relief it brought to them helped to make it work. He admits, had he been by himself, he could never have done it.

Someone, at one of his earlier meetings, had told him that JC's had a little work some times and at the very least, he could do some volunteer work there, be around healthy people, some of whom had been in his shoes one day. It would also give his family a break, knowing Chad was doing something positive.

Chad wasn't paid in cash but was given help to manage his disability income. His family was invited to check out the donated clothing and other things. They were allowed to eat for free at JC's and because by now, finances had become a real burden they were advised, and helped through the many services available to them.

When a new person came to JC's even for a visit, they would be asked their name. Naturally not everyone gave their correct name. Maybe some had a good reason or maybe they were just a little suspicious. The plan was to have some idea of who, when, how many and how often. An inner gate was always locked and the person coming or going would show their JC's ID and were allowed to pass day or night. How much Information they wanted to give was up to the individual and usually after staying there for a while most people would be glad to give as much as they could as it would not only help JC'S but also help the individual move forward a little easier. Things like getting a job, a disability, finding their own place to live, receiving mail, keeping track of medical information and appointments, meeting others they knew, and anything else that might help were all addressed.

Even though he went home every night, Chad had been encouraged to give his family information about what went on at JC's. By now, the center knew that a spouse of an alcoholic would need as much care as the alcoholic. Chad's three children were out of the house in the day time during the school year and it allowed the center to offer his wife, Dian Taylor, work. They would offer her work for five days, four hours each day, giving her ample time to be with her family and doing what she needed to do at home. It wouldn't be a lot of money but the important thing is, it would be hers, to do with as she felt she should and she would be around others who had been through what she was going through and they could give her positive support.

Diane started out at JC's center doing laundry, cleaning or most anything they asked. In less than two weeks she was doing some of the bookkeeping. There was always some kind of work at JC's. The more you organized the easier it was to get things done. If for some reason something more important came along, well you just put off the organizing. She enjoyed the variety and it was easy to see, she understood what fast and efficient meant.

It didn't take long for Frans to notice her either and ask if she would come to work for him in his restaurant. The same hours with less pay but Frans felt with tips she could do much better. She would be given a couple of weeks to see if it would work for her. JC's hated to let her go but that was the way it was supposed to work. JC's would give them a start and others would take over.

The next day, Dian Taylor came in to Frans's Restraint, thirty-five minutes early and started in like a ball of fire. It was as though she had worked there for years and had no trouble getting along well with the customers. She would have a cleaning rag in her hand one minute and the next bringing coffee to someone. A pad of paper laid next to the cash register that she would write on and next to it, a jar with her tips. After about three hours there was a lull in the customer traffic and Frans called her over to one of the tables.

Nervously, she sat down at his urging.

"Number one," Frans said, *"you don't start working thirty minutes before your shift. Today you will go home thirty minutes early."* He went on, *"I suppose it would be silly of me to ask you if you ever worked in a restaurant before."* Before she could answer, *"I know this is your first day here, but some things just won't wait. Do you feel you are being paid well enough?"*

"Yes, I have worked in a restaurant as well as several other places. I am so glad to have a job and one that allows me to be with my family when I need to. The pay is more than a lot of others pay and with my part of the tips It is more than I was making at JC's."

"Your part of the tips?" Frans stammered, *"what are you talking about? Any tips you make are yours and I expect you will do pretty well. Karl told me you were doing some book keeping for them and that is another area I could use help in. For now, just keep doing what you are doing but that doesn't mean coming in earlier than you are signed up for. Already the staff likes you and the customers seem to notice your good attitude. I think you are going to be a great addition to my staff. Remember, work together, learn together. Right now, if you would. Take care of that customer coming in the back door. He's the owner of that large auto parts factory down the road and it wouldn't hurt my feelings if he bragged up our place to all his employees."*

It took a little more than a year for Chad and his family to stabilize and it was a celebration day, when he was able to go into the disability office and say, *"thank you for helping me get through a rough time, and he no longer needed the service."*

Chad had been a welder and rigger, working around the country installing large equipment. He didn't feel it was the best idea for him to get right back into that life style. Being on the road, made it even easier to be around drugs and alcohol. When he started volunteering at JC's it was easy to see how useful he could be. On the road, he had been installing machinery and now, closer to home, he was taking some out as well as dismantling many for the scrap yard. He had the right moves, knew machines, and knew something about avoiding the pitfalls of this kind of work. He loved JC's and they loved him.

After working for and with JC's for a few years, he would hear grumbling from some of the contractors who were in the business of machine removal and demolition. Because of the support he was getting from JC's he was taking a lot of work from these other contractors.

Talking it over with JC'S staff, they came to the conclusion, he should go out on his own, start his own company. They would loan him tools and a vehicle for a small charge and he would work toward getting on his own. The scrap and salvage work, were how it all started here at JC's. John and Karl were getting to the point of not being able to satisfy all the salvage work they had to do so they decided to turn some of their work over to Chad.

When one slides backwards through addiction, the undoing is usually a lot faster than the rebuilding. Like the machinery, taking apart was faster than putting the same together.

Credit stops quickly as the person loses a job, over writes a check or just quits paying bills. Even JC's could not afford to be giving credit. They of course wanted the best for Chad Taylor but this was something he had to work out himself. It was enough for them to help him out as much as they did. Giving him money was something they avoided with all the guests. By now Chad understood that and was happy to know he would one day, have the chance to pay not only for the loan of the truck but give back for all they had done.

Not only a person's financial state was in ruin but also their home, house, relationships with neighbors, family, friends and everything they had touched was a mess.

Dealing with so many things, plus needing to feel humble and tolerant as he was being treated less than other people. He would hear comments whispered from extended family, neighbors, local business people, *"How long is it going to last this time? This is just a temporary thing. I've seen it before; he'll always be a drunk. He's just doing this so people will feel sorry for him and give him more money so he can drink."*

Chad's immediate family was there for him and that was a blessing. Dealing with all his problems had caused a lot of pain for the whole family. Still, his wife's income was a big help to his starting out on his own and she was more than willing to help.

Fortunately, this is what JC's salvage was all about. Time and time again they had seen people in the same position and they were there for a kind of safe place where people were positive, encouraging, and happy. Some days, before going home, Chad would come to JC's after a long day of machine repair or demo and take a shower. Then he would have a cup of coffee and find a needy person to talk with or help out in some way. He found out that helping out was something he needed more than the person or persons he was trying to help. He could meet his family there, sometimes the whole family working in JC's kitchen, serving guests and sharing a kind word.

One day, one of Chad's old friends from work was in town and called at Chad's house. Chad's wife Diane was there and told Mike Murphy that he would be able to catch up with Chad at JC's place. Giving him the address and not much more, she sent him on his way. Chad was just pulling in to JC's with a load of old machinery on the back of his truck when Mike showed up. Surprised to see him, Chad parked the truck, jumped out and shook Mike's hand.

Mike started, *"Were doing a job in town and when the rest of the crew show up, we will be here for a while. I figured I'd look you up. Let's go and get a beer ol buddy before I dry up"*

Chad looked at him smiling and said, *"You may not believe this, coming from a guy who drank the most with the best, but I don't drink anymore."*

Mike just stood there looking and kind of smirking, *"I'm not sure whether or not to believe you. You do look a lot better and you even sound a lot brighter, but if it's true, am I going to have to listen to some righteous, seen the light speech?"*

"No" Chad said *"You never listened to anything I said anyway."*

They both laughed and Chad offered Coffee for a substitute.

"Coffee is for breakfast and I don't usually touch the stuff after eight AM. You sure it's legal to drink coffee this time of day?"

Chad coaxed him to Frans's restaurant and over coffee and cinnamon rolls they rekindled the old friendship.

Chad didn't say a lot about his sobriety and Mike didn't ask too many questions about it. Mostly they talked about the machines they were removing, new tools and methods, safety equipment and rules. They talked about how great it was to see each other again.

Chad told Mike a little about JC's and among other things, it was a place for those needing a temporary home. *I believe we have enough empty beds and when the rest get here you guys can bunk here. There is no drinking or smoking on the property, and all that is required is if you come in drunk you don't bother anyone else. There is some kind of food available around the clock. This restaurant is open at six thirty in the morning. You'll pay the menu prices at Frans's place here but nothing at JC's. Of course, they would be glad if you left a donation of some sort but it's not required.*

Chad insisted Mike stay at his house at least this first night.

"You already know where I live and the front light will be on. Just come in and find your way around. I will leave a note but I don't think you will need it. We have a guest bedroom on the first floor and the bathroom is just

around the corner. No smoking in the house. We will leave a couple of other lights on so please turn them off when you are ready for bed."

"You seem to have all of this figured." Mike said *"How do you know I won't be there before you go to bed?"*

Chad just looked at him and they both had a good laugh.

Chad and Diane were always up by six am and around six thirty they heard Mike, showering in the bathroom. He came out not saying a lot as Chad pushed a cup of coffee in front of him.

"I figured you had to be out early and check the job before the boys showed up so Diane made a couple of sausage and egg sandwiches for you to take with you to eat when you had time. I got you a thermos of coffee for later."

Mike grabbed the bag of sandwiches and the thermos of coffee, thanked them and was gone in minutes.

After he left, Chad and Diane hugged each other, knowing they had done the best they could for someone suffering a hangover.

A few days went by and nothing was heard from Mike or his crew. Chad had left word with the night volunteer people and gave instructions, should they show up.

On the fourth night they showed up. Chad would find out the next morning that they had shown up around midnight quite drunk but quiet. Chad had shown Mike the arrangement and the rooms, the showers and the toilets, smoking outside. They were escorted to two dorm type rooms, three beds in one and four in another.

Chad received a call early the next morning and he instructed the caller to see that they were offered breakfast and pack some coffee in a couple of the old donated thermoses.

Several days went by before Chad would see Mike or his crew again. One day about two in the afternoon, here they come. Three pickups and a larger truck with torch and welding equipment.

When Mike seen Chad, he explained that the trucker who was supposed to haul away a piece of equipment was delayed and they couldn't do any more that day.

Chad knew three of the men and the other three were new to him. Introductions were made all around and finding a place to sit, they drank coffee, telling stories of travels and troubles.

One of the guests came up looking for two people to play euchre, shortly after another needed a partner to play corn hole. Mike and his crew were soon comfortable with the people here and Chad found it easy to leave them to their own entertainment.

They would be on the job in town, for six weeks and Chad would see them at JC's often but keeping up with his own work kept him away also. Often, he would see one or two trucks at the shelter. He heard stories of things they had fixed or projects they had helped with. One day when he passed by the kitchen, he seen one of the men washing dishes. He couldn't believe it. If only he had a camera.

On weekends they would show up early in the morning, having breakfast and interacting with all who were at JC's. They got to meet many of the volunteers, John, Karl and their families and their children,

There would be reports of them coming in some nights, drunk but never of any problems.

The six weeks were over and they were gone. No goodbye, thank you, we are going here or there or much of any of that. They had made a few individual donations but very little and that wasn't really an issue but it would have been nice if they would have at least said goodbye.

Three more weeks went by and a large crate arrived and delivered by an independent trucker. He was able to drop it with his lift gate and JC's people had him drop it on a trailer so they could move it where ever it needed to be moved. With pry bars they opened the crate and in it were several more boxes. A large envelope was on the top.

Chad had been called because his name was on it.

"Dear Chad, an office girl is typing this up for us. We are not the best writers and wanted you to know, how much we appreciated you letting us stay at JC's. What we didn't tell you was, we had tried a couple of hotels before we went to your place. Let's just say it didn't work and we managed to stay out of jail. At your place we met so many people we could talk with. We started looking forward to time off just so we could go there. If we get back there, we will be looking for a place at JC's again and hope we will be welcome. The rest of what is in the crate should be self-explanatory.

Your buddy Mike."

As they went deeper into the crate, they pulled out box after box. Chad just stood there shaking his head. A manual came out for a commercial dishwasher.

One of the people opening the boxes said, "Some of these are parts for that big old dishwasher we removed because the owner said it was too costly to repair and a lot of pieces to keep it going a long time."

Another envelope, a bit dirty and crumbled revealed a hand-written note. *"Don't worry buddy. It's not stolen. This company liked our work and when we explained you had one of their products and it wasn't working, well, I think you will hear even more from them. They said they were going to send out a technetium to help get the machine up and running."*

Another over stuffed envelope was pulled out and opened, reveling a large amount of cash and in rough handwriting, a scribbled note, *"As you know, the company pays for our room and board. We have never been treated so well and had such a great time. It was like a vacation. Thank everyone for their courtesy and kindness"*

All of their names were on the note. Ralph Harris, Russ Deming, Brian Thompson, Mitchell Johnson, Sean McClure, Timothy Buckley and Mike Murphy.

Early in the days of starting up, John and Karl had decided they would only decorate with things pertaining to and of interest to JC's. If someone connected with JC's, painted a picture, that was one thing. To put up a picture just because it looked nice wouldn't do. People would offer this or that and some that were reported to be worth a lot. A lot of ideas of what would look best and what was proper and John and Karl could see competition in the future. Better they thought, wait for things that will show people who we are and give the guests and volunteers something to be proud of.

This letter, like so many others, was framed but this one was hung on the wall outside the kitchen.

One day, Chad's wife came to him in the middle of the day. *There has been a terrible accident. One of the customers at the restaurant brought this news article to my attention. Chad, I have to get back to work but give me a call as soon as you decide what is best to do.*

The article went on to say a machine accident had caused the death of one worker and injured two more. The company Chad had worked for, had been named as the contractors. No details but that was enough.

Chad went to the center and asked if they had any information on the guys who had stayed for several weeks. All had left addresses and phone numbers and Chad copied Mike Murphy's. He called Mike's home and his wife Laura answered.

"Mike told me about your place and oh Chad, they sure need you now. They can't work now or at least until the investigation is over and I'm not sure they could ever work anyway."

She paused, obviously crying

"It is so bad. They won't even come home."

Chad said *"I have your address and I will try to send someone by that you need to talk with."* Chad would let the center know of the situation they would gather as much information as they could. Someone somewhere would know somebody who could go and visit with those who needed a visit. A person who understood enough to listen rather than going on about their own experiences.

The accident had taken place some three hundred miles west. Like so many things, Chad discussed the situation with the people at JC's and everyone agreed he should go and try to look up Mike and the men. One of the volunteers, Charley Dawson, offered to drive Chad and they could take turns with his car as Chad's truck would not be the best to take. They called their families and people at the center pulled together extra clothes, food and a few other things they might need. They were on the road in less than forty-five minutes from the time Chad decided to go. Under different circumstances it would be a picnic vacation. For now, it was, *"be ready and fit for whatever comes along"*.

Taking turns, driving and napping they arrived at the city in little more than six hours. Finding the factory was easy and from there they drove around the area until Chad spotted their trucks outside the Magpies bar.

Michael sat there at the bar with Russ and Tim. They sat there drinking and staring, looking by Now, like they had been there a while because they were doing more staring than drinking.

"What are you boys drinking?" asked the bartender, "Two coffees please" as Chad sat down next to Mike and Charley Dawson sat down on the other end, next to Tim.

They sat there not speaking for some time, just drinking their coffee until Mike made the first move.

"Not a good time for talk Chad but I am glad to see ya."

"This is my friend Charley Dawson. I don't know if you met him at the center. He helped me drive so we could get here a little quicker."

Introductions were made around and that seem to help them to open up.

Mike started in, *"I don't know how much you know or have heard about the accident, but it was bad. It was so bad."* He paused and took a drink from his beer. *"Because of the location in the factory it took a long time for the rescue equipment to get there. It was a heavy piece and they needed heavy equipment to move it. No overhead and no wide isles. All we could do was stand there and try to dream up something while we waited and listened to their screams and moans".* He paused looking into the bar mirror. *"Brian didn't make it and Sean and Russ are in rough shape."*

"Mike, you still won't have to listen to some righteous, seen the light speech, but we, Charley and I are going to say a little prayer and all you have to do is sit there."

With a nod from Chad, Charley started in *Thanking God for a safe trip and how speedily they were able to locate the crew. He thanked Jesus for letting them be available to Mike and the crew and asked for healing for all. Then Chad jumped in asking for a quick recovery for Ralph and Sean and for good friends to be there for the families helping to bring comfort.*

It was short but long enough to get the attention of two other customers and the bartender who bowed their heads in respect. Then, Chad started in with the Our Father, saying it very slowly and gradually everyone including the bartender recited it with them?"

Tim Buckley said, "That felt like when someone hands you the right wrench you didn't ask for or even know you needed just then. Thanks, you guys."

Chad Said, Charley and I are going over to the hospital. You are welcome to come along if you wish.

Russ piled in with Chad and Charley while Mike and Tim led with one of the tucks.

Traffic was heavy and the going slow. Chad was starting to wonder if he was doing the right thing, getting so involved in something he couldn't do anything about. "Would they hate him because he wasn't with them when the accident happened? He might have seen something that could have prevented it. How bad would they look? Could they even talk about Brian and how he died? Crushed, no doubt but how long and,,,,,,,,,,,,,,,,,,,, ,,,,,,,,,,,,,". His brain just wouldn't stop. Over and over, so many questions and most would never have answers.

They made it to the hospital and up to the third floor. Chad and Charley went in first. Ralph Harris had obviously lost a leg. Sean, although he had a lot of bandages, didn't look too bad. The three men looked like they were glad to see Chad and were introduced to Charley Dawson. Russ, Tim and Mike crowded in and found places around the room. *"Can you two hombres believe these guys drove that far just to see ya?"* Tim said.

Ralph said, *"I bet they really came to try and straighten you three out, as if that were possible".*

More and more jabs around the room with a lot of laughter when a nurse came in.

"For some down in the mouth patents, you guys are having just too much fun. Some of the other patents want to come down and join you, so you better keep it down. Yes, call me Nurse Ratchet"

Then, she laughed and said, *"If I can have all of your permissions, I would like to take Mr. Harris for x-rays, that is unless one of you wants to do it and I'll stay here and laugh, with you guys"*

Shuffling around and moving out to the hall while they rolled Ralph's bed away, they heard him tell Sean, *"Please go ahead and tell them that story I just told you. It will be easier for you than me."*

As he was rolled away, they all came back in the room and looked at Sean.

"Let me tell ya, guys, this is going to be a little difficult." He shuffled in the bed a bit, cleared his throat, "Well here goes. *"It seems Ralph was in Vietnam and one day he came back to camp drugged up and weaving. He was in no condition to go out on patrol with his squad. One of the other guys said he would take his place which apparently happened often, one person taking*

another's watch or run. On this day the squad was ambushed and the guy who took Ralph's place got his leg shot off. He made it back to the states but that is all Ralph knows. Just before you guys came in, he told me the story and he said, and,,,,,,,,,,, this is the difficult part. He said all these years I have been feeling guilty, to the point of not being able to sleep or get it out of my head. All of a sudden, I feel what that guy has been feeling. As soon as I can, I am going to look him up. I want to get better as soon as I can. Then he said, I guess God is not through working with me yet."

They all stood there looking at the floor, thinking, holding back tears, how, just a short while ago Chad and Charley had prayed for healing.

Ralph came back from X-ray and they all Stayed around for an hour or more, laughing and planning at least one more trip to JC's.

About that time the owner of the company Jo O'Rourke and his wife Stephanie came in. *"Well, it's good to see all of you together and in good spirits. To what do we owe this to?"*

It was all explained and Joe had heard about JC's when Chad had said he would not be coming back to work, traveling on the road.

"Listen all, maybe there is not a good time to discuss this and rather than some boring needless meeting let me tell you now" Jo said. *"We have insurance and as you have been told, your wages will continue. More importantly you are not all supermen. Staying away from your families and staying drunk will not do any of us any good. I need you guys to come back to work someday and I mean all of you. It will be some time before the investigation is over so you are all on a kind of paid vacation. I'm sorry but I am trying to say this as best and as quick as I can. Of course, you need to see your families and soon. After you spend some time with your families, I would like you to think about visiting JC's and maybe staying there or in the vicinity for a while. I intend to visit there myself. I am curious about a place that has managed to do so much for so many for so little. I believe it can offer the kind of therapy you need and maybe I need. I have already talked with the insurance people and they had no trouble agreeing with me. I expect cost had a little to do with that. Just the same, based on what you guys have told me, I think it is the best we could provide. It will give you a chance to do a variety of positive things, meet with people of all walks of life and have a chance to get, more back than you can ever give."*

Stephanie spoke up, *"Jo and I have talked about volunteering somewhere for some time and we believe JC's might just be the place. JC's has figured out that allowing people to volunteer for even one day or one hour, they often go away feeling like they have experienced some kind of healing. They want to volunteer more and are so willing to support something they are a part of. As you probably know, helping others or putting others before your self has many benefits. Psychological, as well as physical. Many studies and much has been learned. We feel like it is time we cashed in on some of that opportunity to help others and give back some of what we have built up.*

The trip back to JC's was uneventful. Chad and Charley talked about how much had been accomplished. In just a few hours, so many lives had been changed for the good. Well maybe not changed but given the chance to see the better side. *"What if they had not come? What if they had not stopped at the bar? What if they had not gone to the hospital, talked with the other patents or the nurse, Jo or Stephanie O'Rourke or the so many others they got a smile from. They had done nothing or at least very little but what a payoff."*

Back at the center, they received a generous welcome. The media had already picked up a story about the people JC's had sent out to be with the families of the workers and a story had been given, about how the attitude of the patients had improved with a visit from JC's.

Chad and Charley made a trip out to the chapel and stayed for a good half hour.

For a while at least, the volunteer situation would have to be managed well. At least for now there would be more people than needed so they would give as many as possible a chance, even to the point of creating new jobs. A list would be made, being sure to get as much information as possible as well as being sure, no one was left out. Things were painted with half cans of donated paint, tables were being built from old pallets, the trail around the large outside area was being improved, trees were trimmed and donated plants put in the ground. JC's knew there would be times when volunteers would be scarce and good positive volunteers were their best investment.

The King will reply, "You did this for me." Ma. 25:40-45

CHAPTER 6
Fruitcake Folly

"Wow, what was that?" He just stumbled back against the building wall taking inventory. It'd hit him right in the chest and there probably would be a bruise there but it wasn't the kind of hit that leads to bleeding or at least he didn't think so. Felt like somebody punched him real hard. Looking down, he seen a wrapped package and picking it up, found a store-bought fruitcake inside.

He sat down there on the pavement, in a bit of a corner, out of people's way and examined the fruitcake. Not to his surprise, it had never been opened. Although very few people cared about fruitcake, he happened to like it a lot. It was obvious this was not sent to him as a gift in fact it really wasn't sent to him. The person throwing it, must have been in that fast-moving car he heard go by, so he had walked right into it, as the car Sped by. He just happened to be there and was a good target. He remembered a vehicle racing by, a loud radio, a voice hollering *"Merry Christmas wineo fool"*.

Arnie Dexter had been hit with eggs, tomatoes, cabbages, pieces of wood, stones, he had been beat up, urinated on, spit on, stabbed and kicked. He had never been hit with a fruitcake.

Living on the street, one gets used to most anything and you learn pretty early on, there is no one to complain to. Respect is not something you are privy to.

Wouldn't it have been nice if someone would've come up and handed him fruitcake. Such a silly thought but then, well, that just doesn't happen to street people. This is the street and this is the real world.

Arnie new he could not sit here very long. He needed to collect cans, and check out some dumpsters and it was already pretty late in the day. He had fallen asleep the night before in a dumpster behind Bradshaw's hardware and a good thing for him it wasn't trash pickup day. Anyway, the bottle he had found late yesterday, had him sleeping far too long.

A female voice asked, *"are you all-right?"* She seemed to come out of nowhere, well-dressed and acting concerned. *"Those crazy kids threw that right at you and they were going pretty fast. It must've hit you really hard. Shouldn't you go to the hospital and have that checked? I would be glad to give you a ride".*

"I'm all right. Just stunned me for a minute. Thank you for asking ma'am."

He got back up, grabbing the fruitcake in the bag it was in and started down the street. Maybe it was the sign pointing to the hospital on the corner, maybe the church bells that were ringing somewhere, it might've been the pregnant lady that passed him by and smiled, wishing him a Merry Christmas.

Cars and people hurried on by, some going one way, some going another. A cacophony of sounds from sirens, Christmas music, blaring horns and loud voices.

It was all just way too much and he hurried around the corner, across the street and under an old dark stairway leading up to an abandon apartment over an abandoned carpet store. Back in the corner he felt his knees give out, leaning against the wall, crying, vomiting, and feeling like his whole insides were coming out.

She didn't like fruitcake and would make jokes when he ate it. Just playful jokes and she bought him all the special fruitcakes this time a year. She was the kind of person that just beamed when she knew she did something good for someone. Sometimes she would come home in tears and he would hold her while she told him about one of her students that she just couldn't seem to help. All the stray animals knew her and Arnie and his wife were going to move to the country, just as soon as they could, after the baby was born, so that they could take care of needy animals in their spare time.

After a while Arnie pulled himself together. But what he needed was a drink and he was pretty sure Mike was good for it. Mike owned a bar in town and when a customer left a drink, he would funnel it into an empty bottle and set the bottle outside the back door in a corner where Arnie could find it. Sometimes, if Arnie was lucky, Mike might've saved several drinks and the bottle might be almost full. He had to make sure that he left the bottle so that Mike would refill it.

On his way over to Mike's bar, he found an old discarded milk carton. This would work just fine.

Sure enough, back behind the used cooking grease barrel was the bottle. Not quite half full but enough for Arnie Dexter right now. Carefully pouring it into the empty milk carton, replacing the bottle back where he found it, he was on his way. He had taken a pretty good pull on the bottle before putting the rest in the milk carton.

By now it was getting late. He must've fallen asleep back there and not realized it. He really wasn't very hungry but he couldn't remember how many days it had been since he ate. He trudged along through some of the back alleys and back over to JC's shelter, where he knew he could get some hot food. Almost back to JC's, he ran in to Bridget. *What you got their Arnie?* Handing her the carton he said, *"have a swallow I guess it's going to be Christmas, so Merry Christmas."* Bridget took the carton held it up and then stopped.

"Where'd you get this carton Arnie?" Its sure smells like it's got some antifreeze in it.

Arnie stopped dead. He thought for a few minutes as they both stared at each other. They both knew what antifreeze meant. *"I, I, picked it up behind Marks's repair shop".*

"We got a get you into JC's. They'll know what to do. Bring the carton with you in case they want to check it."

They hurried off and in a matter of minutes they were in JC's telling their story. The Hospital and poison control were called and both Bridget and Arnie were hurried off to emergency.

Arnie was in a rather drunken state by now and couldn't remember whether he had drunk from the carton or not. As far as it went, Arnie wasn't sure of anything by now. Bridget said that she had not drank any and did not remember seeing Arnie drink from the carton but who knew what he had done before she seen him.

Tests were made and Arnie was told that he would have to stay for the night. Had he been a little more sober he might have protested but as it was, he had little desire or strength to protest anything.

The next day Arnie found himself on his back in a hospital bed trying to put together pieces of his memory and missing quite a few pieces. There were tubes and flashing lights, buzzing things and everything much cleaner than what he was used to. He laid there a little while, then realizing there was somebody else in the room. Looking over, a well-dressed woman, middle-aged, nodded to him.

"So, Mr. Arnie Dexter, I understand you thought you were a car radiator. My name is Wendy Dower and I'm a psychiatrist"

"You can just leave right now, and unless I committed some crime, I'm going to do the same."

Several minutes of time passed and finally Wendy said, *"Maybe sometime later you will want to talk to me. I can be contacted through JC's. I didn't get a chance to talk to Bridget,,,,,,,,,,,,,,,"*

"Oh God, oh God, oh God," Arnie hollered and started weeping uncontrollably burying his face in his pillow.

Although Wendy had started out the door, she knew this was not the time to leave. Seeing a nurse in the hallway asked if Arnie was allowed coffee yet. "Could you bring a couple, black?" She went back to her seat and as Arnie seemed to calm down a bit, told him, *"Bridget was doing quite well and had been asking about him."* That seem to quiet him. More time passed and eventually Arnie, rolled on his back. *"Is she alright, I mean is she okay did she drink any,"?* his voice fading away.

"Yes" Wendy said, *"She is all right. Bridget didn't drink any of the antifreeze and it doesn't look like you did either. You were both very lucky. There probably wasn't much in the carton when you poured the whiskey in but on an empty stomach, well I have an idea, you understand what might have been. The doctor was in before you woke up and said you were suffering from malnutrition but there were no traces of the poison in your system. You will be able to leave just as soon as you feel up to it and it's in their best interests to free up the bed, that you have no means to pay for."*

She let that soak in a while, cranking the bed up so that he could sit and giving him the coffee, and sitting back down.

All the noises in the hospital seemed to be magnified. The voices, cartwheels in the hallway, machines buzzing and beeping. Wendy knew that Arnie was hearing them also, but he just sat there sipping and staring into his cup. This was good, just maybe he was thinking.

Finally, Wendy got up, *"I am leaving now as I have work to do. JC's knows how to get a hold of me when you're ready and I have an idea that is going to be very soon."*

With that she left.

In a little while the doctor came in, looked at Arnie and said, *"there is not much more that we can do here. The best doctor you can have right now is yourself. I believe you know more than anybody, about what you really need to do if you want to stay well. I have ordered extra food for your meal and I suggest you eat it. After that you are free to go. The nurse will remove the tubes and give you your clothes."* The doctor left.

The meal, a bit large as it was, came and Arnie did his best to eat most of it. He quickly dressed and left the hospital, finding his way over to JC's salvage. It didn't take long for him to locate Bridget and the two of them sat down at a long table with some other people from the shelter. He or rather they talked about what had happened and how they had heard of other people accidentally drinking poisons like antifreeze and not coming out as well as Arnie.

A few days went by but Arnie just didn't seem to be himself. He went out looking for cans but even when he found enough, didn't drink as hard as he had been. Back at the shelter he ate very little and seemed to spend a lot of time sleeping. To those around him, he looked like he was in a trance and was just waiting to die. Some days, he would go out and walk the circle track around the yard, staring and walking. He might sit in one of the many benches in the yard but no one could get him to engage in any of the activities.

After the fourth day away from the hospital he approached a volunteer asking if they could get hold of Wendy for him. Wendy was called and she would be there in about 3 ½ hours, as there was somebody else that she needed to see.

When Wendy showed up, she invited Arnie to follow her to the special room that JC's had arranged for volunteer therapists. It was a rather large but still warm feeling room, they had paneled one wall with of all things, refinished palette wood. There were only two chairs in the room, very comfortable chairs, the kind you fall down into and want to go to sleep. The room was decorated very sparsely, a couple of books on a small shelf, a few scenery pictures, some framed forms that Arnie assumed where licenses. There was no machinery in the room, no computer, no television and only some very large windows looking out to an enclosed garden with a tiny pond.

The minute Arnie sat down he felt comfortable and just wanted to be quiet and say nothing. He could see the door if he wanted to leave in a hurry but he didn't feel like he wanted to leave. It was all just so quiet and so comfortable.

Finally, Wendy said, *"don't think you're going to fall asleep. That's what you were doing the last time I came to see you and I have far too much work to do, to watch people sleep. You called me and this is how it works. You start talking and actually you'll be talking to yourself a lot. There are probably a lot of things you need to hear yourself say. That doesn't mean that I'm not listening but if I keep barging in, you may never get to say the things you need to hear yourself say. I have this pad of paper and will take some notes if I need to but please, start in when you're ready."*

"Where do I start" in a very low voice then clearing his throat a little louder *"where do I start? If you've been around at all, you know more about me than I know about myself. I'm just another drunk. Believe it or not I was once a real person. I don't remember a lot of it and maybe I don't want to. I've been drinking really heavy for several years and that seems to be the only thing I want to do. I would like to get my life back or at least I think I would. How do I even start that? Yes, I know these people here would help me, and they already have helped me a lot. They give me food and clothes and a place to sleep all for free and how would I ever pay all of that back? I didn't pay my wife back very good when she let me get things I didn't need. It cost as much as $100 a day to stay in a hotel. Some hotels, at least some crummy ones are only $25 a day. If you buy a hunting bow, that costs a lot of money, and I would never shoot an animal. She knew that. But that still ends up,,,,,,,,,,,,,,,,,,,,,,,,,,. I have stayed here a long time and I've eaten a lot of meals. The meals here are pretty good and even though I'm not hungry a lot, some are hiding a lot of meals. Big trucks deliver food and you have to watch out and don't take the street they are on. I'm glad Bridget is all right. Bridget is a nice lady. Bridget and I have been*

talking to some of the other people and warning them about drinking things that they're not sure of. The doctor seemed to think that I needed to eat a little more so I've been trying to eat more. I used to like,,,." And then he stopped. Just sitting there for a time and finally saying, *"I think I need to leave now."* Getting up, opening the door and leaving without another word.

Wendy scribbled herself a few notes and leaving the room herself, stopped at the desk and asked them to give Mr. Arnold Dexter a message that she would be by in three days at 10 in the morning and if he liked, she would see him again.

Driving back to her office, Wendy thought about all the things that he had said. A lot of rambling, touching on a lot of different subjects, and not really saying anything. Part of this was because he was nervous and uncomfortable to the fact that he was being seen by a psychiatrist but maybe, in all of it, there was more to it. Right now, she couldn't be sure, what if anything he was trying to say and it would take more time if she was ever going to be able to help him.

On Wendy's suggestion, one of the volunteers asked Arnie if he would like to help with one of the chores. There was always a long list of things that needed to be done and any time, there was a possibility of getting one of the guests to help out, they, JC's tried to provide a chore that would work out best for JC's as well as the guest.

Arnie agreed and started out painting one small wall in a bathroom. Not all the walls but just one. Something he would be able to see the completion of and feel good about the improvement. It wasn't a big job but that was part of JC's planning. If they could get even a small job done by one of the guests that was better than nothing. Furthermore, they had found that by offering the small jobs they often lead to the individual doing larger jobs. JC's had learned that people like to be appreciated and how easy it was to appreciate somebody who was doing work for you for free, even the smallest job. By the next day Arnie found himself carrying out trash, doing a little more painting as he was very good at it, and found himself being introduced to wooden palette salvage and seeing all the beautiful work that had come from what others had thrown away. Some people were flattening out tin cans and using them to roof bird houses and even a dog house. Some were cutting up worn clothing for rags as well as other uses.

Arnie had still managed to find time to get a drink now and then but caught himself trying to slow down. He knew he would never be able to stop. He was smart enough to know that he was addicted and when you're addicted you just don't stop drinking. Sure, he had been invited to the classes, but always managed to beg off. That just wasn't for him.

Arnie told the person at the front desk that he would meet Wendy again and so he was ready when she showed up at 10 in the morning. They went back to the same room and the same comfortable chair with the same relaxing view in the same quiet. Why couldn't it always be like this?

Wendy told Arnie, how glad she was to see him and the fact that he showed up made her feel like her job was worthwhile. Once again telling him she was there to listen and not ready to give any advice so he could start right in as she only had an hour before she was to see someone else.

Arnie went through the things he'd been doing for the last few days. Said he felt good about being useful and even though some of the work seemed to be very easy he was busy. He told about painting the wall in the bathroom and although he was pretty shaky, found a way to make very straight lines. *"Straight lines were important in the painting job and if you took your time and covered up the areas you didn't want to get paint on it always came out good."* He said Bridget was doing well and he was glad that she didn't get hurt because of him. he told her about taking out the trash and how some birds were coming around the trash container and how you have to cover up the trash container because the birds come around and then stray cats might get the birds, and he talked about just a whole lot of things, rambling on and on, one subject not meeting up with the next. He started telling her about the wooden pallets and talked about the creative ideas and things people were making of these pallets. He said they would make a great fence if you wanted to keep stray animals in and safe,,,,,,,,,,,,,,,,,. and once again he froze. Stopped dead in his conversation, sitting there for a while then saying again *"it's time for me to leave"* and once again leaving without another word.

Again, Wendy stopped at the desk, left a small pad of paper with instructions for Arnie to use it to write whatever he wanted to and she would like to read it on her return in four more days. Once again, he was to notify the desk if he wanted to see her.

At the next meeting, Arnie brought the pad of paper Wendy had left. Wendy asked to see it. There were words or maybe writings, excellent hand writing but with little meaning. Sentences running on or subjects running into each other. There were drawings, mostly stick figures, animals, a bow and arrow in several pictures. A picture of a broken car and what looked like a broken truck. There were stick figures of people and one which caught Wendy's attention, A figure which was obviously a woman with a large bump where the stomach should be. There were other drawings and all were scattered around pages and nothing connecting to anything else.

Wendy handed the pad beck and let him talk until he once again, just got up and left.

More and more meetings, sometimes Arnie having notes for her and always a lot of things to talk about but not really connected. At one point he admitted that he needed to stop his drinking and was going to try really hard. He might even go to a meeting.

Sometimes when Arnie came to one of her meetings, he seemed to act like he was afraid. Afraid of what, Wendy didn't know.

By now a couple of months had gone by and each meeting seemed like a lot more gibberish although Arnie did seem to be improving, getting more and more involved at JC's, being more of a help, and trying harder to quit his drinking. This day, like all the other days, he came and sat in the chair but this time he seemed just a little different. Wendy told him to start in whenever he was ready.

He calmly started out, *"I read the paper today and the woman in Mansfield was killed."* And he was quiet. Wendy waited and waited, expecting he had much more to say. This was quite a long way away and what does that have to do with him. She had learned by now that he cared about people and didn't like to see them hurt but this was going on all the time and what would make him pick out this particular incident? She gave him quite a bit more time but her time was getting short and finally she asked, *"so what does this have to do with you?"*

He sat there not moving at first, then finally grabbing his face and like she'd heard once before, *"oh God, oh God, oh my dear God, I killed my wife."* And with that, he got up out of the chair ran out the door and Wendy would find out that he ran out of JC's.

Wendy stopped at the desk as usual, leaving a message for John and Karl to give her a call as soon as they could. She had another client to see but would be free in an hour. It was important.

Wendy met with her client and then returned the call to John. They arranged for a meeting time and together with Karl went into a small private room. They all understood about client confidentiality but they also understood that JC's was responsible not only to the law but to other clients, other guests, and society. Some things had to be shared. Wendy told him what she could, mainly that Arnie had confessed to killing his wife.

Sitting there a few minutes quietly ruminating on the information, Karl broke in first, *"we have learned a lot about jumping the gun, making too much out of too little information. As much as the authorities watch our place it would seem that by now, we would have heard something."* John spoke up, *"he has never shown any fear or acted like he was hiding anything when the authorities have gone around making bed checks, looking for someone they thought might be here. I agree with Karl, we need to do something fairly quick but not so quick that we do more damage to whatever has already been done."*

"All right" Wendy said, *"I think we all know what we have to do, phone calls, the library, old newspapers and the rest. Speaking of rest, don't believe there will be any of that for a couple days. We also need to do our best to locate Arnie and keep him safe before he does something more to himself or somebody else."*

The next four days were very busy days recruiting as many volunteers as they could and still, while telling them very little, were able to do a considerable amount of research. Any clue they could think of, they would follow to the very end.

On the fourth day they got a break. The guests had been asked to watch out for him and one of the guests had seen Arnie hanging out in an old factory. *"I know he didn't see me but I seen him and I didn't say anything to him. I just came right back here to tell you guys. I don't know what's going on but I sure hope you can help Arnie. We really like him and he's a hard worker. Puts the rest of us to shame, and Lord knows we need a little shame."*

Together Wendy, Karl, and John, drove out close to the old factory, walking about a quarter mile so they might have a better chance of him not seeing them too soon. They entered the factory and quickly enough, found Arnold. He didn't make any attempt to run but just sat there as though he was waiting for somebody to arrest him.

A bit of silence and maybe nobody wanted to be the first one to speak but eventually Wendy said, *"we know what happened. We came on a news clipping and looked up the story. It was not your fault that your wife and unborn baby died in an accident."* They all sat there quietly for a while and John suggested they all go back to JC's where they could get a cup of coffee and Arnold could clean up a bit. Without much resistance Arnold went with them, back to JC's and took a shower with very little insistence. He put on the sweats, JC's provided and met with them in a small private room, having coffee and sandwiches. Karl and John told Arnold they were just there to assure him that he was still more than welcome at JC's and would do anything they could to help him move forward. They would leave him with Wendy as this was her work.

"Please stay" Arnold said, *"if you have time, I think it's best that you all here this.*

"I suppose you might say I have been on the run. When it happened and all I could do was leave."

"Can I ask you a question?" Wendy said *"what made you think that you killed your wife? The authorities told us it was an accident that you couldn't have avoided. You were in the right. You weren't speeding, he was in the wrong lane, and there was nothing you could do."*

Arnold looked at her, staring as though he was looking right through her, *"I like to shoot a bow. I don't care about **hunting** and she would've never let me hunt anyway, but I like to shoot. I was pretty good at it and even won a few trophies. I am a designer by trade, designing very high-priced furniture for big hotels. That can get quite boring and so the bow and a little competition used to break up the monotony."*

"What does" Karl started in, then realizing it was not the time to ask questions.

"That day, we were on our way to see a German Shepherd, that we had heard about. It had been hurt and the people could not afford to take it to the vet. Francine was in a hurry to get there but when I pleaded, she agreed it would be okay to take enough time to check out the new bow at the sport shop." He paused for a long time.

Finally, John looked at him, *"I think we can take it from here, I remember from doing our homework and checking the area, there was a sport shop, just off Main Street. You figure by turning off the main Street that it was your fault that she wound up in the path of that vehicle. I'm not in your socks my friend but in this business it's not always easy to be as gentle as we would like to be. You are carrying around an extremely valuable body and one that could be doing a lot for other people. By now you should've figured out that carrying around guilt accomplishes nothing. This will probably not go away easy and I hope you always have pleasant memories, warm memories to remember her by. While you are working on that how about if we all work on cleaning you up so you can give us back some of our investment."*

There were more meetings and more talks, Arnie doing the AA meetings and working hard at JC's salvage. He knew he couldn't move back to his old home and with the help of some people at JC's contacted his family who were very happy to hear how he was doing. They arranged to take care of all of his business matters, sell his house with most of its contents and send him whatever was important. Along with everything else he walked away from was a sizable bank account. Buying a place in the country just like she would've liked and with references from his old employer didn't take very long for him to find a job, or as it turned out, offers for several of them. When he did his interviews, he made it clear that because he had been helped so much, he wanted the best job he could get so that he could earn a lot of money to pay back all the people that needed help. No, he wasn't going to throw it out on the street but there were organizations.

The Place that Arnie bought consisted of 40 acres about 10 acres of which were trees. It was owned by an older couple that had farmed it many years before but could no longer keep it up. There was a large barn and a number of outbuildings with plenty of room for archery and for taking care of any stray animals that just happened to come along.

He asked the former owners to stay on for several months while he made some changes to suit his needs. With the large farmhouse it was easy for all of them to have their privacy and it worked out very well. Mrs. Myers would make his meals for him and Mr. Myers advised him and helped him on a number of projects around the farm. Mr. and Mrs. Myers were tickled to feel helpful and Arnie was glad that they were able to save him so many steps. Arnie told them about JC's and one day a call to JC's got him a van and eight people coming out and help around the farm.

Here they were, these poor, lonely, homeless people, most not acclimated to this kind of living, running around laughing, curious, asking a lot of questions, and being helpful. Arnie had called the local lumber yard and arranged for enough material to clean up the old granary and make it a decent sleeping area. JC's sent him a lot of things that had been donated to them and were extra. This was to become a place in the country for the poor and the homeless, the alcoholics and the drug addicts, some of the mentally disturbed. It wouldn't happen overnight and he wouldn't just turn a lot of needy people loose in an area without proper supervision but this was a start. He had people coming out this time who were suffering from poverty and being homeless. This was to be a little vacation for them only staying as long as they wanted to and only working if they cared to. This was time to take a break trying to decide where they wanted to go from here.

Right from the beginning, Mr. and Mrs. Myers had asked Arnie if he would like to go to church with them on Sunday. Feeling like he needed to prove himself he said yes and found himself being introduced to several people in the community, on their way into church. Of course, there had to be a small brunch after church and nothing would do but they would have to attend and introduce him to even more people. Arnie didn't realize that one day he would look forward to going up in front of the church and telling his story. That would come later. Right now, he was meeting people but more importantly he found he needed to be there in church every Sunday. That took a while also.

On a Saturday evening a call came in. *Mr. Arnold Dexter? This is Sally from JC's; I have a note here for you to call Wendy as soon as you can. She says it's okay to call late. Do you need her number?*

When he called Wendy, she told him how glad she was to hear from him and had heard that he was doing well. She had some information, important information and was not something she could exchange over the phone. *"Could he come in one evening and meat with them at JC's.?"*

"I get off work at 6 PM and you are about a half-hour from my work. Will 630 6:45 tomorrow work?"

103

He arrived at JC's, Wendy, John and Karl all waiting for him in one of the small private meeting rooms. Sandwiches small pieces of vegetables and fruit were waiting and he was glad to tear into them while he was listening.

"We are going to have to bring up old history again," Wendy said. *"This is about your accident and information that you need to have. Some new information has only recently come to the surface in regards to the accident and the young man driving the truck. People came by from the prosecutor's office wanting to talk to you. They didn't have your new address and of course, as we often do, we put them off as long as we could trying to get just a little more information. I was able to get a judge involved in the case and explain not only who I was but what you have been through and how you are doing. That bought us or more importantly you a little more time to figure out what you're going to do or what you need to do. It turns out the truck that hit your wife had bigger intentions. It seems he was headed towards a schoolyard at a very large school to do some horrific damage. This information only came to light recently by way of a snitch wanting some air for his own case. As bad as it is, the accident saved an awful lot of children's lives. They, people in authority, would like to open the case up again. Right now, the young man is charged with manslaughter. They would like to have him charged with a capital crime and arrange for him to get capital punishment."*

"Wow" Arnie said. *"That is a lot to take in. After what I have been through, what I have seen and all the help I have had, it is difficult to think the way I might have a few years ago."* He sat there in silence for a while, finally breaking in, *"has anyone heard what the young man has to say?"*

"We were discussing that, before you came in," Windy said *"and to answer you, no, we have no idea what he is saying. Whatever happens isn't going to happen overnight so I believe we can use whatever influence we can, to find out a little more."*

A considerable amount of time passed and eventually the story came out that the young driver of the truck had been hired by a third party and had no idea what was in the truck. There were issues about the condition of the truck, breaks, steering and so on. The person who had hired him matched the description of a person who had been under surveillance for some time but disappeared. Later a street camera had picked him up in another country. Not much more was said about him but it was apparent that enough was known to show beyond the shadow of a doubt, the accuracy of the young man's story. Because of the length of the investigation and trial, the young man had been given probation and time served.

Wendy insisted on meeting with Arnie again and he assured her that he harbored no ill feelings and it looked like the young man had been through more than he deserved.

One Friday night Jessica from JC's called, *"Arnold we have about five guests here that would love to come out and visit your farm tomorrow. I told them they might have to do a little work and they're looking forward to it. Everybody likes to get out to the country. There is a local lady here that wants to bring them out and is willing to drive the van. She is a Judge and usually volunteers late evenings. I never thought she was the kind of woman that would want to visit the farm but will take any volunteer we can get."*

Saturday morning the van arrived, Arnie was out from the house a way, cutting up an old dead tree and not paying much attention to their arrival. Pretty soon they walked out to where he was working and turning around, he seen a face he recognized. It was obvious that she was the driver, but from where did he recognize her? He was sure he hadn't seen her at the shelter.

Feeling a little uncomfortable, Arnie just moved on to the guests and suggesting some small chores telling them where the boundary lines were and about the refrigerator in the barn if they needed snacks or something to drink. *"The place is yours to enjoy. Be safe and explore."*

Finally, he turned back to this very attractive woman who had driven the van. *"I'm sorry and,,,,,,,,,,,,,,,,,,,,,,,,,,,,,,,,, hate this part. I've been through this before and I don't know how else to do it so I just have to ask. Maybe it's my imagination but I think I know you from somewhere."*

She looked at him, saying basically the same thing. *"Yes, I heard your name was Arnie, mine is Carla, and that is not Judge Carla, at least not right now, and I feel I have met you somewhere. This is a beautiful thing you have going on here. All the way out, the guests were talking about it. The two who had been here before, telling the others. I thought we were headed to Disney World"* she giggled.

Arnie said, *"there are no dinosaurs or space ships but I do have a mouse or two"* and invited her up to the house for coffee. They talked about the guests and how they liked the country, and both agreed it would be nice to have more time to spend outdoors with so many who don't get a chance for this kind of experience.

"I sure wish I could remember where I've seen you."

"Well, I heard you were a Judge and I haven't committed any crimes that I know about but, all of a sudden he hollered, *"fruitcake, I was hit with the fruitcake."*

She looked at him and sitting there in silence as if she were turning pages of a book. Then, she seemed to wake up, as if from a bad dream. *"Is this all some kind of cheap trick?"* She demanded *"yes, I remember you now, dressing up in old ragged clothes, arranging for somebody to hit you with that package, knowing I worked at JC's. I can't believe anyone would do something so outrageous, I should have known."* And putting her coffee cup down hard, started to get up.

Arnie sat back shaking his head, *"no no, please, absolutely not, I guess this is one of those things that some people call coincidence. If you will give me just a minute, I will try and explain some things to you."*

When he had seen her on the street and she had asked him if he was all right, the night he got hit by the fruitcake, he never dreamed he would ever see her again. Much had happened after that and he was trying to be a different person. He told about his wife and baby and many of the things that had transpired before and after their death. He told her how she would joke with him about Fruitcake and do her best to find much of the same at Christmas time just for him. He told her about his interaction with JC's and was surprised he had never seen her there. He told her that it was people just like her, that helped him get back on his feet. His story took quite a little while and before it was through, there were tears on both sides of the table. It was an incredible story, one he wasn't likely to make up and when he was finished, they both sat there staring at each other.

He was starting to feel pretty nervous and it was obvious they were both a little nervous. Arnie said *"I think we better go out and check on the guests, they might be having too much fun"* and they both laughed.

Standing on the porch outside and looking over the less than perfect landscape, they could see a few of the guests. One of the women was sitting in the grass with a mother cat and several little ones. A couple of the men were struggling with some wire and wood, attempting to repair a fence. Another man was nailing a piece of tin over a hole in the barn. Carla asked,

"So where do you go from here? If I can be a bit judicious", smiling, *"It seems like you have a number of projects started and with enough support could be finished quickly".*

"Just like JC's Salvage, I want this to belong to them." Arnie said, *"I want it to be their creation or at least I would like the poor and rejected people to have something they had a part in. It will never be that theme park or some Gentleman Farm, but hopefully a collection of thoughts and ideas, mixed with a little sweat that will always have that sweet sunny aroma of spring hope. Hope is not something we can satisfy and move on but instead, something we must continually feed with our caring. Out here they are given a chance to care for something and better yet, we are given a chance to care for them."*

"Somewhere in all of us is the desire to be better. Better at something. Maybe giving them what they think will make them happy or better is not so good but I believe feeding them hope will help them to make the right choices to get the better which will do the most for them. I can't save the world and as far as that goes, I can't save anyone but I can let them know that I care and do my best to show that. Sometimes that is a lot harder than it seems."

"Do you think bringing them out here and giving them lunch and a place to relax is giving them hope?" Carla asked.

"No, Arnie said, *"that has little to do with what they really need. Sitting with them or working with them and sometimes not sharing even a word. Complementing them on what they do, seeing them on the street, have you ever looked for the poor and marginalized on the street? Once you start looking, they are everywhere. They need to be seen and that is caring. That is the start of hope. Out here they are seen in just a different setting and that is about all".*

Carla looked at Arnie, *"I have been working at JC's salvage shelter for some time. Now that I think about it, they do like to be outside. I have walked with some of the guests on the path around the yard, had hot dog roasts, bonfires and built snowmen outside with them and it has been fun. You are right, sometimes we hardly shared a word but we were communicating. I have to say, your idea of hope and caring must have some substance. I have come away from the shelter many times feeling better than when I arrived. Not sure if it was what I got or what I gave but it seems to work."*

The rest of the day was spent doing small chores mixed with playful activities and ending the day with a bonfire.

Mr. and Mrs. Myers were still living in the house and Arnie was hoping, that would continue for a long time to come. They were invited to join in the activities and nothing would do but she must bring something. Taking one of the men with her, headed back to the house, bringing back out hot dogs, buns, condiments, home-made cookies and so much more.

It was a difficult thing to end but end it must and back in the van, with many, *"thank you's, great time, hope we can do it again."*

Arne asked Carla if she would ever mind bringing a group again? *"I would like to talk with you some more."*

Carla looked at Arnie. *"I would like you to hear my story some time and I would be turning this van right around as soon as I get back, with another load of guests if I didn't have responsibilities."*

"If it's all right with you, I would like to come out as soon as I can get a day off. By the way, The Myers have invited me out to church on Sunday."

The van drove away and Mr. and Mrs. Myers said good night, returning to the house. Arnie walked out to the bonfire, pulling a small cross out of his pocket, sitting down by the smoldering coals.

Arnie sat there for some time just contemplating and listening and finally, looking at the cross he heard himself say *"Yes Boss, your plans are always the right ones."*

CHAPTER 7
A Sound Lesson

This was just his regular Sunday of canning. Sunday was usually a pretty good day to pick up returnable cans, as a lot of people had been out partying the Saturday night before. This day, it started raining. Danny had been up real early because the competition was tough. There were a lot of street people out there trying to get those returnable cans and if he was going to get his addiction satisfied today, he would need at least a couple dozen. He didn't do all that well anymore panhandling. He had long ago stopped trying to look clean and neat or use the same stories about his sick mother and his sick aunt and the operations that people were going to have, as none of the stories seemed to work anymore, anyway.

It started raining early, but now it started raining hard. Danny was used to being wet and used to being in the rain but he thought he might get up against a building maybe behind a bush somewhere at least for a few minutes until the rain slowed down.

Looking around at the closest buildings, he found a spot that seem to be dry, close to the building and some bushes that would hide him from meddling people. Not seeing anybody he pushed his way back through the bushes and into a corner where he was well hidden. The spot was perfect, looking like it had been used by animals as well as other humans.

Danny sat down, pulling out the small bottle he had found, that was almost a quarter full of what he needed. Removing the cap, he took a good swallow and although he was quite wet, this dry place and the warm drink made him feel very good. Danny nodded off and after a while woke up to music. Not just music but church music and after all this was Sunday, wasn't it? Danny didn't care much about music, whether it was Sunday music or any other day music. Danny cared about his addictions and that was about all he had time for.

Sitting there in that dry place, he listened just the same. Some of the instruments, some of the voices, some of it together, some of it individually, had he heard it before? Was it something from another life? And then there was one voice. Maybe higher, maybe happier, what did he know about music? Why was he even thinking about music? Why did one voice catch his attention?

It was time to go. He needed a lot more cans and other people were out there by now, hitting all the good spots. He would go back by the old tubing factory. Young people would go back there at night and drink and throw their cans out. Most of the other canners knew about the spot but what they didn't know, at the edge of the parking lot, in one spot there was a bit of a drop off and many of the cans would wind up down there where they really couldn't be seen. Danny had hidden down there one day when someone was after him to steal his cans and discovered a horde of cans. From then on, he was very careful when he went to that area, not that he was afraid of being beat up but afraid somebody might discover his pickup spot.

The next Sunday found Danny hiding back in the same corner. It wasn't raining and he wasn't tired but all week long that voice kept ringing in his head. This is the direction he usually went on Sundays and now, this was part of his route. What would it hurt to just stay back there for a little while and after a while the music started again? Songs were sung, instruments were played and so often, that voice that was so much different than the others.

This went on for several months, every Sunday finding Danny tucked back in the corner in his own special place listening intently, anxious to hear that special voice.

Like all good things coming to an end and maybe to a good end, one day, one Sunday, while the music was playing, an old man came through the brush slowly and looking at Danny.

"Good morning" he said to Danny, *"I am all alone, my wife died three years ago and although my children come around at times, I spend a lot of days by myself. I have been watching you for a long time from my front porch and I think you are very lonely to. If you would come across the street to my house, I*

would make us breakfast and at least for a little while, we wouldn't be lonely. I would serve the breakfast on my back porch and you don't need to be afraid of anybody coming around."

Danny felt bad that he had been discovered and food really wasn't what he was looking for but thought a little bit, that maybe he could talk this old man out of some money or some empty cans. Maybe he could use his bathroom and find some pills in the cabinet. Whatever he did it was obvious he couldn't stay there in the bushes.

Off they went together, the old man leading, Danny following with his small bag of empty cans, around the back of the house to a clean and cozy enclosed back porch.

"Just Make yourself comfortable while I get us some grub together. There's a pot of coffee over there on the table and some coffee mugs with the fixens. Help yourself and there is a bathroom just inside the door if you need it."

Danny headed for the bathroom but there were no cabinets or pills to be seen. The bathroom was just that and nothing more.

Back out on the porch sitting there drinking very black coffee, once again he heard that voice. The windows were open in the church across the street and the one voice seemed to ring out louder than the others.

It wasn't long, the old man who had introduced himself as Wade, Wade Simmons, came back with two plates of food. Eggs, pancakes, sausage, toast and another trip brought orange juice, butter, jam and syrup.

"I don't call myself the best cook but I usually make a lot to make up for it. Eat what you want and leave the rest. I drive out to the woods and feed some animals. They don't seem to mind what I cook."

"If'n you don't mind, I'll say a thank you for the food." And he started in, *"Bless us dear Lord and this food you provided,,,,,,,,,,,,,,,,,,,,,,,,,,,,,,,,,,"* at the end he added, *"and Donna, I know you're up there listening, and one of these days were gonna be together again, but I want you to know I found a new friend so please help watch out for the both of us, amen."*

Danny felt himself squirming a bit, eating rapidly and eating a lot more than he thought he would. He wanted to run away very bad but something in him seem to hold him back. The old man talked about his wife Donna as if she was right there with them, and he said he went to church on Saturday, and on Sunday, him and Donna would sit there listening to the music. *"Yes, I know she's not right here or at least we can't see her, but somehow that music and that very special singer makes me feel much closer to her."*

"I know you need to leave and I have to clean up here before I go to the cemetery. I hope you'll come again for a little while. You and I don't have to be lonely."

And that's how it all started. Danny had told himself that he would never be back there again, that he would start taking a different direction and all the other things we tell ourselves when we are afraid to admit that we are just lonely. Danny did come back the next week on a Sunday and many Sundays after that. Danny knew that he was not very healthy, all of the years of addiction had taken its toll. In the past he had pushed all of that out of his mind, but lately it was harder and harder to deny it. He found himself staying around Wade's house, more and more and sometimes even sleeping on the back porch on a small cot that Wade provided. Sometimes he helped Wade with some landscaping or cleaning out the rain gutters. He could climb ladders and do some things that Wade couldn't do and he found himself feeling very good about doing it.

A lot of days he would leave and sometimes it would be several days before he returned. One day Wade said to him, *"Danny, I care about you, like my own son. I'm going to tell you something and all I'm asking is that you think about it."*

He told Danny about a place he had heard about, called JC's salvage. If Danny would like, he would go with him to check out this place. He had offered Danny a place at his own house but knew that wasn't the best for Him. A few days went by and Danny came to Wades place and over a coffee he agreed to go. It wasn't but a few minutes with Wades car and they arrived. JC's was not a fancy place, by anybody standards. JC's salvage was an old abandoned airport that had been turned into a center for the poor, the addicted, the homeless, and anybody else that wanted to visit for an hour, for a day, for the next two or ten years. It was run almost totally by volunteers many of whom had known people in need or had been in need themselves. It was a large area with plenty of room for expansion and lots of things to do or just room to be alone if you chose. After checking in, they were given the grand tour by one of the guest volunteers. They were told, people from the medical profession would come around and do minor health screening, people to advise them on housing, managing their finances and just generally many things that they could use, if they chose, to help them towards a better life. The area outside had several small gardens and in spite of not being very neat or looking like wade would have liked to see, they were producing tomatoes, onions, carrots, or at least some nice tops, Leaf lettuce, beats, several kinds of flowers and wade recognized jalapeno pepper plants.

The benches around the yard were very inviting and some were occupied with people reading, sleeping or just staring. Danny could go there, stay for free and try and clean himself up. There were not a lot of difficult rules but a lot of very helpful people, if and when he was ready for them.

Not right away, but Danny did go to JC's salvage, still pretty much living the same life, going out to satisfy his addictions and coming back to sleep and eat. The influence of JC's had an effect and Danny made a decision to try and try very hard.

One day Danny told the counselor, "Today, I'm going to quit" and he quit cold turkey. Detoxing was not easy or quick. At his age it took a toll. Weeks went by and Danny was still suffering. The people at JC's took turns watching him and encouraging him but more than once, thinking they would have to call the hospital. Somehow, someway, he seemed to make it to the other side. "I feel cleaner than I have felt for a long, long time," Danny said.

JC's told Danny he could stay there and they would find him enough to do, to cover his keep and some pocket money, to use or save as he chose.

One day, a man from veteran services came to JC's salvage, to talk about what was available to veterans. Danny, although being a veteran was quite sure that nothing was available to him. Almost the first day, he was released from the service he was on the streets, staying high, as many waking hours as he could. He had not taken the time to inquire as to what if anything was available to him and had never been advised to check. Now, he went to the meeting just the same. As it turned out, there was quite a bit available to him and after a little less than a year was able to receive a reasonable disability, with back pay, along with several other benefits.

At least once a month, Danny would find a way to get back and see his friend Wade and because he had money now, he would find something to buy wade. Once he bought a small barbeque grill and had it delivered. Wade couldn't believe it, When Danny showed up the next time, Wade got after him. *"Why did you do that. You can't afford that grill and JC's is more important than me. If you have that much, they deserve it, not me."*

"Oh no" Danny said, *"You have done a lot for me and JC's is where I got the idea from. I've been doing a little work around there and they said I didn't have to pay anything for staying last month and that I should get you something you could use."*

"Well than let's get to it, I have some steaks in the freezer that I bought just for this occasion. I have been wondering if you were ever going to show up again. I'm just dying to try this out and just dying for those steaks too. Haven't used it yet so let's get started. Need to turn it on and burn off the brand-new smell and then we will be ready. I'l pull the steaks out an I been a readin how ta take them right from the freezer an put em on the grill so we do it right"

From than on, there were many meals shared that had been prepared on the grill. They would talk about what would be good next time and a date, usually a Sunday would be decided, Both Danny and Wade contributing something to the meal.

on a Sunday, they would have breakfast often from the grill and quite often would hear that special singer, with that special voice. Sometimes Danny would show up early Saturday, help Wade with some chores, stay the night, take a shower and change into some clothes he had left with Wade and together go to Sunday service. Not always but once in a while that special lady would sing on Saturday.

Both Wade and Danny had gone through an awful lot and maybe that was why they appreciated what they had. Wade had his little house and Danny had JC's. Wade had his children to see once in a while and Danny had friends at JC's and the family, they were to him. Together, they had each other's company on Sunday and that special singer that they both looked forward to hearing.

Years went by with Danny aging much faster than Wade. The addictions, the drugs and alcohol, the living on the street, had all taken their toll. One day while helping out at JC's, Danny passed out. An ambulance was called and Danny was rushed to the hospital. When he became conscious again, he told one of JC's people that he was all right and he was ready to go home. Danny never did go home again, at least not any earthly home; his liver and kidneys could no longer serve him, like they were intended to. His body was just worn out. Danny was told he only had a short time and was kept alive in hospice care for three and a half weeks.

From the time he was told, he never seemed to show any fear and to more than one, it seemed he was looking forward to the next life. A priest would come to see him during the week, along with many friends from JC's.

Military affairs had been contacted and Joseph, Danial Sullivan's family had been found and advised of his condition. He had accomplished three tours of duty, been wounded twice and the last time, only one of three survivors of an enemy attack. After completing his third tour, he was given an honorable discharge and just left to a town, different than his home town. Nothing had been heard from him since.

"Of course, he should have been given transition time to acclimate back into society, before his separation. He should have been given time with counselors before separation" one of the senior officers said,

"But sometimes they just fall through the cracks"

Wade came to see him and they talked about what they had been through, how they had met, the time they shared and how they had helped each other.

Danny asked Wade if he would take the money, he had saved and arrange for a funeral service. *"I know there won't be too many people there but maybe you could put a picture of Donna there because she always seemed to be there with us. Also, it would be nice if you could get a recording of that special singer's voice and play it. I think that would be nice."*

Wade, trying to hide his wet eyes, said, *"You be sure and tell Donna I'm coming along as soon as the Boss gets through using me down here. You tell her that and give her my love".*

A small service was arranged, which turned out to be a large service, at the church both had attended, across the street from Wade's house. To Wade's surprise, a lot more people attended the service than expected.

When it turned out that Danny had been decorated while in service a military funeral was arranged.

As for the singer, when she was told of the situation and her part in bringing him so much joy in his later years, could hardly say yes fast enough. She would be there and was there, although not always singing her best while fighting tears.

CHAPTER 8
Sharon Terlecki

She had seen the hard times and somehow it had ordered her life in a way, not all would agree with. Always someone to suggest, Sharon Terlecki, should have, could have done something better. People would say things to her, they would never consider saying to another. Insulting things, things to laugh about, at her expense and because she always laughed with them, seemed to make it legal. *"Tough skinned, a lot of fun, nothing bothers her"* all the thoughtless things we say, maybe just to have something to say. It had never occurred to them that Sharon Terlecki had ever been any different or could have had a different life.

She was never asked why or much about her background. Her address had been, a cheap room in town that was home until she ran out of money. After that, for more than the last two years she had just stayed on the streets, finding a shadowed corner, piece of landscaping to hide in, or a 24hour business that she could flop in getting a couple hours sleep. It never occurred to her to consider her plight. Like a robot, Sharon just existed and rationalizing wasn't in the game.

At JC's, doing repairs to the building, its contents, furniture, clothing, bedding, shoes or most anything was regularly discussed. Everyone was encouraged to repair, rather than throw away. Many donations in the way of clothing, poured in and it would be easy to just buy a guest something new or at least, newer but if they could be taught or see what it takes to clean, make small repairs, sew on a button, that would be showing something positive and something to consider. If guests, were ever to be on their own, sewing on a button, mending a curtain, making a pillow cover from old discarded clothing, make a dishcloth rather than buy could be good for them. Also, so many things could be accomplished without spending precious cash donations for JC's.

Leftover food was used for the next meal and guests were encouraged to look up or suggest recipes, based on what leftovers were available as well as healthy.

All of these things were difficult to teach. Most any kind of repair or reuse, had been ignored by most of the guests in their lifetime. Although poor, they had a hard time, understanding why they should repair something when the shelter could purchase or had much better stored. Nor could some of JC's employees and volunteers understand this concept. *"Throw it away"* they would say, *"I will buy you a new one."*

When Sharon had first showed up at JC's, she was just moved around like one might move a lamp stand or piece of furniture around. She didn't talk much and didn't seem to appear too excited by anything she was asked to do. On the other hand, she didn't complain or push away from anything she was asked. Like some kind of universal machine Sharon just did what she was asked and did it pretty well. After some time, she was able to teach some of what she had, not so much learned but by what was needed. If something needed paint, sewing on a button, patching a hole in a shirt, a meal put together, making decorations from almost nothing, Sharon would take the job of showing someone or several, how to do it.

Sharon Terlecki understood trying to teach life values. She had been, homeless and knew it was wrong for volunteers to tell the gusts about their way of buying whatever came along, when the guests didn't have and wouldn't likely have that kind of money for a long time, tell them how you made something out of what you got for nothing. Tell them about the delicious meal you made from leftovers and how much tastier, quicker, healthier, and cheaper, it is than a fast-food place. You won't have to leave home for it, be disappointed by something missing, you can learn to make just the amount you want, at just the time of day you want. If something is wrong with it, you have only yourself to blame and learn from. Tell them about the clothes you got from the thrift store and how you were able to alter them, to work for you. Talk about the five or six shirts you bought for the price of a single new one. Tell them about the things that help to make you non-dependent"

Sharon Terlecki seemed to be one of the few who understood, a little patience and caring, would go a long way. She knew it would pay off, for these people, maybe not right away, but one day.

When JC's Salvage, had started out, one of the first things was to build or at least find a place to be used as a chapel. Specifications were, "A Chapel", Not this or that design to represent something but for now rather than later, a chapel. John and Karl felt it was important enough, to not put off until a lot of people accepted it's looks, parts, pieces, dedication and recognitions.

From that, it never really had all the pomp and ceremony of so many chapels. It was just there; improvements had been made. In time, it grew much larger with a few more comforts but that was about all. It had started, in the corner of one of the old abandoned airplane hangars and gradually took over the entire building or at least a good part of it. There was also a small chapel or grotto, out back on the yard but this inside chapel, was for groups and if the word fits, a little more formal. The building was only heated when used and even then, not heated very well in the coldest months.

As for decorations, just about anything went. The walls were covered with reminders of so many of the events JC'S had seen. Reminders of so many of the people who had passed. Some on to a better and productive life, some on to the next life and some to who knew where. Little stories, pictures and as long as it was thoughtful, it could go on the wall.

The important thing, the chapel worked. By now, from one to a hundred people could go there without it being crowded. Various ceremonies and services had been celebrated there, including births, weddings and wakes. Birthdays, anniversaries. Accomplishments would be recognized there. A Priest or Minister would be contacted to come out and perform the ceremony's and as many as wanted, could attend. There was always a Sunday service, but never was a guest or anyone else told, they must show up. This had to be strictly because they wanted to be there and nothing more.

After Sharon had been around a while and it could be seen that she possessed some real skills, she was given the use of a room that had once been an office. This room was in one corner of the hanger/chapel. It was a place she could save odds and ends of various clothing pieces, remove buttons and enough room to teach some house or home keeping skills. Shortly after she moved into her own office, she started keeping her own records of who, when and where. She kept records of her cash outlay which she would recover at the biannual rummage sale. The room had a door which could be locked and the room was small enough to be heated in cold weather.

Sometimes someone using the chapel would come and inquire about her work and maybe become one of her students. Sometimes one of her students would decide to stay for a church service. Anyway, it was just another, throw together idea, which had worked out well. Just like a cash investment, JC's was always trying to get more back than what was invested and with a person like Sharon Terlecki, this was easy. She was eventually paid but probably just enough to keep up her little apartment, which was in walking distance of JC's. She was allowed to eat, go through the used clothing, take advantage of the showers and laundry, or most anything JC's had to offer.

Because of JC's donations storage, they could pretty well decorate and supply the needs of anyone moving into a new home. Sharon was given the opportunity to use whatever she needed. Once in a while she would see a lamp or wall hanging, she liked and be allowed to take it to her own apartment. It was like a loan and so, in a way, she was always redecorating.

Sharon loved her job and sometimes would have to be told to take a break. Her hours were whatever she wanted and she might be seen there late at night or early morning.

It was hoped that one day, Sharon would break out of whatever kept her at JC's and move out to the real world. She had been offered many jobs, as well as opportunities to go back to school. For now, this was all she wanted and JC's, was satisfied she was moving forward. She was earning a living and giving back, more than her share and that was what JC's, was all about.

Sharon found herself doing some decorating around JC's taking on projects like fancying up one of the small rooms for the guests. Pretty soon some of the other guests would ask her for help. That got Sharon looking at decorating magazines, some, from the donated salvage and some, bought for her by volunteer workers, she had made decorating suggestions to.

One day she, Sharon, was approached by one of JC's demolition people. They were contracting to remove most of two floors of an office building but the manager needed his employees to continue on, in part of the building if at all possible. The cost to shut down completely, or move to a new location would be staggering and JC's was offered a considerable bonus, if the that could be avoided.

They could, of course just throw up a few rough walls, inclosing the appropriate amount of space for the needs but working in the midst of demolition was not like working in the normal daily conditions they had hired in to and this project was going take a while, most likely a couple of years.

A little reluctantly, fearing she was not up to the request, Sharon agreed to at least take a look at what was going on and have a better idea of what was needed.

About a forty-five-minute drive to the sight and up a few stairs to what was a very large office building, people working to remove equipment from one side and hauling it to storage somewhere. People on the other side working in cubicles.

The noise was very loud and although they had made provisions, such as, large vacuum devices to keep the dust down it was going to take a lot more to accomplish better results.

"Not much to look at" Gary said, *"Simple enough for our work but making it look, good and keeping the working office side cleaner and happier, in the meantime isn't going to be easy. If we can pull this off without destroying the equipment that is being used while we are working and not upset too many people, we will be heroes and could do a lot, for our business. So, what do you think Sharon?"*

"I'm sorry" she said, *"This, has nothing to do with what I have learned and I'm afraid I would only take too much of your time to do nothing. You are going to need a whole crew of people who have been trained in this kind of work. I am so sorry you brought me all the way over here but I don't want to mess things up for you. I wish, well I'm just sorry and wish I could say more."*

"It was worth a try" Gary said, trying to hide his disappointment. *"At least you came over and looked at it."*

As they were leaving, Sharon spied a large church she had visited many years before. Gary noticed her attention to the church and asked Sharon about it.

"Oh, just a place I went to, a long time ago and never get over here anymore. It was always so warming and holy to me!"

Much to Sharon's insistence, that Gary's work was too important to take the time, Gary insisted they stop in and take a look. *"And"*, he reminded Sharon, "I am the driver."

Opening the massive doors and then the second set of doors, like walking into a castle. Soon she was back so many years ago and just slowly walking up the center isle to the front, fell on her knees like she was in a trance. Almost forgetting anyone was with her, she started to pray. Memorized prayers, Requests, made up prayers and settling to just listening quietly all the while, tears falling.

Suddenly she remembered where she was and where they were supposed to be going, then, jumping up, almost falling down. Gary, coming out of somewhere, grabbed her arm, saying, *"slow down their lady."*

They walked out of the church in silence but the minute they were outside Sharon started to apologize for taking his time.

"We were only in there about twenty minutes and maybe I needed that stop more than you. That is the last time I want to hear your apologies."

"Oh, I am so sorry" Than holding her hand to her mouth like she was ashamed for saying that.

Gary looked at her sternly gradually breaking into a giggle which turned into a laugh, Sharon gradually going from somber to joining the laugh which lasted for the entire walk to the truck.

On the way back to JC's they were in a lot of traffic. JC's was

Outside the city and Sharon wasn't used to seeing so many vehicles. *"What is that?"* she asked Gary about a large truck hauling large sheets of something blue and some more pink.

"That is insulation for,,,,,,,,"

Excitedly she said, *"Yes I know what it is and that is what you need."*

She was still jumping around too excited to talk. Gary said, *"If you knew what it is then why?"*

"*I can't talk now, wait till we get back to JC's*" From that she was all silence, staring and studding air, like she was in the process of disarming a bomb.

Back at the shelter Sharon jumped out of the truck heading almost running to her little work area. Stopping and turning around, she hollered to Gary, "*don't go home until you see me. I will have something to show you.*"

Near going home time, Gary went out to Sharon's office and work place.

Knocking on the door a call came,

"*Come in.*"

He found it to be a little cool for the kind of work Sharon did.

On her shabby desk, she had some large drawings.

"*Come over here*"

Immediately he recognized a drawing of the office area they had been to. A little rough but the idea was there.

"*This is simple or I believe so,*" said Sharon, "*you are going to have to wall off the part being worked on. Don't start! Just be quiet until I finish.*

You will be walling off the area being worked on. You said, you usually use plywood and build temporary walls. I want you to build two walls allowing for a wide as possible, hallway between, thus cutting down on noise and dirt. On the inner walls I think you can cover them with two-inch insulation board, light blue isn't bad and decorate the walls with whatever we can come up with. This would be a great project for some of the guests if you could arrange it to be done on a weekend.

You know, around here we have pictures, some framed, some not, signs, old license plates, pieces of decorative cloth, ribbons and a lot of things to make fun walls.

I have an idea, that the employees will find the walls and decorations fun and do a little decorating themselves."

Gary stared at her, looking a little agitated "*I sure wish you could have told me this before I called the owner of the business and advised him to go with the other contractor who just happen to be in his office at the time!*"

Sharon winced, wanting to cry.

"*Just kidding,*" Gary said, "*this is so simple and so perfect, I can't believe I didn't think of it*".

Sharon looked at him, by now not sure what to believe.

122

"Seriously, If I must be serious, Sharon, This, is so great and honestly, I would have never thought of that. When I think of all the times, I could have used that Idea, well, that is why you get the big bucks and have this fancy expensive office."

Again, Sharon looking at him. This time with eyes wide, eyebrows lifted.

"OK," Gary said, "I'm leaving and we will talk again in the morning. I will start lining up materials and transportation. Most will be delivered on the job and I am pretty sure I can get a delivery on the weekend and enough help to pretty well get the most of this done the same day. This is done rough and not the same as something that is supposed to last twenty years. Maybe you can spread the word and just maybe some of the gests, will help. Some of the gests might be able to help with the wall construction but others will have to stay out of the way until we can get enough done for the them to start decorating."

Starting to leave, over his shoulder he said,

"This will at least get you a much better office and work space, if I have to do it myself."

By now, JC's had at least 150 people, either staying permanent, or just coming in during the day, as they had their own place to stay. Sharon knew it would be no trouble getting 8 to 10 volunteers.

Gary took a week to get everything arranged while completing work on another job. Phone calls made, delivery and workers scheduled for Saturday. Staging area for materials and parking arranged.

Sharon, with the help of volunteers and guests, had spent a god part of the week putting together odds and ends to decorate the walls. She had a kind of following and much of the work she did was just plain fun. This was fun,

"How do you think this would look?" "What about that" "Wow! I haven't seen one of these for a long time." Her part of the project flowed, helpers getting caught up in it.

Saturday came around soon enough and as it turned out, because there had been so much buzz around JC's about the project. Sharon wound up with more helpers than expected. She had asked for 30, expecting 10 which she felt more than enough to manage.

Guests Showed up at JC's very early and Gary was there to pick up two guests who had offered to help him with his part. Waiting for him were, eight people, 5 men and 3 women.

Packing in four of them and telling the others, *"Someone will be back for you in about two hours. Go back to bed or get some coffee. I will need you badly when this bunch gets tired out."*

Getting to the sight he found his crew already started. The lumber was being delivered and a kind of bridge had been built to carry the material from the bed of the truck, to the large porch avoiding lifting down and carrying up the four feet of steps. The porch area was large enough that most of the material could be piled there and right away, two of Gary's crew, showed the guests where the material was to be placed in the area it was going to be used.

While two men and the driver were unloading the truck, four guests and two of the crew were caring lumber to the second floor, work area. Fortunately, there was a large enough elevator to carry supplies to the second floor and that is where they had started. As soon as 2x4s came off the elevator they were put in place and covered with plywood. The double walls went up like they were being driven by a machine. As soon as the truck had been unloaded and was away, the pair who had been unloading plywood, started in on building the walls on the first floor. The simple construction along with their wordless teamwork made it move along pretty fast. The guests had been told to try avoiding getting in the way but help if you are asked.

Gradually the guests found their place, carrying in more material but only staying ahead of what was being used so as not to clutter the area. If any cutting was done and there wasn't much, the scraps would be picked up and tossed into a container outside.

Gary had called Sharon and told her to make it at least three hours instead of two, and could her driver bring his other guest helpers?

Sharon showed up about a half hour, later than what Gary had asked but knew from what he had told her it was better than getting in the way. With her was a van and two other cars. People started getting out and Sharon asked them to just stay outside until she could find out the plan, if there was one.

Gary took his four guest helpers in, letting them see what was going on and taking over for the four who were leaving.

The helpers Gary had brought were pretty tired and didn't have to be coaxed to go back to the shelter.

By now, it was standard practice to have a great meal waiting for guest workers when they returned, outside of normal meal times. A simple call from their lead person and it was done.

As they were loading up to go back to JC's the truck load of blue insulation showed up. Cat calls and jokes were hollered out from the guests leaving, to those staying. *"You guys got it easy" "you waited for the hard work to be done?" "Bunch of blue boarders".*

Unloading the insulation was pretty quick, considering the large amount that had to be unloaded. Somewhere around midafternoon they were able to start bringing it in and it was being installed almost as fast as it was brought in. Some pieces were covered with a piece of cloth, some of the cloth was used and laundered decorative bed sheets and some from bolts of cloth and all from an excess stock at JC's. Soon after the first sheet of covered insulation was put up, Sharon brought in a box of things to put on the wall. About that time, one of the office workers came in, saying they needed to pick up something from their desk. Her boss had told Gary that she might be in and so was more or less expected.

"What on earth is this"? Tamie asked. *"I knew something was being done but?"*

A short explanation and

"Wow, I am so glad our boss is thinking of us. He has always been so considerate anyway. Which reminds me, He has a birthday coming up. Could I pin a piece of paper on the wall with his birth date?"

Sharon was quick with this Idea. That could make just a lot more fun for this wall, encouraging more employees to do something similar when they came in to work, on Monday.

"Sure, that is a great idea and if you have anymore, birthdays to celebrate put them up also."

"I can do that" Tami said. *"All of us, just happens to have a file in our laptops with all the office birth dates and we try to celebrate them, even if it is just a little cake at lunch. I might have a couple of photos I can down load but you will have to tell me how and where to put these."*

"We have brought plenty of straight pins, double back tape and various fasteners you can use." Sharon said. *"The rest is simple. Separate everything so it will be distributed down the entire wall. Copy them to different colors of paper if you have it. That way, they will have to look a little harder for theirs or whoever they are looking for. Put some near the top and some near the bottom. Our clever construction people have made an insert in the wall for a large coffee pot and snacks. I have an idea many lunches and breaks will be spent out here in the hall."*

By 5oclock, everyone was exhausted. The walls were done and better than Gary, could have expected. With all the help and all the fun, his workers made it a point to do it well. A little extra here and a little tweak there. The construction people looked over and commented on their work as they left and it was obvious, they were proud.

They had put in a long day working early and around and with people they were not familiar with and it had paid off. So glad their part was finished.

Working during the week, while employees and others were coming and going would have made it pretty rough.

Gary said he felt bad that Sharon hadn't been able to finish, but that would be a little easier to do on Monday. Not the surprise element he would have liked, but in reality, the whole project was a lot further than he would have dreamed.

Sharon agreed to stay behind, with two of her guests offering to stay with her, cleaning up. Shortly after Gary left, a van and car, showed up with the workers who had helped in the morning and at least four others people.

Now, Sharon just couldn't leave or maybe wouldn't leave. This was more and more exciting. She ran back and forth supervising, correcting, a little touch here and an adjustment there as they decorated the wall, soon looking like an art display at a museum. The upstairs wall was being finished just as well. Those decorating couldn't believe how she could see the little things which made so much difference.

The helpers loved it, asking, *"Is this ok here? How does this look? Am I putting this in the right place?".* They wound up staying until sometime after 10pm. and no one was complaining. They were just glad to have been part of something which was so much fun and looked good to all.

126

Sharon had been going since very early morning and fell asleep on the way back to her apartment, being woken up when the driver got there. With a quick

"Thank you" and a *"see you tomorrow"*, she made her way, up to her door, rummaging for the key, stumbled her way inside and falling on the couch, asleep in minutes. Later, she wound up in bed, but only after a long hot shower.

The next day, by now remembering it was Sunday, Sharon was up early, going to church and back home for a little more rest. The previous day had taken its toll and it would take a few more days before she was her old self again.

Monday found Sharon back in her little office, long before anyone else and before most of the guests had waken up. She puttered and put things away, still struggling with a little soreness and weariness from Saturday. Somewhere around 9:30am, a phone call came in for her to come up to the main office.

What on earth do they want now, she thought but Sharon wasn't a grumbler or complainer. Someone once said to her, "an elephant could step on your foot and you would just wait for him to move."

Someone from the office building they had worked at, on Saturday, was asking about her and wanted to see her and see her now. A car was waiting and in she got, buckling up as they sped off. The driver said, it sounds like something you did is holding up people from going back to work.

Sharon was scared. What could she have done so wrong? The short trip gave Sharon more than enough time to consider every detail and find fault in so many things she should have done better. What was she thinking about? She should have never taken the project on. Who did she think she was? This would never happen again.

And soon they were there, climbing out of the car, knees shaking, she could hardly make it up the stairs. The driver opening the doors, and in she went, to an uproariously loud group calling her name and saying thank you Sharon. There were people in construction clothes, suits, dresses and slacks, all praising her. Great job, Unbelievable, classy, so comfy, respectable, something we can work with and so many more things being said. The noise seemed to go on for a long time and finally a woman dressed in torn jeans and a camo shirt raised her hand to quiet the group.

Gary came up about that time, putting his back to the woman quieting the group and mouthing, *"Say Nothing for now"*. As he turned around, he introduced the jean wearing woman. *"So, Deb, this is Sharon. Sharon is our design Teck, who sets up these things. We recently found her and feel pretty good about that. Her skills go way beyond what we could have ever hoped for. Unfortunately, she has a tight schedule and could only give me a few minutes but I am so happy she could come for that."* The woman in jeans, Deb, said, *"thank you for all you have done. You being the expert already know how many people are affected by construction changes and how much it can cost with time and attitude. I never knew something like this could be made better than a normal setting. Everyone is so grateful. I won't keep you any longer but be sure we will meet again soon."*

Gary said, *"thanks Deb,"* giving Sharon a chance to shake her hand and off they went.

"Who, was that person?" Sharon asked, when they got in the car, *"Does she work there?"*

"No" Gary said, *"She doesn't work there."*

"Then why, what was that all about and why couldn't I tell them how little I had to do with it.? I was embarrassed and you made me feel like the liar I am."

- Gary asked the driver to wait just a few minutes. *"There is nothing I have to say that can't be heard by Frank here. Sharon, listen to me for just a minute. I have to go back in and discuss things with the office manager but before I go, you surprised me when you showed me your drawings of this project. Your ability to suggest my crew, get a time table that would work out so well and being able to work with people not the least skilled as you are, suggestion of material to have it work out so well, and being able to decorate it, cheaply which isn't so important as quickly. Any other approach to this job would have required a lot more time meaning a lot more time for the owner to have to deal with it and at a lot more cost but much less money for my crew".*

- *"We normally just build a single wall and no decorations unless some employee decides on some personal graffiti. This kind of thing can be very distracting, not good health wise, and people, employees, staying home because of it. It can be just as hard on the people doing the tear out as my crew is and the people doing the rebuild. Trying to get things done, while trying to be considerate of the workers makes for a lot more work. Your design of the walls, addresses health, noise, egress, and attitude issues. The inset in the walls for a coffee pot and treats, that was your idea, not the construction people, as I heard you tell an office worker. They love it. It's close to their work but at the same time, takes them away from their work space for a few minutes. You are the winner. I was just there to fasten it together"*

- *"By the way, that lady Deb, In the well-used jeans, is the owner of the whole building as well as several other buildings around here. When she says she is anxious to see you soon, you must be good. She doesn't say that very often if ever. Sharon, you are good and I, am proud to know you. You are good! Now, take another day off and go home. You look exhausted. I will tell them back at JC's and it will be perfectly all right"*

Sharon decided she would go home, even though she was pretty sure she didn't need to, she would try and rest.

Sitting down on the big soft chair, one of the latest loans from JC's and grabbing a donated, interior design magazine. She could hardly look at the pages, her mind was so full of what just happened. Was Gary serious and what right did he have to judge or was it good of him but what if,,,,,,,,,,,,,,,,

Waking up, moisture drooling from her mouth, not sure where or what, Not really caring but slowly coming to, while just sitting and staring ahead. Now she was moving her head a bit, *"I must have fallen off to sleep"* the magazine still in her lap. Like she was talking to someone, *"I wonder what time it is?"* She looked around turning her head not all the way but enough like she was looking for something and gave up. Then remembering she had a watch on, *"Oh my gosh, I have slept for five hours. I guess I was tired, and maybe I am still tired and I really don't care."* Dozing off a couple more times and then, deciding it was time to at least move.

She pulled herself out of the chair heading for the bathroom. A little water on her face, that was supposed to work.

Sitting down at the kitchen table with a pad of paper and some of her drawing pencils she started making notes.

What had she done? what could she do? What would be best? A few sketches and more notes that didn't seem to mean anything. Then, just sitting there looking around like someone was watching her. Looking up at one of the poster signs she had borrowed form JC's, read, **"Let God do it".** What on earth did that mean? Was he going to make her dinner or do the laundry? How silly but then realizing her exhaustion had dulled her brain a bit and she had always known what that meant. Why would she have borrowed the sign if she didn't. This last project and its success had thrown her off balance. She knew exactly what it meant and what she should do about it. Tomorrow she would go back to her normal operation, repairing and making things for the shelter. Someone would be there wanting instruction on a sewing project and who knew what. She would take what God sent and go with it.

A message on her phone told her not to come to the shelter on Tuesday as there was some work going on; She would be in the way, and she wouldn't be able to do much anyway.

A little put off, decided she might just go and lay down in a real bed for a nap and maybe be able to think more clearly when she woke up.

By Wednesday morning she was ready. She had gotten up and laid back down several times, cleaned places in her little apartment that didn't really need cleaning and read parts of several magazines and books. Sharon was really ready.

Walking back toward her office room she noticed a number of cars and trucks in the yard near her place. When she got to the chapel, opened the door and yet another uproarious congratulation from staff, guests, volunteers and construction workers. Looking toward her office it was obvious it had been made Larger and a lot of work had been done on the outside.

"What is this?" she asked, *"What is this all about?"*

One by one, they explained how they had heard of her great work and its success. They all told her about how it made their life better. More recognition for JC's and more money to those who had worked with her.

A brand-new idea many were anxious to learn, some for their own home and some to use in their own work. What it would mean to guests moving in to their own place.

"Sharon, you took nothing or almost nothing and turned, what was going to be a nuisance into something to be proud of and want others to see. You didn't do it with money but, what can we call it? Street seance?"

"Anyway" one of the guests said, *"Let's go and look at your office."*

The room Sharon had been using was turned into something much more serious and a place one could work in, much easier. A new floor, walls more solid. There was a large table for drawing, sewing or whatever she wanted to use it for. There were cabinets, obviously used but cleaned and painted to look like they had been planned for this space. A sizeable desk no doubt from the recycle and several folding chairs which had also been painted to look happier. An extra door in one wall, open to a bathroom not finished, but with a second door exiting to the chapel area. On one of the walls was a large covered sheet of insulation board for her to use for notes or whatever she seen fit to use it for. On the board was a sheet of pink paper with the words, *"Relax,* **Let God do it***"*.

As soon as she seen the sign, Sharon, motioned to one of the other women in the group, *"Please get everyone out of here."* Peggy understood and shuffling everyone out and closing the door behind her, Saying, *"I think most of you will understand. This is a women thing. Right now, she is in there, crying her eyes out, and crazy, yes, I know, that is her way of telling you how grateful she is. That's just the way we women do things"*

In the days, weeks, and months to come, Sharon received a lot of visits. As much as she didn't want to, eventually, she had to start asking people to make appointments. Guests from the shelter, sometimes just to talk. Workers, others who had heard about her decorating skills, business people She would tell them right from the start how much time she could give them, 30 minutes, sometimes 45 minutes, all depending on how many appointments she had backed up. Some days she would have no one and that was when she worked on many of her other projects.

In between appointments she would often do, little decorations, for walls and shelves, not to clutter but to make her work place, more and more cozy.

One day, there was a knock at the open door. Sharon, caught up in a little project and her back to the door, just said politely, *"please come in."*

Behind her she heard, *"My, my, being in this room is therapeutic."*

Sharon turned around and a little woman was standing there eyeing the walls and decorations. She was a small woman, dressed not well but clean and there was something about her. Had Sharon seen her before?

"My name is Debbie and you probably won't remember me."

Immediately Sharon recognized her, *"Yes, from the office project. I am so glad to see you here in my humble place. I heard about your donations and that is a great thing. You must be a wonderful person to think of these souls. What brings you to JC's?"*

"I stay pretty busy and at times I could use a place like this to just come and sip tea, talk girl talk and forget the rest of the world for a while. For now, I don't have a lot of time."

"Please sit down" Sharon said, pulling out a cleverly decorated folding chair.

Debbie sat down saying, *"I am going to get right to the point. Gary has told me all or a lot about you or whatever he knew about you."*

Sharon flinched.

"It all sounds good or at least what he told me about you. Now I feel the need to tell you about me and it won't be easy."

By now, Sharon didn't know what to say and could only wonder where all of this was going.

"Let me just,, well here goes,, I was born in Cuba and came to the US on a raft. Not everyone on the raft made it. Some of my family was on the raft and some friends and family were already here. There is a lot more to the story but another time. When we arrived, we soon got together with other family and friends as well as other people from Cuba. A kind of community. Early on we learned how much more we could do by doing it together as a kind of business. One person would find a place to get cheap food or free food, another person would find free clothes, some would work and get a little cash and everything would be shared. The cash would be saved as much as we could and it didn't take long for us to get enough for a down payment on a large house. It was a pretty rough house but we all stayed in it and the men and some of the women worked on it making it better all the time."

By now, Sharon could see this was taking a toll on Debbie and wanted to stop her but just couldn't.

"About the time the house was looking pretty good, things happened to raise the housing values in the area. The house was sold at a great profit and we than bought two houses, once again needing repair and repeating the same thing, this time not making such a large profit but profiting anyway. From there it is all more of the same. Some of us went to school learning what we could about business and some were able to do some investing without continuing in a school and did well enough. Of course, there were and are always some who didn't go along with the program and could use a place like JC's to reclaim their lives. It seems for some anyway, once they fall behind, they feel like there is no hope for them and they just give up and wind up with tougher addictions, but that is not why I am here.

I have done very well in these forty years and intend to continue to do well. Will I ever have enough money. As long as there are needy people there is never enough money.

Back to why I am here, I liked you from the first moment I laid eyes on you. When I heard your story from Gary, I liked you even more. I want to hire you and will tell you now, before someone else discovers you, you will be paid well, better than you ever dreamed I am guessing. I have waited this long just like I wait on and study anything I am going to invest in. I need you for your designing and decorating skills. You will be sent to schools but I feel you won't need much of what they have to offer.

Before I go any further, to me, you are a special human with feeling and heart that many folks lack. I need that more than anything. That shows up in your work.

Another thing, I need a sister. Yes, sounds crazy but a person I can go to once in a while and just talk to, without being judged or examined. It seems proper that your office is in a chapel. Expect to see me some times when there is a service.

For now, I have to leave but can I give you a hug?"

Tears flowing, they hugged for a long time saying nothing and finally just parting.

Some weeks went by and a call came in to Sharon from Debbie. *"Hi and I am anxious to see you and if it is OK, I would like to have a meeting with you and Gary and maybe some people from JC's. I would like to start a company, based on what you were able to do in my Oak-Hill office building. I feel there is a need out there and let's get in on this before a lot of others figure it out.*

I will give you several days when I am free and you and Gary and anyone else interested can see if you can work some free times out also. If these dates won't work, then I can just back up and find some other times. If we are going to do this, I believe we need to jump on it soon. Think about it and be ready with any questions you will surely have."

After some juggling of dates, they agreed on a Saturday to meet at JC's from 9am until it ended. Karl and two other people from JC's joined Sharon and Debbie in one of JC's larger rooms.

So, the Saturday came and so started "Remodel in Peace". Tammi, Sharon, Carl, Karl and John Hosmer from JC's Were all there.

Sharon was to be the President and would basically be the mouth piece for all of the design, Together Sharon and Gary would work out time schedules, as well as number of people involved and Debbie would work on the business part of the operation, could they do a non-profit? She would examine wages, benefits, advertising and promoting ideas. They all agreed JC's would be a large part of it but finding out just where they could fit in, would have to be studied. Could they continue to work out of JC's? Would they be able to use guest volunteers? They needed places for storage and could JC's be used for that? John and Tammie agreed to work on those issues. John and Karl had gone through much of this over the years so they would be working with Debbie on many of the questions and at the same time taking advantage of Tamie's knowledge and influence.

As far a personal pay back, wages, at least for now, they were all doing OK. Sharon had the smallest income; well below poverty level, but with the freedom and help from JC's she was lacking for nothing and would not even consider any personal return for now.

The meeting broke up in less than two hours. Karl asked Sharon if she would stay just a little longer to talk with him and John. When Tamie and Carl left, John closed the door.

"Sharon, John and I have something to say to you and I am afraid it is going to be like an arrow in your back. Regrettably something we feel must be said and know no way around it but straight forward."

It seemed to Sharon like a long time went by before another word was said. She had come this far and what had she done wrong? Were they going to toss her out, feeling she had been there too long?

John started in, *"You know we love you and appreciate all you have done for us and all the folks here. We hope you stay with us for a long time"*. Now he hesitated, *"This is hard, We, Karl and I know very little about your past. We don't and never did need to know about that part of your life. We have seen a lot of people and we come with our own past. What Karl and I want to tell you, we feel sooner or later you are going to have to deal with it. Your past that is. Through all your smiles and laughter, it is still easy to see you are carrying a load. We don't need to know whatever you decide and will never need to hear any of it. We are telling you this because we think so much of you and it is something both Karl and I, had to deal with in our own lives."*

"We are leaving now but not going too far. If you ever just need someone to sit with you,,, we understand that too."

With that they both gave her a hug and were out the door quick.

Sharon sat there, hating them for bringing the subject up but at the same time, after being around JC's and all the injured people, knew they were right. Up until now, she had managed to keep most of it suppressed. Pushing it back and doing her best to avoid anything that might remind her of the event. She found herself sitting there in the same spot but it was getting dark. A knock at the door and opening it, found John there.

"My wife came in to pick me up and we are going to drive you home, can I get your coat and do you have a bag to take?"

Nothing was said on the drive home and When Sharon climbed out of the back seat, John's wife jumped out, grabbing her and giving her a serious hug, then without a word climbed back in the car. They watched as Sharon walked up to her door and went in and then they drove away.

Sharon didn't show up for work on Monday but a call came in to John of Tuesday.

"John, I'm not sure what I am saying or at least how but I realize everything you and Karl said to me is correct and for my good. I have decided to take your advice but will need a lot of help."

John could hear her sniffling but just waited.

"I would like to go somewhere with a few helpers and it could take most of a day. I would like you and Karl and Debbi and Gary and Wendy who I met.

135

I believe she is a phycologist or psychiatrist. You can bring your wife if you like but she has not seen me as much and, I don't know what, just if you could do something like that and I would rather not wait too long if you don't mind."

John said, *"Stay right there and I or we will be by."*

In less than a half hour John was at her house, surprising her when she came to the door, *"We are going to do what you would like today. It seemed like something that didn't need to wait! Karl and my wife will not be coming with us; they have things pending. Wendy and Gary will be waiting at JC's."* Picking up Wendy and Gary, Sharon gave John some general directions, saying I will do a little better when we get closer.

For almost three hours they drove along in mostly silence. Then as they got closer to a small town, Sharon told John to turn first this way and then that way. Another forty-five minutes and they were coming close to a large body of water. *"There is a park over there."* she said.

She continued to direct John to a parking place and started to get out of the car. Very slowly she walked toward the beach, Windy, John and Gary a little apprehensive. Where was all this going?

John motioned to Gary to walk on the other side of her just a little behind.

As they got out to the beach, Sharon just stopped. Like a statue staring out at the water or maybe out at some rocks. For a long time, she stayed like that with silence from all, wondering, *"what next"*? Then with a horrible blood curdling scream, *"God, please help me"*. And with that she started to cry, her whole-body contorting, convulsing and shaking. Soon she almost fell to the sand everyone catching and holding her, still deep, deep sobbing and leaning on Wendy, while John and Gary held her up. She reached in her shirt pocket, pulling out a newspaper clipping and handing it to Wendy.

For Wendy the headlines were enough. Jerking and trying to hold back, letting out a tortured guttural sound handed it to John and Gary.

Husband and young baby disappear under waves, never to be seen again, as wife looks on from shore.

They weren't able to look at each other for some time, standing there like some kind of eight-legged animal hardly moving. At some point, john started moving toward a picnic table, partly lifting partly pushing, soon all getting the idea and walking slowly, Sharon still unloading more tears.

When they had sat down for a while Sharon started to unload. Sobbing and gradually getting out broken bits of information, sometimes information they wished they didn't have to hear. Between what Sharon had to say and the newspaper article, the story went something like this.

At one point in her life, Sharon was doing well. Married with a young child in day care, on week days. A job in a fabric store and her husband with a good job. On a long weekend, they decided to take off for the beach. Sharon and Rob loved the beach and when Jason came into their lives, it was even more fun. A great sunny day and a lot of other people with the same idea. Finding a spot close to the water, so they could watch little Jason play in the water, they set out the toys, blanket, sun umbrella, sun block and all the things one brings to the beach.

Her husband Rob had bought a blowup boat, raft kind of thing and he was busy with that. Sharon had brought snacks and drinks and everything seemed picture perfect. Once the little raft was full of air, it was time to launch it. Rob picked up, Jason, putting him on the raft and off they went. the raft was pretty light and designed for not much more than the beach. Rob paddled, first on one side and then, on the other, sometimes going in circles, laughing as he went and Sharon on the shore laughing her heart out. He stayed close to shore and just far enough to keep the little raft out of the sand and floating. Pretty soon a breeze, caught them and they were, very slowly, being blown out and down the beach. But by the time Rob realized it they were a good hundred feet from the beach

He had intended to stay in close where the water was no more than a foot deep. Rob continued to paddle as they were heading toward an outcropping of rocks and Rob knew the raft wouldn't take much of that. Still, in spite of his efforts, they blew toward the rocks, all the time, Sharon watching, realizing what was happening. As the raft touched the rocks, the raft seemed to completely deflate immediately and just as Rob reached for a rock to grab and pull them out, Jason fell from the other side into the water. By now many others on the beach could see what was happening, with some running toward the rocks so they could go out and help. Rob, realizing Jason had fallen back into the water, jumped back in and disappeared under water. It all just happened that fast.

Later when an investigation was done, it was determined that there was broken glass along the jagged rocks, which could explain why the little raft deflated so fast and, when divers had gone into the water, not much more than 6 or 7 feet deep and had discovered a hole or tunnel going through to the other side of the out cropping of rocks. They felt, it was likely, when the breeze came up and started pushing down the beach, it would or cold have caused both bodies to be pulled in if only temporary. When the bodies were recovered the next day, they were covered with cuts, scratches and bruises and only a short distance from the place where they had been seen last.

According to witnesses, at the time, Sharon had stood there on the beach screaming until medicks came and gave her a sedative. From then on, it seems, she just stayed medicated for a long time. When the doctors quit giving out the prescriptions, she found other ways of getting something to ease the pain, until one day, five years later, she stumbled into JC's.

Gary asked to borrow John's keys and John without a question gave them up. Gary was gone and back in no time and back at the picnic table spreading out some newspapers, set up some cups, filling each about half with some wine he had purchased and pulling four coffees' out of the bag.

They all sat there sipping the wine and then the coffee. Some cookies came out of the bag making it a more relaxed time if that was at all possible.

After a long time, Sharon said, *"I think I am all-right now but will you please come with me one more time?"*

She walked back to the beach with all following. Getting there she reached down picking up a stick, drew two crosses in the sand. One much larger than the other. They all stayed there for a little more time and saying prayers, some common memorized prayers said together and some of their own creations. No one was going to forget this day or this place.

Sharon turned, saying, *"I have so much to be thankful for. First to God and then to all of you."*

That seemed to end it as they walked to the car. There wouldn't likely be anymore said about it but especially for Sharon, she had the peace of knowing she wouldn't be carrying this alone.

Wendy, John and Gary had invested the good part of a day but knew they had received far more back than they would have earned, any other way.

CHAPTER 9
So started the new life of Harvey Dowed

Rome was beautiful. How lucky he was, just to be here.

This was not like his home in the US. He had seen the pictures in magazines, movies and other people's travel photos but like so many things, not the same as being here. The tourism was here, the panhandlers, vendors, street food, flyers advertising the things you just shouldn't miss, those selling the genuine, *"made in Italy"* statues, rosaries, watches and souvenirs, they hadn't even taken the time to remove the *"made in China"* stickers from.

Harv was not tuned in to the cultural arts like so many others. When he traveled in the US, he tended to spend more time out of the cities and out of the museums.

Still, this was more than beautiful. Breathtaking and beyond imagination? Sitting there in a street cafe with his cup of tea and looking around. This was a hundred museums turned inside out.

He imagined the artist taking the time to draw just the ear for just one of thousands of statues and facades that he could see from where he was. He wondered what the artist had studied. What would he think about the future of his work? Would he consider the flocks of birds using his orecchio for a needed place of rest? Would the artist sit back with his own cup of tea or wine, deciding what the head should look like that he would attach his masterpiece to or had the head already been created and he needed to get the ear to fit the exact action the head was taking at the time?

Well anyway, here was Harvey Dowd, sitting in a cafe in Rome Italy. A place he had never given a lot of thought to or thought he would ever see. Harv had won some money. Not just some money but Harv, had hit the big one. He had been in the habit of buying not many more than four or five lottery tickets in a year. Maybe just waiting in line to pay a bill and the person in front of him would buy a ticket, kind of reminding him, lottery tickets were even around for him to buy and so, he would buy one. He would stuff it into his wallet and sooner or later, more often much later, check the number, feeling stupid for wasting the money.

This time was different. Although he had never had enough numbers to win even a single dollar before, this time he had them all.

Like so many, long before his win, he had thought about what he would do if he ever did win but thought about it as if a person was advising him to make all the wrong decisions. He had heard the stories of those who managed to blow it all in a short time and were worse off than before they won. He had heard of the families and friends coming to the winner with hard luck stories, the winner could not turn their back on and were sorry later for not looking further into the story, first.

I am not suggesting Harvey planned to win and Harv was not the kind of guy who planned winning anything. If he won a prize at his grandmother's bingo, he was tickled but even that was rare. His life had been one of doing toward the result and not wasting a lot of time dreaming.

When he found all the ticket numbers matched, there had been a bit of the blood rushing to his head. Did he have the right date? Did he get all the numbers right? Was he forgetting something? Looking around, was this a cruel joke? Then he settled back realizing he was at home and no one was watching, decided to do a little practical thinking. In his own way, he had everything he could want already. A younger person might not have understood that but he was sort of settled in. People had said to him, people are crazy to quit their jobs when they win money because they lose all their friends and find they have nothing to do. Harvey knew, if he had any friends at his job, they would still be friends after he quit and as for keeping busy, he had never figured he would catch up with all the things he was trying to do now.

Harvey did leave his job, almost immediately and with very little explanation. After he was sure of the win and consulting a lawyer from church he never returned to his job, calling in one day, telling his boss that he was sorry for giving such a short notice. He would not be in to work that day or any day after and could he arrange to have any papers he needed to sign, sent to his attorney? Gave the name of the attorney and hung up.

The going away party and all of the "what you should do" advice could be saved for a better person. He was not one of those people who believed he couldn't be replaced and knew it was best to just be away for a while, giving him time to think before spending and allowing family and friends to assume he had blown it all. Harvey made a quick exit without telling anyone anything. Fellow workers, family, friends were told nothing other than he was on a mission to find something.

It would be easy to stay around, listening to needs and handing out small amounts while being praised for being such a wonderful guy. He knew too, it would be easy to make a lot of wrong decisions, giving to the wrong person and forgetting the most in need.

Harvey Dowd had a brother who had addictions. Whether drugs and alcohol caused the mental illness or the other way around, it didn't matter to Harvey. He cared a great deal for his brother and had lived through all the warnings, apologies, short jail trips, hospital trips and damage at home. Now his brother Stan was staying at a shelter. They, the family, had heard of JC's Salvage. It didn't look like much but after spending sometime volunteering there, the family agreed it was as good as could be found and a place that Stan should go rather than just put him out on the street. There was no guarantee Stan would stay there but from what they had seen, there seemed to be a better chance of him getting somewhat comfortable at JC's. At times, Stan could be clear-headed enough to realize he couldn't stay at someone's home and understood, a shelter was best.

There wasn't a lot of people running around in scrubs and smocks, with stethoscopes, noticeably drooling out of a pocket but they always noticed someone sitting on a bench or sharing coffee time with a guest. Most of the time it was difficult to tell who was a volunteer and who was a needy guest. That seemed to be the aspiration of JC's. This person is not going to change overnight, why force it? "We try to keep them here under their own volition," John Housler said one day. Of course, long enough for them to witness a better life and one they would not only strive for but be able to achieve. "We would rather our staff or volunteer people didn't come in here thinking they are going to change someone and start telling them what they have to do. Most guests have spent a long time unlearning or never learning what society or just civil order means. Lying, stealing, leaving broken things behind, like credit, family, friends, jobs, and a place to call home is just a part of their lives now."

By now, Stan, Harvey's brother, had been at JC's for over two years. Harvey talked confidentially, with John and Karl who had started JC's, not telling them about his win but suggesting he had a few extra dollars and might be able to help a bit, financially. He was told, *"it sounds like you have just come into some money or you would have suggested this some time ago. Save your donation for now. As much as we would like to take all the money we are offered; we encourage people to look around and look deeply at our operation and then decide what you want to do. You may find something better. Something we can adopt or you may find, just a place your donation would be better spent. We and I am sure you also, want the best for your brother and the rest of the guests. Please don't forget us and if you feel we are serving as we should, then of course, we would love a donation. That way, we may even get a larger one, or at least you may feel better about it."* Harvey, telling them how much he appreciated their advice told them he was going to be away for a while but would get back with them.

With not much more preparation, Harvey decided to take a trip and almost the first place coming to mind was Italy.

Although never being in a foreign country before, he felt it to be the safest place from being recognized as a winner and harassed for a while. As for, why Italy? No particular reason, other than, it was the first place that he thought of and he was pretty sure he had heard most or at least many spoke English and he would need that. Maybe he had heard someone talking about Italy or seen something on Television somewhere.

He had drawn up what he considered a safe simple contract, with the attorney, he had known from church. Together, they agreed on a reasonable yearly amount he would pay for a three-year period, allowing both Mike the attorney and himself time to investigate the best direction for the money, the best way to invest and help him make decisions about his own life style.

He had asked the attorney to arrange for someone to exchange information for him, maintain his home, even staying in part of the house, leaving a place for him and his personal belongings. Harvey's wife had passed away several years before and his three children were doing better than he was. At least up in till now and he wasn't going to rock the boat. He had long ago learned, "whatever we do is going to be considered wrong by some people".

He had found a cheap hotel in Rome and walked, took busses, exploring as many suggested places as he could. Some days he just stayed in his room reading or writing about the things he had seen. The attorney had been his only contact and part of the agreement was that a trusted person would do most of the calling and receiving calls. As it turned out, the attorney's wife filled the bill.

Harvey didn't get lonely as he thought he might. He made friends with people he met, always staying low key. There was nothing to hide, just acting like the person he was before the win. His story was an early retirement, and a chance to see more of the world and as that was the truth, he had no trouble keeping it straight. He was so careful to keep it a secret, at times; he would forget the money he had won, later realizing he had done something to save a few dollars, he wouldn't have had to. He carried a couple of credit cards with low credit limits, so anyone checking would see he had the money to pay for his needs but not a lot more. He used an ATM card at a bank with only a few thousand dollars in an account, and kept just a small amount of cash in his pocket.

Family had been told of his desire to get away for a while even before the win and do a little travel east, which was not necessarily a lie as the airport was east of his home.

After a couple of weeks in Rome he moved out to the country a bit. Slowly he was learning the transit systems, and using the trains and busses became a lot easier. He would get passes and tickets that would get him the most travel for his money, not that he needed to, but then, why not? It was Harvey's way and it turned out the best way to stay unnoticed. He figured that someone out there would want to do a story about his win but he couldn't do a lot about that. If he was discovered he would just deal with it when the time came. Finding him would have been a bit of a job because he didn't have a plan and he wasn't sure himself where he would be tomorrow. He would get a dozen suggestions a day and although he vowed, he would visit them it would only happen by chance. Harvey wasn't a long-range planner on this trip and when something caught his attention, he was off in that direction. After a while he found he just couldn't get enough travel in. He wanted to see it all, taking notes and back in his room would put what he could on paper saving ticket stubs, receipts and anything he might, to send home to His attorney's office to peruse later.

Early on in his travels he was noticing the poor and some just seeming to be poor. There were the panhandlers, the cripples who would not be so crippled at the end of the day, some who would kneel making it look like they had lost their legs and there were plenty of those who looked seriously poor.

He had seen them at home and of course when you win a lot of money, well, Harvey did nothing. He knew he should but he wanted to learn a little first. Knowing his brother's situation all these years, helped. For now, better Harvie looked like he needed it as bad as them. He would do his best to make it right later, after trying to learn the best way to do the best with his winnings.

Maybe because of his brother, along with exploring most anything, he found himself stopping at shelters and places that housed the poor. He would talk with the people in charge and try to get into a conversation with some of the people staying. Basically, they, the people running the shelters, were all trying to do the same thing but there would be little differences from place to place. One might be just a sort of flop house allowing a person a night sleep out of the elements while others served food. Some may insist the traveler stay for a spiritual lecture before meal time and another might require, they take a shower before anything else. Some of the places were just one big room with no privacy, while others had smaller rooms which would accommodate four or six and leaving one individual in charge of order like a dorm captain.

The costs to maintain these places had to be staggering and even with his new and very large won wealth he could distribute it in a few of these cities and it would be gone in no time. Just organizing and doing everything necessary to be legal, would entail people to watch and enforce the rules and as for the rules. How would you ever get these people to obey the rules? The more he seen the more he became determined, not to give up a penny until he could learn if there wasn't something better.

Listening to the stories and being careful to believe only some, he would go away, always feeling like something was missing. They were all doing something good for the poor and any amount was more than what he was doing but still It was almost like the physical body was being taken care of but not the person. Not the heart and soul, not the brain.

One day, he decided to call JC's and see if he could get a little advice on how best to help without giving out too much information of his wealth. When he called, it was almost 7pm. and wasn't sure if he would have enough time or if he would even get through. Right away he got through and asked if Karl or John were in and could he talk to them.

"I am away from the states right now and would like to have just a few minutes of their time." Harvey said.

"Yes, they are in but I'm not sure if they are free right now, Can I have your name?"

Soon John picked up the phone and Harvey apologized for calling so late.

"Late" John said, *"it's only just after 1pm, where are you?"*

"I am in Italy" Harvey said. *"Traveled the country some and now back in Rome. Maybe I am just lonesome for home and my brother but also, I would like to glean some information just because I am curious. I have visited a few shelters on my visits here and of course they don't all do it the same and they sure don't do it the way you do. You seem to pay more attention to the guests and that must be difficult with time and finances."*

"Boy, you couldn't have come up with a better question". John Said. *"And first, how are you? There was some concern here. When your family came to visit, they said you were not at home and they weren't able to reach you by phone. Said you had transferred your mail somewhere. They were not too worried as apparently you have a habit of not telling them when you leave for a while."*

"If you need to tell them something," Harvey said,*" tell them I have fallen into a better position and will call them soon. I should have called before now but have been very busy"*

John said he would if they came by and as for the question, *"That is something we have pondered and discussed from the very start. Believe it or not, that is a subject that has been on our minds and have been wanting to meet on it. We don't very often get people anxious to discuss that part of what we do and especially people who are world travelers. So, it would be good for us to see your side of it. If you are willing, let me get a couple other people in on this conversation and we would call you back tomorrow. JC's will pick up* the phone call cost and with 6 hours' time difference, we will call about 9 in the morning here; it will be about 3pm there. Will that work for you?"

"That will be good." Harvey said, "I'll be looking forward to the meeting."

The next day came and on both sides of the ocean they were ready. Coffee, drinks, snacks, Harvey had gone out and bought a pocket recorder, more pencils paper and was ready.

At JC's John had collected a few friends who were mostly longtime workers at JC's and were the most understanding and sympathetic to the current subject. Besides, John, Wendy a friend and psychiatrist, Karl, Julie Praetor and George Lyle were there.

John and Karl had prepped their crew a bit, telling as much as they could, they would be discussing, on how they felt about what JC's was doing that might make a difference.

Karl started in, "Thanks for your interest, Harvey, that has a lot to do with what we have to say. We watch for people who seem to have a little more than just an opportunity to volunteer. We appreciate all the help we can get and not everyone can dedicate that much time."

"One of the things that might make us different, we talk to our volunteers and encourage them to spend time with our people. We have a kind of informal class on a regular basis talking about how they can get closer to our guests and at the same time, not being too forceful. It is not an easy thing but after some time many of the volunteers catch on. Well let me give you over to someone else and thanks again Harvey."

"Hi Harvey, my name is Julie Praetor. When I first came to the shelter, I was kind of selfish. I wanted to do a little project and maybe I just was looking for the acknowledgement, recognition. Everyone would like a pat on the back and how easy it is to show off if you pick your audience. It doesn't take a lot to impress poor people. I wanted to build sheds and you may have herd of them. Well, I learned a lot from that. When the guests found they could be a part of something they would see the finish, in a short time, it would make them so happy. Without any skills at all, they could be a part of a project and that they would see used for a long time. Sometimes I could use their ideas and suggestions and then, I started to ask for their suggestions. Pretty soon there was a kind of competition for the chosen suggestion. For that short time and their small participation, they had something that they could, talk about, carry with them and that knowledge and pride that couldn't ever be taken away from

146

them. Years later some of them come to me and discuss, "remember when". I try to pass that on to other volunteers."

A few hand signals and George Lyle got on the speaker phone. *"Hello Harv, if I can call you that. My name is George Lyle."*

"I get called Harv most of the time at home. Go with it."

"OK than, Harv, here I go. My turn at changing the world. I was homeless and an alcoholic. Now I am one of those who recovered and found my way back. I will always be an alcoholic, even though I haven't had a drink for several years."

"I can share my stories but always keeping in mind, I must tell them, the guests, of my success, carefully, without attempting to make them feel guilty. I need to use my experience to recognize and remember, just how difficult it is. Let them know there is hope and be their friend, no matter what. I feel, it is my job to pay a little back by being a friend to these people without letting them think I am trying to convert them to my way of thinking. The last thing I want to do is drive them away. I have to admit, it isn't always easy but often after a long conversation, sometimes mostly listening, I feel like I come away with a great prize. I learned this attitude right here at JC's. If I had to tell you who I learned it from, I would be lost for words. I remember the first day I came to JC's and right from the start, they made me feel like I was at home. Not just comfortable but like I was in a place where I owned something. This was my little place of security and I had healthy friends here. No one beat me to death about all that they were doing for me. They seemed to be glad I was here. I have no idea where all this is going and what if anything we are or can do about it but count me in. We truly get more back than we put in. Here is our own, sometimes on board, JC's shrink. I don't know of any woman who makes as much money as Wendy Dower just for talking."

Wendy, laughing, gave George a look as though she didn't appreciate his comments, but of course all in fun.

"Hi Harvey and I don't think that is what my parents had in mind when they called me "Windy" but who knows? I am so happy to be a part of this conversation and not sure if anyone told you but we have been chatting, talking about some of this for some time. Just listening now has given me some ideas or at least opportunities to see some things I overlooked in the past. I'm not sure if we were told to treat the guests the way we do or if we came up with it collectively. My job as you can imagine, goes beyond, just talking, listening and

comes the part about diagnosing problems. We as Doctors, learned a long time ago, people need other people if they are to become healthier or recover from any kind of illness. Having people know that you are aware of their existence and care about them, can do a lot more than pills sometimes. On the other hand, sometimes the guests need a loving hand to convince them, they do need to take their pills. Getting volunteers and people outside the circle to understand these things, can be difficult. If one hasn't been exposed to the problem then that person can hardly be expected to understand that our guests are suffering some kind of illness and should be treated as such. To me at least I see this as we all need more understanding. Learning what we need to do for workers, people who want to be volunteers, paid staff, leaders and guests. Let us not assume everyone understands what sometimes seems so obvious to ourselves, and find they have overlooked something serious. What we are doing here today, call it brain storming, conceptualizing, or just attempting to conger up a helpful inside-out rule book. Whatever we are doing, I feel is in the right direction and very important. If we put just what we learned or recognized today, down on paper I believe we will be on our way to a good start."

John jumped in and said, "we have said a lot here today and I hope we can all go away with something to think about, put your thoughts down and meet again soon." They all agreed, thanking Harvey.

Harvey said, "I would like a minute with just John and Karl but looking forward to talking to all again soon."

Wendy, Julie and George filed out chatting among themselves. As soon as they were gone John said, "I expect you have something in mind already. Lots of people are interested but not usually as much as you. What's up?"

Harvey started in, "I expect by now you have figured out I have come into a little money. Because of my brother, I couldn't help but be interested in shelters. It is easy to see a lot of the wrong things to do but what is the right thing to do as far as investing? Spending a lot of money on things that create the wrong impression, watching that black hole of consumption grow as we donate, finding more and more reason to spend, usually takes us too far away from the real issue. I'm looking for reason and answers before I donate."

John shot back, "Yes, I pretty well figured out you had some cash burning a hole in your pocket. I was on the street a long time and there was a time when I would have done my best to give you a story, so you would cough up some of that green. You are so right about how donations can go wrong sometimes. If *we hired all the staff, we could use, we would lose the opportunity for guests as well as volunteers to be involved. Free involvement creates a lot more caring and an opportunity to see more and hopefully start to see the real problem. Too often paid staff may do their job well but then, just shake their head and go home at the end of their shift."*

Karl chimed in, *"If I could, I feel like we have put a lot in a bag for a make-believe meal. A lot of ideas and we should probably decide not what but how best to use all of what we have learned. So much was said today but I can't help but feel, when we finally decide what we want, it is going to be one of those times when everyone goes, of course, why haven't we thought of this before now. It is going to be a simple solution and all of us will find it much more than what we started with. The thoughts, exchanges and work will be well worth it."*

They closed with that; vowing to be in touch soon. There would be mail, and internet exchanges, all working toward a better plan when they met by phone next.

Harvey felt pretty good, at least at first. They had talked a lot about a subject that he knew little about and seemed to exchange a lot. He met new people and seemingly very nice people. John and Karl, he had met at JC's but just a little more than an introduction and now it felt like he had known them for a long time. He went out on his veranda overlooking the street, taking his recorder, paper and pen, some bread and a bottle of wine he had bought a day earlier.

Using an ear bud he listened to the conversations, over and over, taking notes on high points and anything seeming worth going back to. Over and over, he played the recording and it was easy, feeling like these people were here with him. Pretty soon he found himself waking up from an unintended nap. Papers on the floor, wine glass still full and his recorder still going with only the fallen ear bud to listen. He decided to clean up and go out for something to eat, asking the desk clerk for references. He was told about a place around the corner and looking more like just another very old building with all the beautiful old architecture that permeated the city.

Around the corner and asking at least four people he eventually worked his way up a flight of very old and stained marble steps. Opening a giant door, he found himself looking into an Italian version of what might just as well have been a fine restaurant in any city in the US.

Finding a table, he was addressed almost as soon as he sat down. Ordered water and managed to find an appetizer to order, expressing to the waiter he would need time to decide more than that. Behind him he heard,

"Sir, we might be able to help you make a selection". Turning he found five young people, college age he assumed, looking at him.

"Sorry sir, we are exchange students, three of us visiting here from the US, and two, who live here. We heard your American English and knew the trouble we had ordering when we first came here."

Harvey was thrilled. This is what he always looked for. A chance to meet someone local and exchange information. *"Yes, I would really appreciate that."* Immediately one of the young women and one of the guys came over to his table opening the menu. *"Now Mike here likes this but for me, well sorry, what do you ordinarily like."* Pretty soon all five were round his table making suggestions.

The waiter came with his appetizer and water, Harvey telling him he would like a little more time.

"Do you mind sitting with us, we have a larger table and anxious to hear from someone from home;" one of the obvious American males said.

This soon became a fun party, everyone trying to talk at once. the students, Harvie had guessed right, were anxious to talk about all the things they had learned from each other and how it was driving them to want more.

Sooner or later, it had to come down to, *"So, what are you here for, as if, it is any of our business?"* a young lady, Maria asked."

Harvey was ready for this. As soon as they became the least bit friendly, he was pretty sure the question would come up and one of the things he had learned a long time ago, if you need to tell a story, make it a true one. That way it is easy to remember the facts.

"I am doing a kind of personal study of homeless people and their shelters." He went on to tell them about JC's and his brother and how he loved him but couldn't bring him home with his addictions.

That went so well, Harvey thought. He was right proud of himself, the subject igniting more conversation and after more than an hour of food, fun and exchanged tidbits of local lore a decision was made to go as a group to a homeless shelter sometime soon.

"I don't mean to be so improper but would it be possible to visit one tonight?" The young people looked at each other sheepishly, then, *"sure, why not? We know our way around and a bus ride will take us right there. Never been there but passed by several times. It is going to be in a not so nice neighborhood, but we don't care if you don't mind"*

"Let's do it" Harv said.

Harvey Paid his bill, making no attempt to pay for his company's bill. A bit too early to let them know he had any or at least much money. He asked the waiter where he could buy cigarettes and was told, they had some behind the counter.

To his new found friends, *"excuse me, I need to use the restroom. I will meet you outside."* On his return from the restroom, he bought ten packs of cigarettes and adding an extra hundred euros on the credit card saying, *"I will be back for more tomorrow but I need to pay now before my wife takes my card."*

The waiter looked a little surprised but put a note in the cash drawer.

Stuffing the smokes in his jacket, shirt and pant pockets, Harvey met the group out on the street, hoping they didn't see the cigarettes.

They walked to a bus stop, a few blocks away and shortly a bus arrived. Off they went, Harvie thinking, *"I don't even know these kids and I am trusting my life to them. Come to think of it, that works both ways."*

"By the way, my name is Harvey. I know you are Maria, you are Giada, and I believe this is Angelo. That's where it stops."

"Not quite, this is Francesca and I am Angelo, that's Mike" Mike said, *"Yea, don't get me mixed up with that name. He's got rough people looking for him."* Laughing, Maria said, *"you mean, sister Mary Roberts, don't you?"* More laughing.

In twenty minutes or so, they arrived in a neighborhood that was not kept up too well and one that Harvey was sure he hadn't been in. No sooner had they got off the bus, then they were approached by a woman in rags, very few teeth and looking like she hadn't had a bath for a long, long time, *I haven't eaten anything today and I am on a special diet can you spare,,,,,,,,,,,,,,,,,,,,,,,,,"*

Harv reached in his pocket pulling out two packs of cigarettes, *"You probably don't smoke but you can sell these for enough to buy a meal. What is your name?"*

"I'm Geeta and I can't thank you enough. Bless you sir."

"Bless you Geeta, I will pray you always get a bed to sleep in." Harvey said.

"Wow, that was something." From Angelo, *"You did that like she was giving you something"*

"She was" Said Harv, *"Now let's find that shelter."*

Off they went, down the street in the direction they were told. People sleeping on the walk-in doorways, standing around like corpses that didn't realize they were already dead. Occasionally Harvie passing out a pack of cigarettes, telling the recipient to share.

One man, was sleeping right there on the walk. A pant leg was torn from his foot up, past his knee exposing a leg covered with sheets of peeling dirty skin. Others would be missing a shoe or sometimes both. There feet would be so calloused and deformed, they hardly looked like human feet. Some with their feet or stomach severely distended. Some would look quite normal, or at least until they started to talk. Then it was obvious there was something wrong. Intoxication was ramped.

Getting to the shelter they talked their way in, Harvey passing out a couple more packs of smokes. After a little pushing and shoving, trying hard not to step on anyone, they found a Nun who was in charge. Taking them off to a small cluttered office, not much better than the area the guests used, she asked, how can I help and so great to see people who are not here because they don't have a home.

Once again, Harvey told his sorry and they exchanged information for most of an hour, the young people jumping in at times with their own questions and all the while, the homeless guests coming by with their questions. Sister Veronica said she had worked at a number of shelters in her life, this one being one of the worst. Poor neighborhood to start with and if they do get anything decent, it is stolen from them. Clothes are hard for them to keep.

Maria asked about those not having shoes. Sister Veronica said that when they did get shoes it was very hard to get a pair the right size and some are so desperate, they would just wear one until they could get another and maybe by than the first would be lost or stolen. *"They can usually get a few cents for a shoe, and if their addiction is more important, they will sell anything even their shoes. If we could just move the entire operation, this raged building and these poor raged people to an area, just a little cleaner, where people at least accepted them without hurting them or stealing from them, well, that would make a big difference. It wouldn't due to move into a fancy neighborhood but something with a field and a fence around it. Something a little better than this. I know that in time, God will provide what is best.*

Harvey took her name and the name of the shelter, promising, to use the information as best he could and would try to get back with her.

The group found their way back to where they had started, this time very melancholy with far less conversation and more than a few tears.

Harvey told them where his room was and he would be turning in. *"I hope you five will be around for a while and I would like to see more of the area. I have traveled a lot but having someone who knows the area makes it much better. I would pay all expenses and you would be great tour guides. Here is my phone number if that is something you would like to do."*

Francesca spoke up, *"I think I am speaking for the group when I say we would like that too. We have some time off school right now and even if we didn't, I'm pretty sure we could swing it. What we seen and learned tonight, is more than we are going to pick up in school for a long time."*

Taking the phone number, they all agreed it was quite an experience and one they would never forget. *"We might be seeing you here in the morning."*

"Come and have breakfast with me. Around 9am." Harvie said. *"Same place."*

Back in his room, Harvey sat down in the big soft chair. Just staring at nothing and going over all that had passed, he wanted to cry. What was he doing, and how did all this start? How did he ever think he could do anything? All the money he had won, wouldn't put a dent in this or that part of the problem. A few million here and a few there and still the problem would be there. What good could he do?

Just then, there was a small knock at the door. Harvey wondered who could possibly want something this time of night? Maybe it was one of the five, but they had his phone number. Slowly leaving the chain on, he opened the door. A hand was passing a glass in his direction and a woman saying, *"Hi, my name is Margaret Epner, could I have a glass of water please".*

The woman in a wheel chair started to laugh and said, *this must look pretty peculiar and I doubt if you could believe my story but if you want.*

"*That would be good*", Harvey said.

"*Sir, they had a plumbing problem in my place today and didn't get back to fix it. They left me buckets of water but for my pills I just need a little to drink and don't think I should trust the bucket water.*"

This wasn't a first-rate hotel and the story sounded a little strange but then a lot of things were starting to sound strange today.

Closing the door, disconnecting the chain and opening it again, he asked the lady to come in. What are the chances this could work out well? Now laughing to himself.

In she rolled seeming to be very efficient in the chair. Going to the small refrig, he pulled out two bottles of water, and gave them to her.

Taking the water bottles and still laughing, she thanked him and said, "*its ok if you don't believe my story. I hardly believe it myself. Maybe we can discuss this some other time. Right now, I need to get to bed and pretty sure from the way you look; you need the same. Remember, it's the little things we do that seem like they don't count but sometimes they make a much larger difference then we will ever know. Maybe I can tell you later but you may have just saved my life. God bless you and get to bed.*"

She wheeled around and was gone as fast as she had arrived.

Harvey re-locked and chained the door and going back to his chair, looking in the mirror on his way by. He did look pretty bad, shirt pulled half out, hair a mess and one shoe covered in dirt, he sat down laughing, trying to remember where he was before that event. Then he remembered asking God, "*what good could he do?*" and Harvey started to tear up.

The next morning Harvey sat out in the street cafe attached to the hotel. He was hoping the five-student group would be back and from there he could watch much of the street. He hadn't realized how lonely he was and the young group were so healthy and positive. What a joy it had ben to spend time with them. Sitting there alone, Harvey was starting to get a little chilly so decided to go inside. The young people would have a lot of friends their own age and without a doubt be a lot more fun than Harvey. Grabbing his cappuccino, he slowly and sadly got up and started in to a warmer place. At least he had last night to remember them by.

"Hay Yank" came a loud cry from down the street. Like five-year-old children, here they came, laughing and giggling. Pocking and bumping in to each other. *"We didn't expect you would be here. Thought after last night we would have turned you off"*.

"Let us go inside." Harvey said. *"It's kind of chilly out here."*

"Chilly? Its real cold" Angelo said. *"If you didn't notice, that you were the only one out on the entire street, I guess you wouldn't notice how cold it is."*

The other four booed Angelo, saying he needed to live in Alaska for a while and they all laughed some more.

They moved into the restaurant finding an adequate table.

At Harvey's insistence, they all ordered breakfast. While they were sitting there chatting Harvey felt a hand on his back. In an obviously lowered voice he heard,

"Mornin stranger. I recon yall saved ma life last night. That was quite a time we had, weren't it?"

Harvey turned around to see Margaret Epner in her Wheel chair. She laughing and Harvie, chiming in with *"Yes we did."* while the five students tried to look busy with their drinks.

Introductions were made round and an explanation of last night which seemed to relax the young students. Margaret ordered and the conversation rose up about the shelter visit of the previous night. Margaret seemed very interested and asked many questions.

Soon the food came and Giada asked if they could say grace. Grace turned out to be the same one most had learned from birth and it seemed to help the group feel even less shy.

Breakfast lasted much longer than one would usually spend. Margaret and Harvey learned the five students were attending the Pontifical theological Faculty in Rome and were currently on a holiday.

"So, do we have religious vocations in mind and any particular Order of religious?" Margaret asked.

"Not yet" Francesca Said, *"This is our first year and we will need some time to make up our minds. Even if we did come with a set direction, we would be encouraged to take time to decern what is best."*

The conversation changed back again to the events of the last evening. Margaret asking even more questions and seemed surprised at how easy and thoroughly the young people could describe what they had experienced.

Mike blurted out, *"Harvie wants us to show him around and he is going to cover the cost. You should come with us"*

The minute he got it out he felt like he had really messed up. *"I am so sorry, Harvey. I am just so excited"* Mike said.

"Don't try to clean it up now, mouth" Angelo said, *"You just sent us back to an empty school room.",* knowing it would in its own way turn a mistaken word into a funny word.

"Try not to be too hard on him" Harvey said, *"were still going but we know who is going to carry all the bags."*

"Oh, come on" Mike said *"you haven't seen the bags these girls have."*

"So", Harvey said to Margaret, *"what do you think?"*

Margaret sat there, quite unprepared to say anything.

"My life has been pretty quiet. Scaring Harvey last night and this breakfast is about the most fun I have had in a while. Before I start blubbering let me make a suggestion. You can hear and learn more about me later." She went on, *"I have been in Europe for some time and have gotten to know drivers who can carry me around. They always use a van that is wheelchair accessible. If you are daring enough to take a late-night stalker with you, I would be glad to pay all the expenses. What do you think?"*

"Let's get rolling," and looking at Margaret, *"If you and I are going to share expenses. I want to suggest we start out doing a one-day excursion today and that will help us decide how things will work out and where we would like to go."*

"That's a good idea" Giada said, *"I would hate to have Mike throw his back out the first day, carrying my bag. I won't need it for one day but look out tomorrow if we are going for longer."*

They laughed.

While Margaret was making a call to a driver, Harvey handed a credit card to the waiter and asked for an empty envelope and a receipt. *"Who is going to be the treasurer. This is how I used to do this with friends. We both put a small amount of cash in the envelope and then put all the credit card receipts in there. We can use my card and only one card. Using more than one makes it too confusing. If there is something so personal someone doesn't feel it should be purchased out of the kitty than that is on the person buying that one thing. I will stop once in a while to be sure it is covered. When we are all done or any time in between we add up the receipts and amount of petty cash used, split it and everyone is happy. Margaret will pay half; I will pay the other half and Mike will carry bags."*

"What about Angelo," Mike asked, *"What is he doing?"*

"I get to push Margaret, if she will let me." Angelo said.

"She looks like she can take care of herself pretty well and smart enough, not to take chances with a lousy driver like you." As they left, Mike and Angelo were still going at it, everyone laughing and Margaret looking like she was having the time of her life.

Starting out the first day for just about eight hours was a great idea. That found them back at the same Ristorante as they had breakfast in. More water bottles were suggested by Maria and should be bought in quantity where they could be purchased the cheapest. Angelo suggested some snacks or premade sandwiches avoiding the need to stop for all the meals and have to pay the higher prices. Francesca said she would bring a plastic bag from her room for trash and Mark suggested they take any small cardboard boxes they happened to find, cutting them up for cup holders or just keeping things organized. Margaret said she had some shipping tape. *"It's not duct tape but works almost as well and doesn't leave the glue behind."*

And that is the way it went. Everyone seemed to need to out due each other helping all they could and excepting whatever came along. Of-course the young ones, realizing they were getting a pretty nice vacation for free did even more to show their appreciation.

When Harvie and Margaret were away from the students for a while, Margaret said to Him, *"For some reason I trust you and this whole thing seems predestined. I was pretty depressed last night and just about ready to take my pills without water and all of them. That is the only time in my life I ever felt like that. More on that later."* Harvey agreed there would be more to say later.

"It doesn't seem like any of us will ever see each other after this vacation if I can call it that. Even before my accident I was doing pretty well financially. Now, since the accident, I am doing even better and will never be able to use what I have. I don't want you to pay a dime for any of this I have it covered and more. I would like to encourage the kids to buy a few souvenirs for friends and family. If you see me pushing them to a souvenir, I don't want you to feel I am using your money. That would be wrong."

"I was too busy looking to see" Harvey said. *"I would have thought just the opposite and maybe you would be strapped because of your condition. As for confidence goes, I sure hope you are telling me the truth because I am doing at least as well myself. Not something I want to talk about or let out right now but we may have yet more to talk about later. Right now, here comes the group and I am loving all this."*

Margaret smiled and said, *"Did I mention my time in Leavenworth Prison?"*

Both were laughing when Giada arrived. *"You two look like you are having just too much fun. Is that because you didn't have to put up with us for a while?"* As the others arrived Harvey said, *"That is exactly why we were laughing but now we have had a little rest and we are ready for more torture of dealing with you, theology termites."* With that they all hugged.

By now, almost three weeks from their start, they had toured a large part of Europe. They would pick a destination. Sometimes as far as the driver was willing to go. Sometimes the driver would only drive for a day and more than once in a while, a driver would sleep in his handicap van and they would go for two or three days. When the driver would tell them he would be done at the end of the day, they would use that for their destination that day. Margaret would reserve four rooms, find a driver to take them around for the next part of their trip and, in a way, that decided their route. It worked like, as they say, "clock works." Planning and discussing, taking notes, making calls while they drove and having their destination ready for them if they happened to have one.

In their travels besides many wonderful sights, they toured many shelters of varying degree. Some more poor than others. No one seemed to tire of talking with the poor and addicts. Margaret seemed especially interested and said more than once, *"I never knew. This is a whole new education for me."* She was surprised to see many of the ragged people they met showing compassion for her as though she was worse off than them.

The young people all agreed, they were storing up information which, guaranteed, would be accepted and appreciated. They had been in touch with parents and school. In both cases there was obviously some apprehensiveness, but after a few days and more and more colorful, jaw dropping, eye opening reports to home and school, they were praised and encouraged.

"Yes, we are safe. We are a group of eight including the driver. The drivers know the areas we go to and always are there, watching and waiting for us, if there was to be any kind of trouble and there never is."

One day, Harvie came up with an idea and discussing it with the students let them take it a little further.

The students liked the idea and the school did also. They, the five, had talked with the school and they were going to be able to use a room and some equipment to meet and talk with the people at JC's The school would provide all the audio equipment and students to operate it. Harvey insisted no video right now and no personal names mentioned. It was going to take two hours. Both groups would be set up with recording devices to replay later. The school felt it was so important, they would allow a local Christian radio station to listen and record if they liked, to be aired at another time.

Several days later, back in Rome, the audio meeting day was at hand. Everyone very nervous, not sure what to say or if they could say anything knowing all these people were listening. Even Margaret had tried to beg off saying the others would have enough to say. Maria said, *"we are in this together and we will go to the end together."*

Angelo said, *"isn't that what the Christians said before the Lions ate them?"*

Only you could come up with that" Francesca said.

Mike chimed in *"We either hang together or we hang separately."*

They all laughed and Francisca said, *"I heard you failed American history. If that is the best you can do, I understand why."* More laughing.

The day came and all went well. At times a listener would be able to detect tears or sobbing when one of the young people was telling their experiences with the poor and marginalized. There were so many stories, told just, matter of fact, it would be difficult not to be dragged in to the circle. Many of JC's volunteers were invited to join the group to hear from these unknown travelers and several of them were in tears.

When Margaret spoke, she was strong, saying, *"I didn't think I would have anything worth saying but now I realize there is so much and it is so important for people to hear this, I could go on forever. This from one who knows and has seen. Some of us are calling our condition "handicapped" I'm in a wheel chair and that is nothing to what these people have to deal with.*

People see me and want to help me with things I am perfectly able to do on my own. People see these poor wretches and want to run the other way, just because like me, never took the time to try and see them as they are and in their predicaments. We only see what we want to see but put right in front of us with our eyes open, makes it much different."

Questions were coming from JC's and somehow the word got out and people were calling JCs on their other phone wanting to ask questions.

Harvey chimed in, *"at least three things we all agreed on for a shelter, number one, proper location, where they, the guests, would be treated as Ill humans and not looked down on. Number two, a large fenced outside area for recreation, a safe place to be alone, for emergency tents or overflow storage, and number three, caring people. Probably mostly volunteers, who are good listeners. Food, clothes, bedding and all the other things would and seem to be out there. Just not enough area to collect and organize it."*

Two hours went by fast and didn't seem like nearly enough time. Karl said they would go over all the recordings and thanked the group, inviting them to drop in if they were ever in the US.

Harvey thanked everyone and said he would be away from the states a while yet but give his love to his brother and family.

It was time for Maria, Francesca, Giada, Mike and Angelo to go back to school. Parting was hard with a lot of hugs, tears and of course promises and endless thank-you's from the students. Addresses were exchanged including parents addresses in case they couldn't get ahold of the each other in school.

Margaret and Harvey watched them heading down the street laughing, poking and bumping in to each other as they went. Almost at the same moment they both said, *"I'm going to miss them."*

"We praise someone for always saying things so poetic but at times their words are so profound." Margaret said.

"What do you mean?" Harvey asked.

"Parting is such sweet sorrow" Margaret said and they just sat there for a while in silence.

Harvey invited Margaret up to a room, on their floor, the hotel had provided for guests and it had its own large veranda. They could watch the street and just try to come down from all that had happened. *"I believe there is a cold bottle of wine in the refrigerator, if the fridge is still working.*

160

We can order something to eat or just munch on. I'll even let you have some of my water. What do you think?"

Margaret agreed and they soon found themselves, relaxing and just enjoying each other's company.

Margaret started first. *"We might just get this out of the way early because I think, hope we are going to be friends for a long time. Part of my life is private and I would like it to stay that way for a while. I will not be able to get really close to anyone for a long time if ever. The time I have spent with you has been some of the best ever, and that without any exaggeration. The fact that we were new to each other, in new places, could afford whatever we wanted and the kids, all contributed. Thank you."*

Harvey looked at her, *"Do you mean we can't run off and get married tonight?"*

"I hate men. They always know how to say the most difficult things the easiest."

They laughed as Harvey lifted the glasses, giving one to Margaret and, *"A toast to friends".* He leaned over and gave her a kiss on the cheek.

"Does anyone ever call you Marge and do you not like the nick name?"

"I am so glad you brought that up. To tell you the truth I hated it," Marge said. *"I noticed you did your best to step around it when the young ones started calling me Marge or Margie. That more or less, represents the things we cling to, that we think are important. Since you invited me on this fantastic trip, being able to see society in the raw, I am a different person. Maybe not better but with different thoughts and ideas. I feel very small but want to do something about the world we live in, if no more than wash a few feet or, or sit with a homeless person for a while. I am blessed."*

"I appreciate you giving me all the praise and credit for this excursion" Harvey said, *"but really, I am new at all of this too. I've had my brother to watch and study and I think he is one of the lucky ones who found a place to take care of him, as much as he can be taken care of. I would have thought by now, we would be advanced enough to do a much better job of taking care of our people than most of the shelters we visited. With all we seen, I am still at a loss as to how I could help but don't feel the necessary financial structure is out there to address the problem. How do we fix the problem is one thing? How do we fund it without wasting a lot of money that sooner or later runs out? Someone, says to us, for instance, that shelter needs shoes. We find them*

enough money for new shoes. Go away patting ourselves on the back and the shoes get old, get stolen and some never get there. We have worked inside the problem without ever addressing the big part of the problem."

"In one of the places I worked for, we had a position for a teacher." Margaret said, *"In this case, it was a woman, and her job was to teach new employees just what was expected and how to approach each and every individual as if they were the only one on earth. I watched more than one person take the job and seem to learn themselves. It was great and customers would comment that this or that person, in the company was so nice they couldn't wait to return. As for the finances, I think that needs a team but also some rules and requirements from those who are making things work. Not just a single well-educated treasurer but several, with some street sense as you say, who would be able to head off problems. Also, I like the idea of storage and giving out, but not recklessly just because the shelter received it for free."*

"Exactly, I believe that part needs study but necessary and the other part, appropriate spending.

"Sister Veronica was like that," Harvey said. *"Who wouldn't want to go back and talk with her?" How about we build a big school and have these people come to it."* Margaret said. *"Teaching volunteers, the best way to treat the guests."*

"I think you have a great plan or at least one to be explored. You said earlier you had a little cash. This is where you find out what kind of crook, that I really am. Could we put up enough money, well let me back up a bit. What if we were to start with something small? A little building separated from the main shelter or building and accessed only by the instructor and students.

In the military they use some kind of system to bring you down so they can build you back up their way. Something to be considered. We or they would be teaching simple everyday things that we often forget but necessary to survive in a decent way. Of-course I would be funding right along with you and I'm not sure I couldn't out due you"

"Sounds like a challenge but, seriously I do want to fund something that will go toward the kind of needs we saw in the last few weeks." Margaret said. *"We would be doing an experiment and if it works, share the idea with all the rest of the world."*

"Would you ever go back to the states?" Harvey asked, *"and meet the folks at JC's. I feel like you are interested in the poor and marginalized and*

that would be a good place to start if they are up to it and they seem like they might. Also, I'm sure you will be impressed by their arrangement and all the stories. It sure isn't the fanciest place and maybe not the best organized but clean and caring."

"One day, maybe one day, I will need to give it some serious thought. It has been on my mind ever since our phone conversations with JC's." Margaret said.

They continued to tour, but not as a couple of older tourist's but more like students, wanting to ingest as much as they could. Every driver and everywhere they stopped, they would ask about shelters, numbers of needy people and were there thrift stores around. Usually they could find a few Vagrants, Un Vagabondo in Italian, hanging around the thrift stores. Traveling without the students wasn't the same. It was still fun but missing some of the camaraderie. They agreed it was time to move on and try to implement some of what they had learned. They would continue to communicate and Harvey wasn't the least worried, Margaret wouldn't keep her part of the promise to share expenses when Sister Veronica's plans were figured out.

The End or at least for now.

CHAPTER 10
Schools and Humanitarian tools

"I can meet you there in the states one day, but before I leave Italy," Margaret said. *"I would like to make one more stop. I would like to go back and visit your Sister-----?"*

And Harvey jumped in, *"Veronica! How could I know that? Let's get going."*

And that is how their journey started or maybe one would argue, continued. They had met in Italy and spent some time touring with five exchange students. Feeling they had said all they could for now, Harvey Dowd was leaving to go back to the US where he was facing the problem of announcing, he had left because he had won the lottery and needed time to think about what he was going to do with it.

Harvie Dowd had been on a journey to, some would say, *"find himself"* He had won a great deal of money and wanted to decide what to do with his life, now that he could do almost whatever he wanted. He had met Margaret Epner in Rome. Along with her and some exchange students, they had toured much of Europe or at least as much as they could, in the time the students had, stopping at homeless shelters which Harvey was trying to learn about. After the first visit to a shelter, both Margaret and the students were anxious to visit even more. As bad as some of the places were, it was easy for them to feel compassionate and need a little more exploring. In a crazy way, much had been accomplished as far as learning, considering what time was available for the students and so on. Margaret Epner was wheel chair bound but she refused to let that slow them down. Plenty of handicap services to help and with Harvey and the Students, it couldn't have gone better. It all came together like magic, only by now, they weren't calling it magic.

With the students back in school now, it was time for Harvey to return to the US. One last stop before he left was on both their minds.

Sister Veronica ran a homeless shelter and they had stopped there weeks earlier with the students, to explore her homeless shelter. It was by far, one of the worst and sobering events, for Margaret and the young people.

When they arrived, Sister Veronica was obviously pleased to see them.

"Margaret and Harvey, how are you? You told me; you have a brother in a shelter who is an addict. I have passed that along to my sisters and they are keeping him in their prayers. Do you have time for tea, I will put it on?"

"I'm Sorry sister but we cannot. Let me come to the point sister. Both you and us have just so much time. I would like to make a donation but first if you don't mind what would you do with it?"

"Well, we always need clothes and." Harvie stopped her, *"Is there a building better than this one, we could help you purchase?"*

"O my, I wasn't ready for that. There are many churches that have closed and some have basements that could be fixed up and come to think of it, some have accompanying schools and school yards, that would work well, but you are talking a lot of money and,"

"Sister, as I said we don't have a lot of time right now but let me tell you what I am going to do. I am going to pledge five hundred thousand for now and we will be in touch. I have an idea those students we brought here will help you find the right place and do some research for you about contractors and other necessities.

We must leave now and thank you for giving me this chance. I hope another time we will sit in your finished clean office and enjoy you and your graciousness"

Sister Veronica just stood there not knowing what to say. *"Rest assured"* Margaret said, *"he is telling the truth and I will back him up with another Five hundred thousand and for now, I have a check here, for one hundred thousand to get you started."*

Harvey looked surprised and Sister quickly put the check in her pocket without looking at it. *"I will start a special account today and there will be a conversation with my superiors but this is the kind of miracle we do not experience, often enough. God bless you both and to be sure our prayers will go with you on your quest."*

Hugs and a few tears, back in the van that had been waiting and off they went.

Later they, with the help of a phone call to Sister Veronica got the necessary phone numbers to check and be sure this would start well.

Eventually getting to Cardenal Be tori Angelo, Harvey explained his desire to donate and gave a short version of what for and how much. *"I want to be sure; Sister Veronica is in charge of what and where, the donation is used and for her to have complete control of its use. Will there be any problem?"*

The Cardenal laughed and said, "you must have enough faith in God and Sister Veronica to be donating that large amount of money. I assure you; we will not interfere nor would we want to if we didn't have to. The donations are how God's work is done but sometimes we are criticized on how we use them. We prefer donators of larger amounts of money to do what they can to direct it to their desired application. Bless you my son and you have my word as God's servant."

Later on, feeling like he had done as much as he could for now, here in Europe he said to Margaret, *"I need to get packing and get to the airport,"* Harvey said, *"I hate to leave, but it must happen sometime. I didn't feel like I could tell people about my winnings just yet and I probably shouldn't have treated my family like I did but there was nothing else to do."*

"How about we fly back together?" Margaret asked.

Harvey looked and then, tried to hide his delighted surprise. "When did you decide to fly back?"

Harvey asked. *"I think it was about the time you told Sister you had five hundred thousand to give away. Margaret said. Or it might have been when you told me you were a crook. I need excitement in my life. By the way, my bags have been packed since last night."*

"So, where are you flying into?" Harvie asked.

"Usually Newark Liberty in New Jersey" Margaret said,

"But that is not necessary. Any place close will be all right. With not having a lot to do, I enjoy seeing the country and finding drivers is not too difficult. What about you?"

"I usually go home to the Midwest." Harvey said, *"landing in O'Hare International in Illinois but like you, it isn't that big a deal. I'm still a little*

nervous about explaining, well explaining. Here it is, I won some money. Not some money but a great deal of money. That is not something one can tell everyone and I am only telling you because I feel you will understand. Wow what a relief to finally tell someone."

"It sounds like we are both in the same boat." Margaret said, *"I won't explain how, why and what right now, but I want you to know, I have more than I would ever have dreamed and can't spend all, the way I am going. I don't intend to get crazy gambling, or buying a large house to pay someone else to keep up. It's funny how, once you know you can have something, it really losses its appeal. Working on this homeless business has me in the best mood I have been in for some time. I finally have something to work on and weather I had a lot of money or none, the challenge is still there and I can at least do something."*

"So," Harvey said, *"I believe I know the solution to flying together. How about we fly to Seattle-Tacoma International, and rent a van, to go the rest of the way."*

Margaret started laughing and Harvie thought she was going to be sick, going on so long. When she could get her breath, she said, *"I expect you were never a taxi driver. It's a shame there is so much water in the way. We could have gone to Hawaii and driven back from there"* and they both were laughing.

Sharing the plane ride and always taking notes about the things which came up in conversation made the trip seem much shorter. Renting a vehicle to facilitate Margaret turned out much easier than they thought. They stayed two days at the airport hotel calling a car rental dealer. The dealer said *"We have three handicap vans, with the front passenger seat removed so the passenger can sit next to the driver and be able to see.* Having the ability to rent something, that in their old life would have been an outrageous cost, made all the difference.

From Washington and through Oregon and then into California the sights were always new. No matter how many times they had seen pictures or been there, they still enjoyed the scenery.

All the time they traveled they were making plans or arranging things talking with people and working as they went. Even though all of this was new to them, it was as though, their whole life had been planned for this. They had talked to their student friends telling them about their meeting

Sister Veronica again. Told them a little about their plans and could they get their friends to help if something in the way of a building came along? They asked them to be sure that they had talked to Cardenal Be tori Angelo, and to be sure everyone of Sisters superiors knew that She was to be in charge and the one making final decisions, if it was to be financed by Margaret and Harvey's friends, still not wanting to tell of their personal wealth.

Margaret talked to Maria, *"I believe some of you students have come from nice homes for your parents to be able to send you to such a great school. You know how you felt the first time you seen these poor and addicted people. You were probably thinking, something like, why don't they do this or that? Get a job or go to school? After seeing so many and seeing their surroundings, you learned just like I did. I am hoping you and your friends can make sure they get a nice place and that no one takes advantage of Sister Veronica. Please, just try keeping in touch with her once in a while. Get other students involved if you can. I'm not talking about moving in but just a five-minute conversation with her and if as many as twenty students are involved, well I know and pray it will go well."*

Maria said, *"Ever since we came back to school that is all we have talked about. When you called the other day and talked to Angelo, we have been making plans and with the help of our instructors, we are planning a group trip with several older adults in a week to see Sister. You wouldn't believe the clothes and food we collected. Not everyone knows but Mike has managed to hustle several packs of cigarettes from some of the secret smokers but he isn't telling to many about that.*

When Margaret had a chance to talk with Francisca she heard, *"Ms. Epner, you don't need to worry, this is a big school and with just a little suggestion, much can be arranged. Every kind of professional person is going to school here somewhere and when they hear about what you are doing, they all want to be involved. It sounds like they have, with the ok of Sister Veronica, already looked at several properties and as you suggested, all have a large empty property attached. We should hear more in a week or so and it sounds like a fencing company has been located, who will hire a few students to help put up a decent fence as soon as the location is decided. For now, there are some things to work out. There are Priests here who are former engineers and some, here who started their education in that direction."*

It seemed like they had started a whole avalanche of involvement and it was wonderful. Margaret knew it wouldn't always be like this, people would forget, some would tire out and some find other duties or necessities to take them away. For now, she just thought about it and marveled at the progress being made in one little corner of the world. Margaret always thanked the students and did her best to go beyond, just a show of appreciation. She would try to remind them of the lasting effects of their work and at the same time reminding them to keep up their studies. "Remember," she would say,

"Knowledge is the answer if it marries the right questions"

Sacramento and on down to San Frisco were some of the hardest places for them to visit shelters. No one wants to believe there can be so many people on the street in their own country. Zigzagging across the country they found the problem everywhere. Each shelter seemed to be specialized, having rules, hours of operation, sizes of rooms or no rooms, and arrangements, of their own. Some of the shelters had rules that must have seemed good to the staff and people running the shelter but not so good for the guests, causing the guests to stay away, even in the worst weather. Thievery was ramped and the health conditions were such, some of the shelters couldn't keep up. Some were cleaner than others yet the cleaner shelters were not always the best. Some places had more cooperation from guests to do chores and some hired everything done.

They took time to visit many of the national parks and scenic attractions along the way, that seeming to make the visits to the shelters a little less punishing, emotionally. Unfortunately, they would hear of homeless camps, even in the National parks.

They were surprised to find homelessness so high in New Mexico. Stopping in Albuquerque, they took time to visit several shelters. What they found were very different opinions between staff, management and those staying there. Some praised the help they received and others claimed the shelter was just there to make money. Margaret said to Harvey, *"one wonders what or how good should conditions be, if the poor are staying there for free, but then, the whole part of moving forward is that they be treated as good as reasonable so they learn, what treating people decently is all about as they attempt to move up. They are most likely to copy what they see.*

They called Angelo in Italy knowing he only had one class this day and anyway it was late there. *"I never would have thought I would get involved in something like this. It has been fun and we are learning so much. Sister Veronica has a place rented for now and depending on her approval could and probably will be purchased in a week. She said, they have been offered a huge donation and are praying it is for real. Another thing we have going on, the school has let us use a pretty small room to teach or at least tell stories of what we seen and what we are learning as we go. People who are wanting to volunteer are required to listen and ask questions before they can come on board. We tell stories of what did happen and what is going on while learning from their questions."*

"One more thing Angelo" Harvey said, *"would you tell Mark, if he could, go to the restaurant we were at with you. I have called the owner there, left money and told him to give Mark several packs of cigarettes for the poor. I know it is not the best thing for them but it is most likely the least of their problems and it helps with relationships and gives them a moment of peace. He knows not to advertise that."*

Statistics said that Mississippi had the least homeless in the states due to their arrangement of housing. Other southern states had low homelessness and they discussed the possibility of the warmer climates making it harder to count, as many of the homeless and marginalized would not come into a shelter. When they arrived at JC's there wasn't a lot of fan-fare. They had called days before and asked to be treated like new volunteers or just curious people. Only a few had been there for the interview and most of the subsequent meetings had been with Windy, John, or Karl. Some knew Harvey from his visits to his brother but as far as anyone knew, he had just been away for a while as usual.

Immediately there was a meeting, food was ordered and coffee brought. Wendy, John and Karl were there looking anxious for their stories.

They started right in. Telling stories and going over and over their notes, which, thanks to Margaret, were extensive.

They told about meeting each other and about meeting Francisca, Maria, Giada, Mike and Angelo who were exchange students going to school in Rome, studying Theology. Getting the kids involved was by accident but turned out to be a great idea. They loved it and have a lot of great ideas.

"*You know*", John said, "*I believe you are right and we haven't looked at that idea enough. Wendy, would you make a note for me to call Franz Muller and ask him how his working with students went?*"

Harvey chimed in, "*At least three things we all agreed on for a shelter, number one, proper location, where they would be treated as Ill humans and not looked down on. Number two, A large fenced outside area for recreation, a safe place to be alone, for emergency tents or overflow storage, and number three, caring people. Probably mostly volunteers, who are good listeners. Food, clothes, bedding and all the other things would and seem to be out there. Just not enough area to collect and organize it.*"

Harvey said, "*Margaret and I feel that there needs to be some kind of school for volunteers where they can be taught, showed or just explained to, that these are real humans and need to be treated like any other human who is suffering some kind of disease or illness. People with so many ailments who are bed ridden or just not able to carry their load are usually felt sorry for. For some reason we have always looked down at addicts and mentally ill people, always accusing them of doing just what they want and putting themselves in these positions. People need to be taught that things are not always what they seem and I would hope some of the volunteers and workers would begin to be a little more compassionate.*"

Their idea of a school for volunteers was picked up immediately. Karl said, "*I have an idea we can get Julia Prater to build a temporary version of just what we need and she can probably have it in service in less than a week.*" Harvey and Mildred laughed and John just said, "*Karl knows what he is talking about. Just wait and see.*" With that, Karl got on his phone, "*Julia, can you do a school building, maximize to portable building allowance. Need a rush on it and have Luann call in your material order as soon as you get a list together. There is an after-hours number if she needs it so I'd appreciate any thing you can do on this one.*"

Karl just came back with, "*now, where were we?* Margaret and Harvey just sat there questing weather or not this was supposed to be some kind of joke, yet at the same time, Karl seemed serious. "*I will or better yet you will see later. Surprises are always fun.*"

Just like that, they were into another conversation.

They both wanted to know about how the things they were doing at JC's were any better or worse than any others. John and Karl had explored other shelters for years but there was always something new to learn and could they do something better.

The food came and John's wife joined them. They talked about so much they had seen, not only overseas but in the US cities as well as in the country.

I'll bet you guys could do a travel log program. Luann said. *John and I have traveled around the states just a little but that's all.*

"*I don't think there is anything more satisfying than travel but a person usually choses destinations.*" Harvey said "*Just doing what we did, caused us to fall into some places we could have done without but still, we visited a lot of places and things we would never have known existed, and would never have seen if we merely went to chosen destinations.*"

"*Another thing, while you are here. all of you have been too polite to ask, Margaret and I are not holding back any announcements or plans. I think as much of anyone could about Margarete but there are too many things and too much to learn about each other to make any commitments now. We still honor and appreciate each other's independence and if we were to commit, we would not be able to bring as much to each other. For now, separate rooms and separate ideas.*"

"*I don't think I can say it any better*" Margaret said, "*We talked and both said we were worried one of us would pop the question and the other would have to find a way to say no, or at least not now. It may sound silly or you may not believe it but we feel like the siblings both wished we had earlier in life.*"

A little more than a week had gone by, when, Margaret and Harvey were called at their hotel. They had been visiting a few shelters about two hundred miles from JC's and were told, the school building was close to being finished for now and Julie Prater wanted them to see it, before they went any further.

The next day they left early and arrived at JCs about 11 in the morning.

Not really expecting much, but thinking, they should at least go, just to be civil, and see what had been created

When they went out to see this building, they were shocked. "*This has nothing to do with what we were thinking about*" Margaret said to Harvey. Julie Prater, standing behind them, wanted to just run away. She had tried hard and had several of the guests to thank for the hours they put in, starting early and working late. *What could she have figured wrong?* Then they asked to be left alone while looking it over. They walked around the building, Harvey pushing some times and sometimes Margaret moving around herself in her chair, going back and forth. Sometimes seeming to share secrets, moving inside, using the short handicap ramp they closed the door behind themselves and seemed to spend an unexpected amount of time before coming back out.

By now all was quiet outside. Nobody wanted to be the first to ask, to ask what? *Would it do? Was it too small? Did the color work?*

Stepping out and looking around Harvey and Margaret noticed the start of what looked like another.

Approaching Harvey and Margaret, Julie Prater asked *"maybe you can tell me the worst part or if there is any possibility of saving part of it.*

Looking at her for the first time since touring the building, it was obvious she was serious and upset, her voice low and shaky.

Margaret said, *"what are you talking about? Did you think there was something about this building we didn't like? O, my dear sweet lady, carpenter, designer and, and wonderful person"* Margaret reaching up and giving her a hug, holding on for several minutes. *"I am so so sorry, we are flabbergasted. There are so many how's where's what's and when's we don't know where to start. I have no idea what John and Karl had in mind but this is so much more than we ever dreamed."*

"O thank you" Julie said, *"I was so worried you wouldn't understand. Portable, temporary and permanent make a large difference and considering what information I had, well",*

Harvey stepped in, *"Like Margaret said, the building is perfect and a lot more than what we could ever have expected"*

Julie started again, *"The building is built so it can be moved, in this yard or on a truck on the highway. Materials are selected to keep it as light as possible while not sacrificing strength. Someone has already asked us for one, just like it, to use as a construction office about a hundred miles away. They, are doing an addition on a school and felt this would temporarily serve the office people and look good at the same time. The little room on the roof can be called a Cupola or in this case left open and we will call it a bell tower.*

We do it just for the touch and it can be removed easy for moving, everything has been duple glued, nailed, screwed, stapled and strapped. When you are ready, we can build benches inside or if you prefer, or just leave it open and use folding chairs.

The more shed type buildings we build, the more ideas we come up with, making the product better, lighter, stronger and cheaper to build."

"A few other things" Julie said, *"The inside of the building is not finished the way we like to have it finished. It is insulated with foam and could be heated pretty easy if one wanted to, but we left that for later. Usually when we build these buildings, even though they are just for storage, we give them some kind of identifying points, a personality of sorts, like the big plastic bell you see on the roof. It won't ring but it looks like a bell that would have been on an old school house. We can do one wall like an old chalk board, paint a big clock on the wall, and some signs like you might have seen on the walls of an old school house."*

Harvey looked at Julie and said, *"how about a sign,"*

"An idle mind is the devil's workshop?"

"There you go, that's the idea and I like that" Julie said. *"Your idea of a school has given us one more project and that is, how many of our people learn to move up. A little sweat, they feel appreciated, they are proud of a good-looking project they had a hand in, even if they just shot a half dozen nails and know its sale will help support the shelter. By the way, did you notice we have another one just the same already started. It is a lot easier for the helpers if they have another to copy.*

There was a pause and Julie started to go, saying *"I better get going, I have a lot to do."*

"Just a minute more if you would Julie. Margaret and I were talking while we were poking around your building. We both have some retirement money burning holes in our pockets and rather than spend it all on doctors and bingo we would like to pay for you, to go to Italy and spend two weeks with a friend of ours."

"Are you, really? but, I'm not the only,, really? I've never been to Italy. Are you sure? Is this to see that Sister friend of yours?"

"Yes, it is and we would like you to help her get started with one of these school sheds. We called her and have already told her how handy it is going to be. That was one of the calls we made inside. I think you could give her a lot of help and I know she could be a great help to you while you can get a chance to explore Rome. If you would, could you do a sort of blue print and a sketch and put a material list together, so we can send it to her?"

"I don't want to sound condescending." Julie said, "but today we use Computer Aid Design and there is a person here in the shelter who is pretty good at it when he is sober. This will be a simple project for him and if Sister Veronica has the internet, Mel can have it ready and sent in no time."

Margaret said, "I'm so glad you told us that. I kind of knew that, not how to do it, but I have seen that kind of blueprint drawing, somewhere. Thank you for reminding us. So many things that could be a help to us if people would only tell us. Not sure if she has the internet but I believe there is someone she knows that does have it. O, and by the way, your fiancé doesn't know it yet but he will be going with you."

"Oh no," Julie said, "Nicky is working, selling cars right now, before he goes back for his last year in college. He wouldn't be able to leave but wow, wait till I tell him what he is going to miss."

"We had heard you were engaged and when we were inside the building, we were talking it out and making calls. You better just tell him to make sure both of you have your passports up to date. We already talked to his boss and the boss is delighted for Nick to have the experience."

Julie, grinning ear to ear, starting to ask, "How did you know? never mind, I'm afraid to ask" and walked away shaking her head. Margaret came over. "All I know is, I need to make some reservations, get an emergency on those passports, call Sister, tell her what's up, call the students and have them prepare for a couple of visitors, and call in the material list as soon as I get it."

"No, the students will call in the necessary materials." Harvey said, "when they get the prints and the material list and that should be soon. As for Nick and his Boss all it cost us was an overpriced new car that we will probably just give away. That part, Nicky's boss has to keep his mouth shut about."

"I never could have thought, giving away money would be so much fun." Harvey pushed Margaret on to the trail around the yard.

"I think it is time for this. I told you one day I would tell you a little about myself." Margaret said,

"Grab a seat, cause, here goes. I had Polio when I was real young. By that time, they had made a lot of advancements in the cure but I was missed. Either the vaccine was wrong or just didn't stick. The reason was never discovered. My parents did their best to take care of me when I lost the strength in my legs and I managed with it. School was not too bad at first, although there were not a lot of handicap facilities then. Other students and teachers would help me as much as they could but sooner or later, I became a burden. As I grew, I naturally became heavier, and harder to deal with. Parents never had a lot of money and they couldn't always use our one car to drive me to school. No school busses in our area back then. You just had to do what you could. It wasn't easy to have friends so I was alone a lot at home. My mother, home schooled me as much as she could, the school providing all the books but her day was already pretty full with the house work and taking in laundry to help out with the income. My father was at his job, all week and sometimes he would take a second part time job at Foxhall's butcher shop.

I guess and sometimes I forget, once in a while the church would send over someone down on their luck. We would take them in, not for long periods but maybe just a meal or a couple of days till they could get situated.

There never seemed to be real bad times but sometimes there were really good times. On some weekends we would all be together and once in a while we would take an all day, trip to a park. It was always supposed to be a surprise for me but I would see my father from out my bedroom window, cutting roasting sticks from the wild bushes at the back of our little property. I never let him know that I was suspicious but I was pretty sure what was coming. The waiting was pretty hard for a young person who didn't get out much.

My father would come charging into my room like he was a knight on a horse, the roasting sticks ahead of him like a lance and go at a teddy bear or one of my dolls. "Give me your allegiance or your life knave or ill run you through."

My line would be something like,

"O, spare me my lord. You can carry me off to your kingdom and I will read to you, stores that will thrill you and give you rest."

Margaret paused at that, making it obvious that this was very hard to recall.

Harvie started to tell her it wasn't necessary, Margaret putting up her finger indicating she just needed a minute.

"*At the park, we would roast hot-dogs that the butcher shop let my father have because they were too short or had some kind of flaw, and sometimes our neighbor would give us a half a bag of marshmallows if she knew we were going to the park. Mother would usually make potato salad from the potatoes stored in the basement, that my father had grown in his backyard garden along with, green onions, carrots, parsley, rhubarb and so many other things.*

My father would carry me around, pushing me on the swings or carrying me up on the slide and telling me to hold on until he got back down to catch me. Those were wonderful times but they were also hard times, watching all the other kids do things I couldn't.

Because I was alone so much, my school work became my friend so I was able to achieve a great education early, moving on to college and beyond. With that, I had no trouble getting a great job, finally being able to take care of my parents, unfortunately, not long enough before their deaths. During all that time, I collected very few friends as you can guess. As I said, people being handicapped weren't always considered capable of much and besides that, my time was limited, keeping up with school and so on.

Eventually I met and married a doctor who had grown up in a town far away from our area and oh, you will like this. Donald's father was a butcher. Donald, was a wonderful person, doing more for me than any one should ever have to do. By the time of our marriage, I had a great paying job and become independent enough to help around the home with cooking and household chores and although we could afford to pay someone, we enjoyed each other, cherished our time together and tried do a lot on our own. Just the way we were raised.

I had gone to work for a broker before I met Donald and I had learned some about investing. While still working, we traveled a little, taking cruses, long before cruses were so popular, and long before they were considered so common. Due to our naivete we thought, that was the good life and one day we would do a lot more. Our expenses were minimal so, we managed to sock away a pretty good pile. The plan was for both of us to retire early and just travel, lavishly. No one ever thinks they are ever going to die.

That sir, may give you some idea of why all of this has so much appeal. I love to travel, meeting new people is always wonderful at least most of the time, but the really best part of all of this is being able to help or maybe, to learn how to really help. Even with a lot of money, we could not do anything right if we didn't understand these folks a little better."

"It won't be easy to teach volunteers, what we are learning." Harvey said, *"How do we teach them that some of the guests will cooperate and some will not, so it is our job or theirs, to turn it around by our actions? We can have a place for the ones that appear to understand and fenced off from those who just refused to cooperate but we have to love and care about their future equally. Instead of making rules they could never follow, we need rules for ourselves so we can learn how best to serve them without, ruining them.*

Doing that in a house where there are only six or eight people is one thing but due to the large numbers out there, we need to do that on a very large scale with much larger shelters and allowing and encouraging them to stay at the shelter until they are mature enough and well enough both mentally and physically to keep up their own living area and give back to society.

A little more than two years went by and although all was not perfect, many of the people making JC's their home had moved forward. Sadly, some went to their next life home, while some advanced enough to keep their own home and keep it in a way to be proud of. A few had recovered from various addictions and were doing very well and, they seemed to celebrate their recoveries with even more hard work as well as a strong desire to give back. The little school building with a few small changes, had proved worthy and had seen a lot of volunteers pass through. Five copies of the building had been made and sold to help support JC's. Summer would see more volunteers on freshly built wood-pallet park benches on the porch of the school building out by the chapel, along the trail or just under a tree in the yard. Talking and sharing a soft drink or coffee, with one of the guests.

A wedding had taken place and actually three weddings and all at the same time. Julie Prater had become Mrs. Nicolas Saro, Sharon Terlecki had finally given in to Gary Tomlinson's wishes and Margaret was changing her name to Mrs. Harvey Dowd

The weddings had taken place, where else but JC's. Chapel. O, there were complaints from family and friends who had long since, learned of Harvey's winnings and insisted they needed something lavish with the biggest party. Margaret and Harvey just said we have a large place and more guests coming than you could ever imagine. As it turned out although apprehensive but none the less curious, most of their old friends and family turned out. Nothing about this was like any other wedding anyone had ever attended, but it did go on for three days. One of Gary Tomlinson's friends complained, I can't believe I am at a wedding that doesn't serve or allow alcohol, and the darnedest part, I am having the time of my life.

The beginning ceremony was somber but serious and longer than some would prefer. The local priest had agreed to do the wedding Mass, telling, several stories about Harvey and JC's, keeping the wedding guests laughing for the best part of an hour. Other than that part, the rest of the ceremony was very solemn. The entire wedding party and many of the visitors had seen a lot of life, making this event, even more serious and meaningful by adding some of their teary stories.

From there on, after the service, it was a kind of happy chaos.

They didn't have a hall or room, large enough for everyone and that made it better. Earlier there had been a threat of rain so they just decided to send people to any one of the buildings around the yard they could get in to, and someone would see, that they were served something. As it turned out the clouds moved away and the weather was perfect.

Shelter guests and volunteers or anyone who wanted to, would carry soft drinks, coffee, tea, water around while others were taking hors d'oeuvres and various appetizers so the wedding guests had a chance to try many things. Not only had many things been prepared inside the shelter kitchen but beyond the fences of the shelter many passing dishes had been prepared.

JC's had been an ugly duckling story, starting out, for those too afraid to get close, like a washed-up leviathan that would never swim again and wind up leaving a bad odor for them to clean up. As JC's showed more and more promise, many more people were curious to get involved. Eventually they had volunteers just hanging out. Maybe not everyone but many people in the area loved JC's and the people involved and were always looking for something they could do. Out in the yard, a pig roast was coming to an end and starting to be served, four roasted turkeys were on another table being caved and with a chef looking person ready to pass out whatever was asked for. Food was everywhere and so many different recipes, one could walk around talking, or sit at one of the many, home-made tables, enjoying the day and always in a place where someone was offering some additions to your plate. One could just sit with food constantly being brough past for you to try. Silverware or flat ware sure didn't match but it was everywhere. Cups plates and saucers were not only from many different patterns or completely lacking a pattern but not all the same size. If you got a dish with a chip, it helped to remember, how silly we can be or how unimportant some things are, that we worry about. On the other hand, JC's had always made a fuss about cleanliness and just as soon as you emptied a dish, someone would be there to exchange it with a clean one. Food was kept covered and there always seemed to be enough ice for where ever it was needed.

Many stayed late into the night and some of the heartier visitors got up early the next day to continue on. Although it wasn't planned, shifts were created. When someone serving, got tired, another person would take over. The hotel had been warned to make sure all of their rooms were ready and many personal homes instantly became Bed and Breakfasts although JC's had warned people not to spend on breakfast because they had been planning for that and it turned out to be as big a sumptuous repast as the wedding meal.

Harvey and Margaret received a call from Italy and asked if they could call back as soon as they could find a quiet empty office so they could get the most out of their phone call.

"Ok," Harvey said, "you are on the speaker phone," After making sure Margaret was comfortable and loaded with copying tools. "So, how is all in Rome?"

"So many things to say. First, your wedding, everyone and I mean everyone wants to congratulate you two. Mike said to pass along, "It's about time." You guys are more popular over here then you will ever know. We five are still hanging around but not quite as much, as we move into some sort of direction in our lives. That explanation will come later. As we have told you in the past, Sister Veronica's shelter is working out very well allowing her, with help, to care for many more of the people she loves so much. The fence has become two fences, one inside the other, just like you suggested and filled in to block some of those who are trying to sell drugs to our people, as you said might happen. They can still go out on their own and get whatever they want but the fences slow that down a lot. The yard gets better all the time going from broken asphalt and *cement, to some gardens and a gravel walk around. Also, Per. Your suggestion we, they have a small chapel and one day Cardenal Be tori Angelo said Mass there. Talk about putting Sister on the front page, it sure didn't hurt on the donations.*

We have a big surprise for you and wanted to save this for whenever you return to Rome but together, we felt this would be the best gift we could give you for your Wedding. I am sure you remember Geeta and she sure remembers you.

She started to clean up after we met her that night and as it turns out, someone else must have been watching out for her. She was called or I guess, Sister was called and a donation was made at the local dentista to repair and make her teeth. She was a little reluctant at first but looks like a movie star now. Some of the girls at school come to the shelter and show the guests how to put on just the right amount of makeup. It sure made Geeta a new person. You wouldn't believe it. Not only her looks but her demeaner has improved dramatically. She has gained self-confidence and is so considerate to others who are where she was. Turns out she had a successful background in book keeping and has found a great job in a prominent shipping company. She has been working for most of a year. Sister lets her stay at the shelter, helping as much as she can and says she wants to save enough money to go to America and work at JC's. You and Margaret should be so proud of all you have done. Even the proprietario del ristorante, remembers you and asks of you two all the time."

Back at the wedding party things were still moving along, some complaining about their overeating the previous day and some moving right back into the huge spread that was constantly changing.

Some of the visitors from out of town were starting to leave because of responsibilities but all had so much good to say. The design or purposeful design of the shelter created a lot of conversation and there had been many explanations of how it all came to be, no one person willing to take the credit.

On the back fence were silver crosses made from aluminum drink cans, everyone was encouraged to visit the area, The crosses represented all the people who had passed through JC's. Some were painted with a yellow spot, indicating they were still there. Some were light green indicating those who had gone and were doing pretty well. There was light brown for those who had left, and never heard from again and then there were some painted dark blue for those who had passed to the next life. A sign there told their meaning and all had stamped numbers that went to a file. It was a sobering sight and especially seeing those who were never heard from again and those who had passed.

Everyone who visited the "Recording fence," came back, as Karl said, *"a little wiser."*

There were also a lot of visits to the chapel to once again see the prayer can and say a prayer of their own and as the sign said,

"Leave your troubles in the can with a prayer, when you return it will be empty."

John and Karl stood away, looking back at JC's. It still wasn't the greatest to look at but it was much more than when it started. There were nice rooms, a good kitchen, laundry facilities and plenty of space in and out if one needed to be alone. JC's was always open, day and night. Like an old motel commercial said,

"we'll keep the light on for you."

You would only get as far as a cot after a certain hour at night and you would wait until 9 in the morning to move into a better part of the operation but anytime you could find a cot and a warm place out of the elements. You might even find a hot cup of coffee.

Karl said to John, *"If we were to run a news article asking about that person who threw out the plastic bag with the hundred dollars, it would make quite a story. I have an idea that many people reading that, curiosity seekers, would show up just to see our place and who knows? We might get even more, volunteers. More donations wouldn't hurt either. I would like to think this place will be able to take care of itself, at least partly, after we are gone. Also, I wonder if we were to put together some of the things the shelter has prevented, like hospital visits, jail times, court costs and so on and put a cost figure on that. Maybe we could get something on the ballet that the voters would see that a tax going toward this kind of project would be as a savings."*

John jumped in; *"I believe it is time to take a little stroll out to the chapel and see if we can figure what the Boss has in mind next."*

WHAT SHOULD A SHELTER BE?

Research, research, research! I don't believe enough can be said about this but on the other hand, the idea should be simple. Is this the best piece of property, based on location, cost, long term availability, room for expansion, attitude of neighbors, and more? Any one person, honest, willing to give up the time, with a desire to get the best for the least could accomplish this with enough phone calls, internet lookups, conversations with others and inspections. This same idea should apply to everything from dishwashers, beds, and down to free tooth brushes. There will always be cash donated but not always enough. That should be handled carefully and invested as much as possible, planning for future.

There should be no age or education limitations on the person or persons doing the research. The names like expert and professional sometimes set us off in the wrong direction. A young person or child might come up with questions an older professional person may just assume they had the answer for. Then sometimes too late comes the questions, from the professional. "Who would have thought?" "They didn't used to do it that way." "I couldn't be expected to know that!"

Using or copying what already exists is not always the best idea eighter. I have seen many shelters and I believe it is time to look for something different, maybe drastically different.

Housing is naturally a need. One will have to determine the building requirements before a location can be decided on, unless the location is right and large enough to handle any and all requirements that may arise in the future.

Size

I like the idea of having enough space, in both the yard and or building, for the unknown future needs. Opportunities might come along to rent, share, provide for other services like Veteran affairs, AA Counseling, Cosmetology, Volunteer medical staff, Housing help, Classes by retired or volunteer teachers, Job placement classes, Carpenter shop, Metal working or Machining, Mental health counseling, Decorating, culinary,

Arranging services so the guests travel is made easier and more likely to achieve whatever goal is required.

Board members

Oh, so important, but Someone once said, **"Listen to the sweeper!"**. So important that the members be sympathetic to the homeless issues if not from experience but at least from academics.

Legal support

From the very start, of course, legal help will be needed. This is not a "show us how". It should be, "This is what we propose, can you make it work legally? Are we doing this part or that part right and if not, what do we have to do to make it legal?"

It won't due to have people, outside the understanding of what is needed to be giving direction and making decisions. We are not housing people in expensive hotels for profit. We are attempting to **save lives** and there is little time to quibble over what would be nice, **rules**.

Housing

The idea of a home for the homeless needs to be given considerable thought. From what I have seen, all too often they, the guests are stuffed into an older house in small numbers and treated well enough or so it seems but in such small numbers.

Then there are the large facilities that usually do not address the individuals well enough. Some of the shelters are merely places to sleep. In most places, guests are chosen or the restrictions decide who and why. That can hardly be the way to make the problem go away or even decrease. Every individual is different and with different problems.

OH, before we go any further, who are these people using these places? These are most often, the ones left behind. All of us can think of a time, when we had it rough and had to work a lot harder to make it.

Easy for us to ask why can't they? I am convinced that this is a very difficult question for many, and a problem for so many more to understand. It seems like when we arrive at a certain place in our lives where we become confident of what we feel is our accomplished success, we forget the past or at least the part we did wrong. If you get an opportunity to know someone homeless or doing poorly, and you spend some time around them, you may find it a little easier to understand the predicament of the homeless, marginalized, addicted and mentally ill.

On the other hand, I have met so many who are still saying, "Why don't they do this or that?" Get a job, Live at home, go back to school, ask a friend and more.

If we are honest with ourselves, we may find we had a lot more help than we want to remember. Someone had to help us get to the place where we could realize what we needed to survive. Then we had to learn what was acceptable to society. All the time being told, the things we would like, even though they were fun and felt good, were not what we needed. From there on very few were perfect. Some got caught and paid the price. Some who are doing well today, won't want to remember their faults and avoided getting caught and were considered clever while being praised for getting away with something, society was against.

How much thievery is too much? How much addiction is over the line? How much lying and cheating is acceptable, if we didn't get caught.?

Anyway, this is not about judging people who are trying to help the needy but rather determining needs required and solutions available. I like to refer to the needs as energy. Weather it is actual electric or gas energy or the food, volunteerism, transportation, paid staff.

Let us assume it has been decided that anyone needing shelter will be allowed, encouraged, coaxed to have a place in the shelter. That should be the standard if we are ever to help this problem. Instead of tossing them out for this or that reason, we should be out looking for them and be trying to bring them in.

> **"Go out, therefore, into the main roads and**
> **invite to the feast whomever you find."**

There are those who have mental illnesses, addictions, abuse at home, have lived in poor and inhumane conditions, or unhealthy conditions at home. They may only need a place to sleep less than seven days a week. Maybe just a place to get away from what they are dealing with and able to return to what they are used to, after a break.

The structure should be so arranged that any and all can stay there for any length of time. Men, women, children, segregated or separated to be clean, safe and not hassled.

Of course, there will always be those who have or can afford what is needed for a decent life and are only taking advantage to save more money. Maybe working away from home and want to stay, avoiding the cost of a motel or B&B. We have all seen the Cadillac or fancy car at the dumpster or in the free food line. That can and should be addressed later.

Some say about the homeless, *"If they get too comfortable, they will never want to leave"*. If you are saying that, you are missing the whole point. I agree. Moving them to a single room in a house or large building is not likely to motivate them. In this design, they are encouraged to mingle, experiencing healthy people and witnessing a healthy society in a place where they are not looked down at.

The people staying would be given a chance to identify themselves, helped to fill out an application, learn the rules, learn what is expected, if they have income, given opportunities to pay a sort of rent with a percentage, returned to them after a year or so from their first arrival day. A "nest egg". Any of the information taken should be done with their understanding and full permission of the person staying. The utmost care and privacy must be given the information and only available to a minimum of staff.

Yes, that would require as many things will, legal interpretations and feasibility.

Part of the building would need an open area with cots or single beds, where initially all would or could go before being called to fill out an application. We might call this a ***holding area***, or staging area, preparation, determination and decision area. Prior to registration Area.

This area would be open, day and night with coffee and maybe sandwiches offered 24 hours a day. Very sparce, with the minimum of rules, for those who refuse or are not ready for a more regimented stay. Any and all, would need to come in through a watched entrance any time of day or night and break off to the applicable area.

If for any reason, a person has been accepted into the regular center and refuses to accept rules and conditions, they can be given the opportunity to go back to, or stay in the **holding area.**

A person might be sent to the holding area because of Intoxication, miss treatment of other guests, avoiding medication or just having a bad day. Many things may cause a person to return to the center in a bad mood and become disruptive. Just sending them back out to the street is helping no one and may cause even more problems at the center or out on the street. Every time they go back to the holding area or staging area, they will, in a sense be starting over but with the knowledge of what is a little better.

This should be considered, control for the sake of the majority and never construed as punishment.

<u>*On Visiting a shelter, we were told about an impressive point system.*</u>

As for the main sleeping area, this to be set up Dorm style, with one, two or four cots to a room. Bunk beds in some. Every bed having some wall space with a place to hang a picture or something personal. Maybe a very small dresser or container but most belongings including medications, clothes, electronics, stored and locked, outside the sleeping area with access by owner, guest while accompanied by staff or volunteer only. Number of trips to storage, closely monitored. Staff and volunteers cannot be tied up making constant runs for the guests.

Location of shelter or center

The location of the building will need to be determined by several things. On the edge of town or in a lesser part of town, seems to be the best. I have never understood why shelters or facilities for the purpose of housing poor and homeless adults, would be put in places where society does not want them. We can argue that no one should have the right to refuse them in their neighborhood but what about the people needing the shelter. These people are already dealing with rejection and probably have, all their lives. If there is any chance of helping them to a higher place, they need a place where they can feel the possibility of achieving reasonable goals while being treated as they are equal.

Shelter people, poor and marginalized, will want to go into a town, to a store, maybe a movie, once in a while. Some every day. Some for good reasons and some for not so good reasons.

Putting a shelter, too far from the things a city has to offer, will only cause the guests to look for an alternative place to spend their nights and days. Once again, the location should be a place to offer opportunity and not for punishment. In my fictional story, I chose an abandoned airport. I'm not sure why but as the story went, I found more need for that arrangement and it worked out well. The biggest part is or was, in my story, a large area to work with.

A partner and I were once looking for a building and outside area, as an improvement to what we were using as a shelter. Coming on one building we found a much larger space as well as much larger building than what we thought we would need. The building had been trashed by young people and looked pretty sad. Turning our backs on it, we continued to look at other places. Thinking about it just a little more, I went back and realized it was more than perfect for our needs. By then it was too late, as our group had decided on something cleaner, much smaller, and in town. The future would have its laugh.

The location should have a large outside grounds. Not necessarily landscaped and maybe better if it isn't. Some landscaping can be done cheaply, people donating clips or pieces of this or that plant to be nurtured and planted. Outdoor games, places to walk or sit, a fire circle, maybe an outdoor bathroom. Connecting property might be considered for the future if the price is right. Once again, a few cement blocks and an old sign will make a table or chair until something better comes along. The right people can do a lot with just a little, making what one has thrown out, into something others covet.

The worse the property looks, the easier it will be to improve and impress those pessimistic passerby's looking for an excuse to say negative things or ready to knock it.

The entire area should be fenced well, leaving the exit through the main part of the building where it can be monitored.

An exit or entrance, from the main building, to a much smaller yard within the larger yard, should exist and be open 24 hrs. for smoking, leg stretches or just fresh air. The smaller yard will allow for easier monitoring during late hours or times when monitoring, the large area is difficult.

The main building entrance should have hours so that coming and going is limited to certain hours, such as, 7am to 7pm. Or whatever works in the area.

The staging area, repeating, should be open 24 hours a day, but allowing those returning after closing to go no further than that area until opening in the morning and then with a re-evaluation and enquiring about their late return on the previous evening.

Patterns of frequent coming and going, causing burdens to staff will need to be checked. Once more, the point system was suggested.

Sleeping area

Sleeping areas should be arranged with dorm type settings, possible one person or groups of two to four persons to a room, with the required number of baths, showers and laves, for a floor or approved number of beds.

Areas and monitoring will have to be set up for the various needs and consideration given to things like egress, privacy, and so on. Single women, single men, men and women, families, children and their ages. Health issues and Handicap issues.

Recreation areas

I feel Television should not be allowed at all, as it causes arguments as to what should be on and when. Far too many will have it on first thing and going until late night. This includes staff and volunteers.

TV, will cause people to just sit and do nothing but stare and if any part of the guests staying in the shelter, is to encourage their moving forward, they will not need just another opportunity to sit and stare. Staff might appreciate the sedentary mood the TV can bring but it is doing very little, for the guests. If there is no TV in the area there is less chance of turning it on "Just for an hour or this important show or event" resulting in longer and longer TV time. Researching the best kind on music for this situation might reveal some warming surprises. For sure there will be complaints about music over television at least at first but in time will be forgotten. There will always be a TV going on in some other area of town or city, if it is that important.

Kitchen

Kitchen should be designed with ease in mind; probably larger than first ideas. The best and maybe not the newest equipment should be sought after, research being considerate of cost and reliability and of course the Health Department. Almost anyone can be appointed to handle any part of the kitchen project. Someone can find out the latest Health Department rules and put together a file of the information. Another person might be given the job of finding a dishwasher, calling first to find the best kind for the needs, best size, where they are likely to find used and comparing with new. In many cases, food service equipment might be available for free or minimal costs in commercial places being torn down. This is the kind of project some are better qualified for. Asking for donations and being able to determine whether it is worth the effort to at least explore the donation, what it will take to acquire it, cost to have it in place and working, and how long will it likely last. A young person, volunteering, might work out well for that.

Access to the kitchen by a separate location other than the serving and eating area, considering hygiene, washing on entering as well as leaving.

The Kitchen workers will have access to the kitchen during their shift and only then, not coming and going. That must include staff and volunteers. Kitchen workers should not be given privileges, such as more food or allowed to carry food out. As important as help, staff, volunteers are there needs to be compliance and although they need to be rewarded for their service, they are being watched by those using the facility and calling it home.

I believe the only way to give out food is to have designated servers. A predetermined reasonable portion or portions adhered to closely with leftovers given out as seconds. Or kept for just that, "leftovers". Leftovers, after all have been servesd, can be the start of many recipes.

I expect most will recognize a lot of what I have written but we can't all have the same background history so we must not assume. Let us not assume what others know nor should we assume we have complete understanding. Working together learning together, growing together, no matter our age or position can be the only way.